The Sweet Revenge Files

...A WILL JAMES MYSTERY

by Martin Herman

194 Rodney Press

The Sweet Revenge Files
...A WILL JAMES MYSTERY

ISBN: 978-1-945211-02-7 PRINT
Library of Congress Control Number: 2017900297

First Printing - May, 2017
Second Printing - October,2017
Third Printing - July, 2018
Fourth Printing - December, 2019
Fifth Printing - December, 2022

Printed in the United States of America

CHIEF CREATIVE & CONTINUITY EDITOR:
Allan Pepper

ALSO BY MARTIN HERMAN
The Jefferson Files
The Jefferson Files - the expanded edition
The Hidden Treasure Files
The Return to Sender Files
The 1st Tuesday of the Month Murder Files
A Very Special Dress & Other Stories (written with Aimee Herman)

Published and Distributed by:
194 Rodney Press

521 Simsbury Road, Bloomfield, CT 06002

"Before you embark on a journey of revenge, dig two graves."
— Confucius

In *The Sweet Revenge Files*, the latest in the current series of *Will James Mysteries,* the resourceful investigator and his crew chase after three different, seemingly unrelated killers each seeking revenge, and all but obsessed by a need to dramatically settle old scores.

- *A television preacher who claims to be doing God's work by ridding the land of sinners ... transgressors ... non-believers ... but whose real driving force is to enrich herself while she settles old scores regardless of the death and destruction left in her wake ...*

- *An art dealer with a dark and well-hidden past as well as all the resources necessary for getting what he wants, regardless of who or what he destroys in the process ...*

- *A former KGB contract killer on a lifelong search for payback from the person who made it more challenging for him to ever rape another woman after he raped her ...*

Each of these criminals seems to be willing and able to do whatever it takes to get their revenge, even though it can and does threaten their own survival.

If you think you know how it will all end, guess again. It is all but guaranteed that you will be wrong — so very, very wrong — because in a *Will James Mystery*, things are very rarely as they first appear.

As with every *Will James Mystery*, you are about to be strapped onto a roller coaster with no end in sight. You will feel as if you are moving in various directions at the same time but will refuse to get off until the end.

Prologue

Wednesday, November 21, 2018 – 8:14 p.m.
Pueblo Memorial Airport, Pueblo, Colorado

Former Military Police Officer, Sgt. Joe Cruz, U.S. Army, retired, walked slowly from the passenger terminal toward the long-term parking lot. He nervously looked around and when he was fairly certain that he was not being followed, he put on a pair of plastic gloves, took a brown envelope out of his jacket pocket, ripped off the top of the envelope, and turned it upside down into the palm of his hand. An automobile key dropped out of the envelope. He pressed a button on the key and looked around the parking lot for sounds and lights to signal where the car was parked. He was told that a black, 2016 Toyota Camry would be waiting there for him. He had received the car key along with a round trip air ticket, a set of detailed driving directions, a laminated card with the words, "the Lord she is angry," in block letters, four thumb tacks, floor plans for the house on Desert Candle Drive, a shiny new house key with a tag attached that said "remove and dispose of this tag before you leave the airport, jettison this key as soon as possible before you enter the house," a security panel entry code, a series of photographs of Angel Cardona, and a bundle of money, all in old, non-sequential $20 bills, as per his initial request. One thousand dollars in advance with the balance to be paid as soon as he turned over the "item;" that was the deal. Although he thought he really drove a hard bargain, what Cruz did not know was that they would have paid him far more to get this job done … much, much more.

He was told that they knew he was not a criminal and probably would not have been interested in taking on this assignment if it weren't to reverse a terrible wrong to a

United States Army veteran's widow. He was also told that prominent gun collector Angel Cardona was an arrogant and corrupt former Navy man with little or no respect for anyone in the Army. Although Cruz never asked, and was never told who he was working for in this assignment, he assumed that he was doing this *good deed* on behalf of a patriotic benefactor seeking to fulfill a dying wish of this widow's husband.

Arturo Hornedo did thorough research on both Joe Cruz and Angel Cardona and knew that such a description would make it easier for Cruz to do what they needed him or someone like him, to do. He told Cruz to enter Angel's house and remove — or as it said in his instructions, *liberate*, what was the rightful property of this widow.

Cruz was now aware of blinking lights in the next aisle. He pressed the button one more time to make certain he had located the car and began walking toward it. When he reached the car, he opened the front passenger door, got in and settled into the seat, pushed the seat back as far as it would go, then leaned all the way back. He looked at his watch. *Much too early to drive there now,* he thought, *I don't want to get there too early; it might make the neighbors suspicious. This is no time to be reported for loitering.* He closed his eyes and within minutes he was sleeping soundly.

*****

He woke up and glanced at his watch, it was a little past midnight. Still too early, but he was hungry and needed to go to the bathroom. He got out of the car, stretched his arms up toward the sky, and then walked around to the driver's side. He got in, adjusted the seat, started the ignition, and slowly drove out of the lot. Shortly after he entered the main road, he saw a sign for Pete's Landing Bar and Grill. He parked, got out of the car, locked it, and then pulled off his plastic gloves and pushed them into his shirt pocket as he walked inside the restaurant.

"Still serving food?" he asked the old man at the register.

"As it says on the menu, we're open till 3 a.m. The grill man left early, but I can get you a sandwich or piece of pie. I just made a fresh pot of coffee."

He quickly scanned the menu and ordered a club sandwich, "Easy on the mayo. Meanwhile, where's the latrine?"

The man pointed towards the back, "Want coffee too?"

"Yes sir," Cruz said over his shoulder, "light and sweet, please."

When he returned to the front of the restaurant, his sandwich and a cup of coffee were waiting on a corner table. The man behind the counter tried to start up a conversation but Cruz pretended to be concentrating on his cell phone messages. *No need to make it easy to be identified later,* he thought.

The man kept coming back to him. When it was clear that the counterman was not going to leave him alone, Cruz asked to have the sandwich wrapped up and the coffee put into a takeout cup. He paid the bill, leaving a $3 tip, and returned to the car.

He put the plastic gloves back onto his hands, entered the car and drove around until about 2:30, and then headed toward the house on Desert Candle Drive.

He passed the Colorado State University campus, then the Walking Stick Golf Course, and finally reached his target. He drove slowly past it, drove another couple of blocks then turned around and doubled back to the university campus where he pulled into an open parking space and turned off the motor. He removed his watch and placed it, along with all the contents from his pockets, into a plastic sandwich bag. He removed the house key and slipped it into his shirt pocket, zip-sealed the bag, and put it into the car's glove compartment. He got out of the car, locked it, placed the car key under the driver's side front tire, and after one last look around he started walking back towards the home on Desert Candle Drive. The three miles or so took him a little less than an hour to walk.

He casually looked from side to side and then walked up to the house from the driveway. He took the loose house key out of his pocket, opened the front door and just before he entered the house, tossed the key into the surrounding shrubbery.

The alarm panel was just off to the side of the door jam, right where they told him it would be. He typed in the security code from memory. There was a low beep and then the flashing red light changed to a steady green. He smiled, listened intently for any sounds from within the house, and when he was certain there was nothing out of the ordinary, he removed his shoes and walked up the carpeted stairway to the upper floor, third room on the left.

There was just enough moonlight coming from the windows for him to be able to make his way toward the wall covered with framed photos. He saw the one framed item he had flown halfway across the country to liberate. Stopping once more to listen for any sign of movement within the house he then reached for the item and gently lifted it off the wall. Carefully putting it on an end table, he reached into his jacket pocket and using the four thumb tacks he filled the now empty space with the laminated card.

---///---

Thanksgiving Day,
Thursday, November 22, 2018 — 3:27 a.m.
Desert Candle Drive, Pueblo, Colorado

Chief Petty Officer, U.S. Navy retired, Angel A. Valentin Cardona was sleeping soundly, or as soundly as anyone can sleep after the better part of 20 active years in the naval nuclear submarine force.

He joined the Navy to see the world and personally experienced many of its wonders. But 20 years was a long time, and toward the end he could think of nothing else but life after the Navy.

As his retirement day got closer, he began looking forward to a calm and peaceful place to spend the rest of his life — or at least the next few years. He felt that 20 years, most of them crammed into a submarine far from home with the daily possibilities of flooding, fire, radiation leak, reactor scram, hitting or being hit by something in the ocean, or a torpedo explosion from outside or within, earned him the right to spend his remaining years in an open and worry free environment. He didn't know where, but he definitely knew that it had to be as far away from an ocean as possible. He had heard that Colorado was one of the more picturesque landlocked states; it had a large collection of lakes and beaches, but no ocean. In fact, it was a thousand or so land miles from the nearest ocean. When he read that Colorado had a relatively dry low humidity climate most of the year, he stopped looking. That was it — Colorado would be where he would settle down. Now all he had to do was choose the city and street and specific home within this state.

He engaged several real estate agents — each in a different part of the state. Finally, he received an e-mail with photos of what was described to be a "once in a lifetime dream house." The note, attached to pictures of a house and surrounding areas, arrived by express mail. The note was from the real estate agent in Pueblo, Colorado. Angel read it several times through, "For less than $700,000, here is a massive home, built only a couple of years ago, with the kinds of features you only hear about in homes for the very rich and world famous. The value can only go up! Why not treat yourself to this wonderful piece of real estate in an area with glorious year-round weather."

He spread the photos out on the floor. *I'm single, I have a nice Navy pension, I have lived frugally all of my adult life, it might pinch a little financially at the very beginning, but why not,* he thought.

Why not indeed?

He was attracted to Pueblo's quiet, small-town life atmosphere. In recent years, the once steel-producing town has been transitioning toward ranching and farming and was even attracting major investments, especially around the Arkansas River waterfront.

According to the real estate broker, the cost of living in Pueblo was well below the U.S. average, double digits less; the climate was always pleasant, and the home on Desert Candle Drive was an absolute steal at $699,900. "This is by any definition a magnificent home. Everything about this home says quality and style. If you don't grab this luxurious beauty now you will simply hate yourself for the rest of your born days," the broker said.

His accountant saw it differently, "This will take all of your life's savings. Even if you put down a sizeable down payment, you will still be mortgaged up to the hilt and the mortgage is only the beginning, think about the upkeep of such a place. You need to also consider that the median home cost in all of Pueblo — not just on the street where this house happens to be — is a little more than a $100,000 and you will be paying seven times the median? You just spent half your life in the Navy, by definition that makes you a wandering man, who are you going to sell it to when you decide to move on?"

Ultimately, it was the clean fresh air and the mind-blowing mountain view that sold him.

Although he signed the papers for the sprawling 41-hundred square foot structure earlier that summer, he didn't rush to move in. As a result of having spent 20 years in a sardine can, most of his worldly possessions fit neatly into a couple of sea bags. Now he wanted to expand — in addition to rooms full of furniture he was on the hunt for, he wanted, as he called it, *the kinds of stuff that make a house a home*.

He went to flea markets and specialty stores, and even attended auctions. At one of the auctions he was attracted to a custom-made shadow box with an antique gun mounted inside. That alone made his closest friends wonder if he had lost his mind; he never owned a gun, he didn't like them around him, but this one caught his eye because of its place in history. According to the auctioneer and the supporting documentation, this particular gun with an identifiable pearl grip and metal eagle emblem, belonged to Sheriff George J. Carroll. Carroll had been featured in several historical fiction books and at least a hundred detective and crime magazine articles. Carroll had been a member of the posse that caught the infamous Ma Barker and the Barker-Karpis Gang, whose spree of kidnappings, murders and bank robberies put them on J. Edgar Hoover's FBI most wanted list. Carroll was also the one who got Joe Arridy, a mentally disabled 23-year old to confess to the rape and murder of a 15-year old school girl in Pueblo in the 1930s. The final ingredient that pushed Angel's hand up to bid on this item was one of the documents which came with it authenticating that it was personally presented to Carroll by Hoover, himself.

The bidding was started at $2,500. When there was no interest from the gallery, the auctioneer dropped it to $2,000, then $1,000, then $500, hoping it would go back up after a few people showed interest. Angel raised his hand and yelled out "I'll pay $250."

"Do I hear $350," the auctioneer yelled.

No one responded.

"Do I hear $300," the auctioneer yelled.

No one responded.

With a grimace and obvious lack of enthusiasm the auctioneer said, "Going once," he waited as long as he could while frantically looking around, "going twice," he again looked around, "if the rest of you out there let this one of a kind piece of early American history slip away you will beat yourself up about it for years to come."

No one responded.

"Okay, stay silent now but weep about it tomorrow," one last look around, "sold to the man in the third row for $250. Pay the cashier over there."

*****

This was only the third night he had actually slept in his new home. There were stacks of unpacked moving cartons in the garage and several rooms waiting to be painted and carpeted to his taste, but as far as he was concerned, *when your photos and "hangable pieces" are on the walls and foods of your choice are in the refrigerator, the house can rightfully be called a home — your home.*

*****

Something woke him; he wasn't quite sure what it was, probably nothing, he was still getting used to the normal squeaks and other sounds a house makes in the middle of the night. He reached for the red remote and pressed the *on* button. A series of closed circuit television scenes moved onto and off the huge television screen on the far wall of the massive room. He pressed *stop* and went back two images. Still half asleep, he rubbed his eyes and stared at the screen. There was someone in the den ... his den. *I didn't hear the alarm go off; could I have forgotten to turn on the alarm?* He wondered.

He slowly got out of bed, reached for a baseball bat that was leaning against the wall and tip toed down the hall toward the den.

Now standing at the door he could see someone holding his new prized possession, the shadow box with Sheriff George J. Carroll's pistol and its pearl grip and metal eagle emblem. He stared at the intruder and yelled, "Hey — what are you doing in my home? How did you get in here? What are you doing with my gun?"

Cruz froze in place.

Angel swung the bat, smashing it against Cruz's head. There was an eerie sound similar to a watermelon splashing on a slab of concrete. Angel leaned back and pressed the *panic* button to the right of the door jam.

Cruz fell forward, collapsing in a pool of blood. The shadowbox went flying out of his hands, landing with a thud on a small glass end table, sending chards of glass in all directions. A huge piece lodged into the back of Angel's head.

Minutes later, when the security guards arrived they found the front door unlocked. After a room by room search, they came across the lifeless bodies of the two men.

Part 1

Chapter 1

Monday, December 24, 2018 – 8:19 p.m.
Radio station WWTK, Norfolk, Virginia

"This is Bill Story speaking; you are listening to *The Big Story* on WWTK, *'America's soap box of the air.'* Just three hours and 41 minutes from the dawn of a new day. Not just any day, it is almost Christmas Day, 2018. Soon there will be the sound of Christmas giftwrap being ripped to shreds. But for now, it is just you and me, sweet callers, sharing the joy of this holiday together. I am your partner through the solitude of the moment. Next caller, Atlanta – what's your name and what's your gripe?"

"My name is of little importance," a gravely man's voice with a hint of an Irish brogue came through the speaker, "And as far as having a gripe ... I don't gripe, only the fainthearted gripe. I don't moan or grumble or waste my energy in such ways. Let's talk about today, a wonderful day, the eve of the Lord's birth."

"So you called to wish me and my listeners a Merry Christmas," the host said off handedly.

"No, today demands much more than hollow overly commercialized words; today screams out for more exciting words ... words like 'explosive' and 'never to be forgotten' ... and 'partial payback' ... oh, I know, and words like 'explosive.'"

"You already said 'explosive,'" the host said

sarcastically.

"So I did, so I did," said the caller, "Okay, how about these words ... today is the day we give babies away at 19-84 and five cents a pound."

"Nineteen what? That doesn't make any sense," the host broke in.

The caller laughed, "Sense? You want me to make sense? Do those with power ever really make sense? What makes sense to me is that the Lord, she is angry ... very angry ... and she will make that anger felt. This will be a very sad day indeed for those who wield power over the least powerful among us; who destroy the simple-minded ones as well as their descendants, this *will* be a wakeup call for true justice. It is inevitable that there will be innocent bystanders who will find themselves in the wrong place at the wrong time; unfortunately, for them this will be their very last day of life on earth," the caller laughed again as if he had just heard a funny story, "Yes, a divine day like so many others, when some will get to live and some will live no more. For those who fail to pay notice it will be just another example of how abruptly life can be taken from the evil and the innocent alike because *their* time has come. In future years, this day will become a mournful and noteworthy anniversary."

"Noteworthy and mournful, quite a combination; so why *did* you call?" the talk show host prodded.

"I am sitting on a bench just outside of the really good seats of an absolutely beautiful and historic building here in Atlanta," the caller said, ignoring the host's last comments. "I am enjoying a small snack; just an apple and a small container of cranberry juice. It says 100 percent juice on the label so I guess I can call it a healthy snack. However, I don't really know how it can be 100 percent cranberry juice; cranberries are so tart that even the label says that the juice *should* be mixed with other types of fruit juices to add sweetness. This tells me that you can't always believe everything that you read." There was now a bit of excitement in the caller's voice, "Did you know that cranberry juice helps prevent urinary tract infections by blocking bacteria from attaching to the bladder wall?"

"This is a very slow night, Atlanta caller, and so I will be more patient than usual. Let me recap," the host said, "you did not call to wish me a Happy Christmas but you did call in tonight in hopes of helping us all prevent urinary tract infections?"

"Not really," the caller said with a chuckle, "Actually, not at all. The first blood lost was mixed in with the turkey dressing; the Lord, she was not at all happy about that. I have to admit that I brought my own food into this building. Those in power tend to frown on such things around here, but what good is life if no one ever challenges those in power?"

"Get to the point," the host said, beginning to lose interest, "Why *did* you call tonight?"

"I just couldn't justify paying $8.50 for a really small box of popcorn and a tiny soft drink," the caller continued, "I have been thinking about the George Orwell book, *1984*, 5 stars, a must read."

"I will ask you one more time, why did you call in tonight?" the host said.

"Oh yes, the reason for my call, *welllll*, in exactly eight minutes and 42 seconds, this absolutely beautiful building with everything and everyone in it will be blown to smithereens."

Bill Story began waving his arms to get his engineer's attention. The engineer was stacking up the next callers and so seemed to neither know about the bomb threat nor that Story was trying to get his attention; finally, in desperation, Story threw a pencil holder against the glass separating him from his engineer. The engineer quickly looked up and read the note that Story had scribbled on the back of his commercial script.

POSSIBLE BOMB THREAT ON LINE 4!
NOT SURE IF THIS IS JUST
ANOTHER CRAZY OR SOMEONE TO REALLY
WORRY ABOUT – QUICKLY, CALL 9-1-1
DO IT NOW!!!

Story said into his microphone, "Say caller, wanna repeat that?"

"Tell me, Mr. Radio Host ... is it right for us to celebrate the Lord's birth by building up the money lenders and the trinket merchants? Must we own the same things our neighbors own? Isn't that just *envy?* Envy is one of the Lord's seven deadly sins ... did you know that?"

There was a brief silence, then the caller added, "Proverbs 6:16-19 names six things God hates, seven that are detestable to her: '*Haughty eyes, a lying tongue, and hands that shed innocent blood; a heart that devise the wicked purposes, feet that are swift in running to mischief, a false witness that uttereth lies, and he that soweth discord among brethren.'"*

The caller gave out a huge sigh, "'*Then will I also walk contrary unto you, and will punish you yet seven times for your sins.*' Leviticus 26:24." The caller's voice was now getting louder with each word, "I promise you seven plagues."

Then the caller's voice softened again, "You know, Mr. Host, the Quran and the Old Testament list almost identical plagues to get the attention of the morally bankrupt – tonight you can look forward to a thunderstorm of hail and fire – Exodus 9:13-35. The Lord, she is very angry and that anger will be felt."

The line went dead.

*****

The engineer quickly dialed 911. On the second ring he heard, "9-1-1, what is your name, your location, and what is your emergency?"

Barely waiting for the 911 operator to complete her standard questions the engineer said, "This is WWTK, the Bill Story Show; we just had a bomb threat called in."

"Is the caller still on the line?" The 911 operator asked.

The engineer looked at his computer screen and grimaced, "No, it looks like the caller hung up. But I can quickly rewind the call and play it back for you."

"Cue it up while I patch you into the local FBI office."

"It could be some wacko but we didn't want to take any chances," the engineer said.

"You did right by calling it in, better safe than sorry." The 911 operator said; moments later, they both heard, "Federal Bureau of Investigation, Norfolk office."

The 911 operator quickly identified herself and brought the FBI operator up to date.

The radio engineer asked if the FBI operator was ready to hear the tape, he said that he was, the engineer tapped into the backup tape and turned on the reserve machine.

At the end of the call the FBI operator asked, "Do you have any additional information which could help us track down the source of this call?"

"No," the engineer responded, "this is all that we have."

"Okay," the FBI operator said, "just let us know if you hear from this caller again. For now, we'll take it from here." He disconnected from both the engineer and the 911 operator.

The Norfolk FBI operator called the Atlanta FBI office and played the recording.

"What do you make of it?" Atlanta asked.

"It could be a crank call but you know the drill — 'In a post 9-11 world, don't take any threat lightly!' Hey, it's Christmas Eve ... most churches are about to fill up for their midnight services ... the caller quoted from the Bible ... he specified a historic building ... if it was here I would immediately get anybody and everybody that is even close to the area and dispatch them to every church that fits the general description ..."

"He also talked about the Quran."

"I don't think Muslims celebrate Christmas — maybe the small number of Christian Muslims do. Hey, I don't want to tell you what to do but I would concentrate on churches if it was here.

"There are a lot of churches in and around Atlanta — even if we limit our initial efforts to churches in *historic buildings* — it could take days." The Atlanta FBI operator said.

"You got a long night ahead of you then," Norfolk said, "don't let me hold you." The line went dead.

*****

"Okayyyyyy," Story groaned into the microphone, "I guess we are all healed now. Moving right along, next caller, Denver — what's your name and what's your gripe?"

"Hi Bill, first time caller, long time listener; my name is Marsha and I'm from Denver. Who or what was that? You really attract more than your share of wackos, don't ya?"

"It takes all kinds, yes it does?" Story responded with a heavy sigh as he read the note his engineer was holding up against the connecting glass.

It's now in the hands of the Atlanta F.B.I.!

"You don't think he was really going to blow up a building, do you?" Marsha asked.

"Give me more credit than that, Marsha from Denver." Story shot back, mopping the sweat off of his brow. "If I did, I wouldn't be chatting you up right now, I would be on the phone with the FBI."

"Well," the caller said, "it is always nice to hear passages from the bible, especially on Christmas Eve."

"Yeh," Story responded, "a great use of the people's airways. So, what's on your mind tonight?"

*****

The man on the bench put a cell phone into his right pants pocket. Then, putting all of his weight against a thick walking stick, he slowly stood up from the bench. He picked up a small decorative pocket knife. Held it up as if to inspect the blade, then dropped it into his other pants pocket; his shoulders stooped so far over that his upper torso was at almost a 90-degree angle to the rest of his body. With apparent discomfort, he slowly hobbled towards the nearest garbage can where he opened the lid, with some difficulty. Leaning against the can he threw away the remains of his snack. He turned to fully face the closed-circuit security camera on the opposite wall and nodded towards the camera. He turned and slowly walked towards the exit.

Several yards before the door his foot caught on a loose tile and he almost fell, but was able to catch himself with the help of his walking stick.

*****

One minute and 17 seconds after disconnecting from WWTK ...

The man slowly walked out to the curb and reached for the door handle of the first taxi cab in line.

In a thick German accent, he said, "Take me to da Atlantique Greyhound Boos Station, please."

"It's only a few miles from here, buddy. You could probably walk there in 15-20 minutes; lights and all it's only a few minutes less by car. If I take you there, I'll lose my space in line and it really doesn't pay for such a short fare. It is busier than normal on the street tonight because of the holiday celebrations; I don't want to miss out on the long fares to the suburbs."

"So double da meetah," the man insisted, "I don't want to miss da last boos out."

"Come on buddy, give me a break," the taxi driver said, "I'm just a working stiff."

"I am *not* your boody, I am your coostomer, or at least I am trying to be your coostomer. Triple da fare den — or vood you rather I make it a complaint with da city's consumer affairs department? Choose your fate and do it quickly, I have a boos to catch."

"Okay, okay, boss," the driver muttered, as he started the meter, "the customer is always right, that's my motto."

Now inside the cab, the man took the pocket knife out of his pocket and dropped it on the floor. He then removed a small plastic bag from his pocket, opened it and allowed a Cross fountain pen and a hair comb to slip out of the bag and onto the seat.

*****

Four minutes and 14 seconds later ...

The taxi moved south on Peachtree Street, turned right onto Forsyth Street, N.W., the passenger removed a small blue plastic box from his coat pocket, glancing quickly at his watch; it was 8:28 and 33 seconds. He waited for 1 minute and 5 seconds and then pressed the red button on the blue box. The taxi almost shook out of control as they felt and then heard a loud explosion; just then, the sky lit up like a giant birthday cake covered with numerous shimmering candles.

"Hey," the driver yelled, "what was that?"

"I vood say da Gods seem to be particularly annoyed, tonight," the passenger said in a calm, matter of fact tone.

"How about I drop you off at the curb and turn the cab around. I had disaster relief training in the Army and might be able to help in some way. You're almost at the bus station anyway," the driver said, excitedly.

"You can do anything you vant to do *after* you get me to da boos station." The man said, calmly, "I told you, I don't vant to miss da last boos out."

Shaking his head, the driver sped up until he reached 232 Forsyth. He came to a screeching halt in front of the bus station. The man calmly stepped out of the cab, handed the driver a crumpled $50 bill, and walked slowly into the station.

The driver stuffed the bill into his shirt pocket and quickly turned the car back towards the direction of the explosion.

*****

The bus station was almost deserted; the man glanced discretely from side to side, and then walked directly toward the restroom sign and into the ladies room.

He looked under each of the stalls, and when he felt secure that he had the restroom all to himself, he entered the last stall on the end and locked the door behind him.

He pressed a small button at the top of the walking stick and it collapsed down to a four-inch tube, which he slid into his shirt pocket. Standing now, fully erect, he pulled off the rubber covering that had been on each of his shoes, carefully turning each one inside out and then stuffed them into his coat pocket. He then removed his black overcoat and turned the sleeves inside out, exposing a bright yellow raincoat. He hung it on a hook on the back of the door, removed his hat, turned it inside out, then placed it on the same hook as the coat. He reached down and pulled up the bottoms of his pant legs as far as they would go and then put a large rubber band over each shoe, rolling the band up to his thigh to secure the pant leg material in place. He reached up and carefully took off a nylon skull cap exposing a full head of long bright red hair.

She shook her hair free, running her fingers through it, placed the skull cap into her coat pocket and removed a small makeup case; carefully but quickly applying lip stick and a bit of rouge.

She put on the hat and raincoat, yellow side out, took a quick look around the stall to make sure nothing was left behind, and then one last check in front of the mirror by the sinks before she walked out the door and into the station.

Looking straight ahead, she headed for the main exit.

By the end of 2018, almost all American cities had closed-circuit cameras placed on the outsides of most buildings ... light poles ... street signs. However, those who took the time to check them out knew that in order to allow the cameras to clearly identify license plate numbers just past the curb, there was a universal blind spot — the eight to 11 inches closest to the sides of the buildings.

She walked out of the bus station and headed straight for the building line from where she proceeded several blocks, turning quickly into a dark alley. As she entered the ally, she removed her hat and red wig, stuffing them into a pouch that hung around her neck. Without slowing down, she leaned her face into the pouch and pulled off the prosthetic skin covering the lower portion of his face, revealing several days' growth of beard. He was particularly careful to place all the hardened theatrical gel from his face into the pouch; there wasn't a question in his mind that the best available forensic investigators would soon be scouring this trail for evidence and he wasn't about to add these pieces to what they would find. However, he was comfortable in knowing that the combination of accumulated dirt, grime, and debris covering much of the alley floor mixed with the blended bleach mixture now being released from the specially treated heals and soles of his shoes would quickly dissolve any loose pieces of the cosmetic gel that might accidently drop on to the floor, adding to the general confusion about the meaning of any specific piece of evidence the authorities would find. He removed a black soft plastic disposable raincoat from his back pants pocket, shook it out and put in on, over his yellow raincoat, snapping the tabs from his chin down to the hemline without slowing his stride. He exited the ally, now with a spring to his step. A black limo pulled up alongside him. It stopped just long enough for him to get inside and then sped away.

Finally, inside the safety of the limo, he carefully removed and folded his thin plastic gloves, placing them into a thick plastic bag which had been stored in a side pocket on the car door. He reached for a metal box on top of the side bar and carefully removed the cover, dropped the bag inside the tin, and watched as the bag and its contents dissolved in the odorless acid solution. He closed the lid and after wiping it clean returned it to the side bar. He reached down and placed each foot into a heavy plastic bag, then eased out of his shoes, leaving them in the bags at his feet. He leaned forward and removed his hat and his various outer coats, stuffing them into the plastic bags that now held his shoes; pulled a draw string on each bag, tightly closing them. Moving the bags to the opposite side of the car he leaned down and slipped on a pair of furry pink slippers. Moving to a cross-legged sitting position he smiled contentedly.

He picked up a small hand mirror, looked intently at the image and then peeled away another layer of face gel, revealing an attractive and well-tanned female face.

She picked up a small napkin from the side bar and wrapped it around the crystal drinking glass carefully placed there for her just minutes before she entered the car. The glass contained two perfectly formed ice cubes, two fingers of Kahlua, and three fingers of heavy cream, which had been meticulously prepared for her. She removed a spoon from a vacuum sealed pouch and gently stirred the drink. She put the spoon and its wrapper into her shirt pocket and then took a small sip from the glass. Satisfied that it had been prepared exactly the way she requested, she loosely wrapped her middle finger within a napkin and pushed the button to lower the glass divider between the driver and the passenger compartment. The driver glanced into the rearview mirror and said, “Any surprises?”

“Surprises are for amateurs Scully,” she said, in a low Southern drawl, “and we are definitely *not* amateurs.”

“Yes, Sister Joan,” the driver responded.

“Tonight, we moved another step towards *payback* Scully ... this is a very good night for those of us blessed with *her* love and guidance, very good indeed.”

“Yes, Sister Joan.”

“Now take me home,” she said as she held the button down until the connecting window returned to the top of the well. She took a full swallow of her drink, dabbed at the corners of her mouth with a different silk napkin, folded it neatly and placed it on the shelf, positioned her drinking glass on top of the silk cloth, carefully wiped the outside of the glass as well as along the rim, shook off her slippers and then stretched out on the luxurious leather seat and was soon fast asleep.

Chapter 2

Monday, December 24, 2018 – 8:42 p.m.
The governor's mansion, Buckhead District of Atlanta

Virtually every Georgia state employee understood that there would be hell to pay if Governor Beau Harper was not the very first to hear about anything of consequence that happened in *his* state. Even though Harper had less than three weeks remaining in his second term at the time of the Christmas Eve bombing, he had no intention of relinquishing power a minute before he absolutely had to. Under the 1865 state constitution, he could only serve two consecutive terms but it was an open secret that he was planning to insert a *compliant* candidate to be the titular head of the state for one term so that he could return in four years for two more consecutive terms. "This is my little sand pile," he liked to say, "don't never mind who calls themselves govnah, I am in charge of this here state and *will* be in charge until my very last breath; and even then, I expect to have something to say 'bout who runs this here place. So don't nevah let me find out from some damned reporter what *you* should have told *me* fust."

The 911 operator who took the first call about the explosion at the landmark theater dutifully called the governor before she even informed the police or fire officials. That was simply the way things were done in Harper's state.

As soon as the news reached him and well before the feds were notified, the governor declared that all physical reminders of the blast be moved from the crime scene to a location — any location — out of downtown Atlanta. "Let us not give fuel to the ever-diligent press and blood sucking reformers, souvenir seekers, bad actors still on the loose, anyone else with mayhem on their mind – and did I say the 'ever-diligent press and blood sucking reformers?' We cannot guarantee that evidence will not be lost or compromised or used just to make this great state, or me, look bad; it is just too much of a temptation. I want the remains of this disaster off the busy streets of Atlanta; I want the space boarded up; I want some fancy dancy mural quickly painted on those boards – some happy holiday design – to greet the holiday tourists. Let's not fill these holy days with gloom and doom." He made this all perfectly clear to his wife's nephew, Georgia's senior military officer, the state adjutant general.

"You're asking me to tamper with evidence, Uncle Beau; there may even be federal statutes governing what can and cannot be done with the contents of a possible terrorist crime scene."

"It's govnah, you weak turd, *the same govnah* who got you this cushy job and the same govnah who can take it away; and I don't give two shakes about what the revenue agents do to rob states of their God given rights; or more simply put, don't you dare stand in my way on this. This is Christmas time in downtown Atlanta and I don't want no pity party on those streets chasing away all of those lovely tourist dollars. I want the National Guard activated on this and I want it done *now*!"

"But Uncle Beau ..."

"I told you, it is govnah, now get to it!"

The governor slammed the phone down, confident that his order would be honored.

Within an hour of the bombing and while first responders were still searching for the dead and injured, the members of the Georgia National Guard began moving sections of the bombed out theater to a secluded area of the Atlanta Airport; *It isn't healthy to make the governor angry,* the head of the Georgia National Guard kept thinking as the governor's words rang loudly in his head, "I don't care where you put it, just get it off of the streets of downtown Atlanta."

Chapter 3

Monday, December 24, 2018 — 8:53 p.m.
Crime scene, downtown Atlanta and emergency complex, Atlanta Airport

A group of National Guardsmen had been participating in a downtown Atlanta Christmas Eve event, so they were able to get to the theater within minutes of receiving the governor's orders. The local commander quickly took charge of the crime scene, commandeered as many vehicles as he could and established a temporary morgue along the outskirts of the Atlanta airport. Crime scene investigators complained but their protests fell on deaf ears. To ensure that the governor's orders would be followed to the letter, a dozen or so of the physically largest, most muscular looking members of the State Police were also sent to the scene. Like it or not, evidence was now being shipped to the northernmost section of what was the old Atlanta Speedway — a 14-acre section of the initially abandoned 287-acre auto racetrack that more than 19 years before had been set aside for Atlanta's first airport.

The movement of evidence created a need to split the available investigators into three separate working groups; some remained at the bombed-out site, most were assigned to maintain the chain of evidence by traveling with the National Guard units as they packed and moved evidence, leaving barely a skeleton crew to set up camp on the outskirts of the Atlanta airport. What could have been a massive investigative force was now scattered to cover the multiple points of interest, with barely enough at any one location to be effective.

The governor had his way, but at a huge cost to the investigation.

*****

Volunteer electricians, plumbers, and carpenters were quickly assembled by the local unions and bused to the airport location; equipment and supplies were seized from nearby construction sites, and soon a series of bare bones working and storage spaces were built in the old hangar and brightly illuminated by powerful Klieg lights. A temporary morgue was set up along one side of the massive shell and the remaining two thirds of the space were quickly filling up with the twisted remains of the theater and surrounding structure.

As best anyone could remember, this hangar was last used to house surplus military vehicles in the mid 1950s. A few of the National Guardsmen tried to clean up the area, but time and neglect made it an almost impossible task; time was running out before the first buses were scheduled to arrive with family and friends of the missing victims. Authorities were anxious to do whatever they could to identify those within the swelling temporary morgue.

One of the detectives complained about the filthy conditions and was told to go to the governor if he had a complaint; he called Ivy Chan instead. She drove out to the hangar, quickly looked around and then called the head of Atlanta's health department at home. Together, they called the mayor and threatened to put a lock on the hangar if he didn't assign enough workers to immediately scrub the area down. He told them that his hands were tied; the governor was making all these decisions, but volunteered to join in with them on a three-way call to the governor for whatever good it might do to get him to move on their request.

An aide answered; at first, he said that the governor was in a meeting. When pressed by the mayor, he said that the governor refused to come to the phone. Ivy asked the aide to tell the governor that her next call was going to be to the Secretary of Homeland Security followed quickly by a call to her old friend currently in charge of CNN's Atlanta Bureau. The aide asked them to hold on and in a few minutes the governor picked up. He told them to mind their own business or call Santa Claus or anyone else if they thought it would do any good and slammed the phone down.

Less than an hour later the governor's private cell phone rang and one of his largest political contributors told him to quickly turn on CNN. A reporter was delivering a scathing editorial about the unclean and possibly contaminated location chosen as the temporary resting place for many of the victims. While the reporter was speaking a series of photos of the known victims were flashed onto the screen. Most of the photos shown were mangled children's bodies.

The governor cursed under his breath, "My luck this thing had to take place within spittin' distance of the CNN world headquarters." He watched the editorial come to a close, followed by what was being billed as a commercial free vigil asking viewers to call their local, state and federal elected officials. Along the bottom of the screen were home and private cell phone numbers for the Mayor, Georgia's congressmen and women, Georgia's two U.S. senators, and finally, the governor.

He made an obscene gesture towards the television set, and then picked up the phone and speed dialed the state adjutant general.

"Yes, governor?"

"Clean the hangar up and make damned sure CNN knows that you did."

There was dead silence at the other end of the phone.

"I want it done *now*!" the governor yelled.

*****

As all of this activity was taking shape it attracted the interest of civilian drones and traffic helicopters from the local television stations. It only took one call to the FAA to make certain that nothing, other than regularly scheduled commercial and U.S. military aircraft would be permitted to fly over the rising complex at the airport.

*****

As the National Guard began erecting a wall of 4 x 8 plywood boards to what was left of the exterior of the theater, a specially trained contingent of first responder rescue workers, military trained volunteers, and a K-9 team with explosive-sniffing cadaver dogs worked through the night, risking their own lives as they methodically sifted through the collapsed building. There was still hope that they could recover additional survivors.

Although each crime scene is unique, most investigators begin with a commonly accepted course of action; they close and secure the immediate area, reducing the chances of contamination or loss or movement of evidence. The governor's insistence that all evidence be picked up and moved before a more careful analysis could be conducted did not help those charged with solving the crime and in the hands of an experienced defense attorney could result in having key evidence thrown out when the case reached the courts.

A reporter saw what was going on and quickly called the state's attorney general, Wanda Parent. "Do you have any comment on the movement of evidence to a different site this early in the investigation?"

"It isn't the process I would have preferred," the attorney general said, "but I will have to look into the matter before I can make any on-the-record comments."

Parent first called the mayor and then the governor asking if either one knew what was being done with the evidence. The mayor said it was all in the governor's control; the governor told her that of course, his first priority was to save as many of the poor souls trapped inside as possible but then he needed to be mindful of the tourist ramifications should they not move the investigation away from downtown Atlanta, "and pronto."

"But that can hurt us when we go to trial, governor," she said.

"Oh, Wanda, I have full faith in you. You will bury the fiend who did this. Don't worry your pretty little self about it."

"But ..."

"Now Wanda, you know that you were my handpicked successor, don't you? I expect you to just work around it, and I know you can and will. Now have yourself a good night." He hung up before she could respond.

She stared at the disconnected phone for a while before she shoved it into her pocket, cursing under her breath.

*****

At his first press briefing, the Homeland Security secretary told reporters that no one would rest until they identified the perpetrator, or perpetrators, and brought them to justice. He also made a point to say that there were no monopolies for *smart*, and so he wanted as many as possible of the best and the brightest working together to help solve this crime, sooner rather than later. He asked for anyone with information about this crime to come forward. He announced a no questions asked $50,000 reward for anyone with information leading to a conviction.

Crime Scene Investigators, specially trained state and federal law enforcement officers, and forensic scientists from the U.S. Army Criminal Investigation Lab (USACIL), in Metro Atlanta's Gillem Enclave worked in teams of three. USACIL, formerly Fort Gillem, generally recognized to be *the* authority for battlefield forensics, had been initially set up to supply worldwide forensic support and train special agents for all branches of the U.S. military. It was decided that effective immediately, a branch of USACIL, the only Department of Defense full-service forensic laboratory in the world would be temporarily located into the formerly abandoned airplane hangar to assist in this effort.

The Atlanta Police Department crime lab already had an internship program for college students. The initial objective was to develop a strong next generation of capable CSI candidates. Requests went out to the various Atlanta area community colleges which offered degrees in criminal justice, forensic science and related fields as well as all accredited four-year colleges and universities seeking advanced students working towards master's degree programs in chemistry, forensic science and other natural sciences. All comers were quickly put to use.

Within a matter of hours, those who would soon become a field force numbering in the thousands, had gone from celebrating Christmas Eve with their friends and families to a scene of terror, death, and destruction.

Chapter 4

Monday, December 24, 2018 — 8:59 p.m.
Camp David, Catoctin Mountain,
Frederick County, Maryland

The president was about to sit down to the quiet dinner she had been looking forward to all day. Her husband was traveling with the vice president to attend the funeral of Chancellor Wilhelm Krüger in Germany. Her daughter, son in law, and grandchildren were going to join her for Christmas gift giving at Camp David in the morning. For all intents and purposes, Washington, D.C. was closed for the holidays. All but the most essential services were now on Christmas break even here in Camp David, the presidential retreat.

The president's helicopter landed just before 6 p.m. and as a unique gift to herself, she did not pack any of her ever-present briefing books. Tonight would be low key and uneventful. Other than a skeleton crew and her personal security detail, she had the entire property to herself.

She insisted on giving the kitchen staff Christmas Eve and Christmas Day off. The staff prepared a number of meals and stored them in one of the huge refrigerators before they left. Lunch had been a quick salad at her desk and so her stomach was beginning to grumble. She was hungry but none of the prepared meals seemed to interest her. She rummaged through the well-stocked kitchen, quickly found what she needed and almost as an afterthought, grabbed a handful of jalapeño peppers which she threw into the pan along with several lightly scrambled eggs. *I'll pay for the peppers with a night of heartburn,* she thought, *but what is life without a little heartburn?*

Her plan was simple, a light and leisurely dinner, followed by a long and relaxing bath, and then some mindless television. Contrary to most other days for more than the past 30 years, she planned to sleep late in the morning, well past her usual 5:30 wake-up call and maybe do yoga, or take a long walk before her grandchildren arrived. She had already arranged for her morning security briefing to be at 9:30 instead of the usual 6:30. *What a rare treat,* she thought.

Her personal cell phone lit up; the number on the screen was all too familiar; the caller I.D. number belonged to the director of the FBI. The president picked up on the first ring, "Hey," she whispered into the phone, "it's Christmas Eve — I would have thought that you got more than enough of me the other 364 days of the year?"

"I am so sorry to disturb you, Madam President, but this can't wait."

The president sat up, "Okay, what is it?"

"Shortly before 8:30 this evening, a bomb went off in a crowded movie theater in Atlanta, no one has claimed credit for it yet but the Homeland Security Secretary says that until we have reason to believe otherwise, we need to consider all possibilities to be likely and so, we should treat this as a possible terrorist act."

"And the casualties," the president asked.

"Too soon to know, but those on the scene think it will be significant — including a fair amount of young children — it was family night at the theater and from what we have heard they had a packed house tonight."

"Oh my God," the president gasped, "Well, quickly organize a National Security Council Principals Committee meeting."

"That is my next call, Madam President."

"I also want a Deputies Committee meeting to be scheduled, independent of all other meetings on this matter. I have been in government too long to think that we will be able to cut through the interagency turf battles to get to the *who, what, where, when,* and *why* fast enough to please me. I want more than the usual finger pointing I want to zero in on bringing whoever did this to justice and we need to make whatever security changes necessary to avoid a similar attack anywhere else on our soil. I will be looking to you and these committees to generate more than just a neatly bound report. I want a speedy and productive investigation ... and I want it sooner rather than later."

"Yes, Madam President."

"Was there any advance warning?"

"Absolutely none, Madam President, everyone was taken by surprise, there was no chatter leading up to the bombing which is why all departments are now scrambling."

"Sooner rather than later, John, the clock is ticking. If it is a terrorist attack someone in the world should have picked up early chatter."

"If they did have an early notice, we need to know why no one saw fit to give us a heads up. Will you be calling the Israelis or will the Secretary of State," he asked.

She thought about his question for a few seconds and then said, "You mean Abimelech Böhmer, don't you?"

"That was exactly who I meant."

"Let me think about that one for a bit." she said.

"Of course, Madam President."

"First I want to bring the opposition up to date." She hung up and began dialing her chief of staff, Mindee Danielle, who answered on the first ring.

Still thinking about the FBI director, the president grabbed the napkin from her lap and threw it on top of her dinner plate, angrily pushing the plate aside.

"Good evening, Madam President," came the crisp voice of the president's longtime aide.

"There has been a bombing in Atlanta," the president said, coming right to the point, "I need you to organize a teleconference for me so that I can quickly get word to everyone on the National Security Council, plus House Speaker Ravins, Representative Blanchard and both the minority and majority leaders of the Senate, the governor of

Georgia, and the representative from Georgia's 5th Congressional District. Have the other 13 representatives from the Georgia delegation decide among themselves who will represent them. Make sure they are all linked in on the tele-conference. We don't need some disgruntled political hack complaining to Sean Hannity that they were left out by *that woman* in the oval office."

"Some will be *en route* to church for midnight services so it might take a bit longer than normal but I will get right on it."

"Meanwhile I will call the secretary of Homeland Security," the president said.

"Do you want the vice president to return to Washington?"

"Isn't he already in Germany?"

Mindy looked at her watch and then said, "Of course, yes."

"Make sure he is linked into the tele-conference in a secure location, whenever it takes place."

Chapter 5

Tuesday, December 25, 2018 — 2:13 a.m.
Camp David, Catoctin Mountain,
Frederick County, Maryland

The tele-conference, the third in so many hours, was coming to a close. "Finally, Fritz," the president said to the secretary of Homeland Security, "I want this done by the book. I *do not* want whoever did this to get off because of some legal technicality or procedural error or violation of a civil right or *any* mistake on our part. I want whoever is responsible for this to suffer the *full* consequences of the law. I would also like the fiends responsible for this to be taken alive if at all possible – we have to know if this is a 'one-of' or the opening volley on a whole new battlefield."

"Yes, Madam President," the secretary said, "but unfortunately, much of the crime scene has already been moved to a secluded portion of the Atlanta airport."

"By whose orders?" the president asked.

"By *my orders*, Madam President," Gov. Harper said, calmly, "And with the courageous actions of the patriotic members of the Georgia National Guard."

"Damn it Beau, at the very least there are clues, possibly DNA, maybe even fingerprints, who knows what may now be lost for good that *could* have helped us unravel who did this, and what about maintaining a chain of custody, preserving evidence from the time it is collected to the time it is presented in court?"

The governor started to respond but the FBI director broke in, “Fortunately, Madam President, some of our agents arrived fairly quickly on to the scene and were able to accompany the evidence from the crime scene to its current location and they are maintaining a chain of custody.”

“Thank heaven for little gifts,” she said. “by the way, who is representing Georgia in this investigation?”

“I have assigned that responsibility to the state’s attorney general, Madam President,” the governor said, “She will be the local *public face* for this investigation.”

“*Fisher woman*,” the president asked in amazement, “What does Wanda Parent know about investigating a possible terrorist bombing?”

“It is what it is.” The governor said.

“I don’t know, Beau, seems to me that federal beats state’s rights in this matter,” the president said.

“Now, now,” the governor said, “With all due respect, Madam President, let’s not get into a pissing contest, pardon my French. The good people of Georgia expect their leaders to make decisions and that is exactly what I did. I was on the job while some others were enjoying the holiday in the comfort and seclusion of their country retreats.”

“Describe it any way you like, Beau, but this president’s wishes just might hold a bit more weight than those of an outgoing governor.”

"Be that as it may, Madam President, however, I still happen to be held in very high *regarrrd* by the good people of Georgia. I expect I will be as popular, if not more popular, in three weeks after I pass the baton to the next govnah," the governor said softly, "and you might need to count on that popularity in the dark days ahead, if you know what I mean."

"Don't threaten me, Beau," the president said.

"I wouldn't think of doing any such thing, Madam President," the governor said.

"Don't patronize me," the president added, sternly.

"I wouldn't think of doing that either, Madam President."

"This is *not* going to be politics as usual. A lot of people died tonight, Beau. I won't stand for anyone playing politics with this. Is ... *that* ... clear?"

"Yes Madam President, *crystal* clear."

After a long silence the president requested all participants on the call to maintain public silence in order to keep those responsible for this crime guessing. "No need to fill in the blanks for these monsters." She also said that she would distribute whatever information surfaces in the hours and days ahead and disconnected herself from the call.

The president sat fuming, "The 'good people of Georgia' wouldn't hold you in such high *regarrrd* if they knew about your many episodes with little Filipino girls," the president said, half under her breath. She then reached for her phone and dialed the Homeland Security Secretary's private number. On the second ring he answered. "One more thing, Fritz, I have given this a great deal of thought and I would like you to reach out to Abimelech Böhmer. It would take days, at the very least for our own people to set up an emergency field hospital in the size and scope we will need; Abi Böhmer and the Israelis have already shown that they can do this in hours."

The secretary started to respond but the president cut him off, "Look Fritz, I understand how far back you two go; I also know that not all of the history between the two of you has been pleasant; would you rather I reach out to him?"

"No, it's my responsibility, I'll do it," he said.

"You know that Abi can help," she said.

"I do," he said.

"After 9-11, it was Abi who had all of the terrorists profiled and individually identified before anyone else — including our own agencies. Abi may be the holder of one of the most effective rolodex files in existence and there is no question that eventually he will do whatever we ask of him in a situation such as this but he can also be vindictive and might prefer to watch you twist in the wind for a while and we just don't have any time for that."

"Warning noted, Madam President," he said with a barely audible sigh.

"Keep me posted, Fritz. I don't want to be out of the loop for a second."

Chapter 6

Tuesday, December 25, 2018 — 3:24 a.m.
ICE Field Office, Ted Turner Dr. SW, Atlanta

The secretary dialed Abimelech Böhmer's personal cell number. He didn't have to look it up, it had been burned into his memory many arguments ago. He looked at his watch, it was a little before 10:30 a.m. in Jerusalem.

"Gut yontif Mr. Secretary of the mighty United States Homeland Security Department," Böhmer said into his cell phone as soon as the caller ID told him who was calling. "Or is this just one of the mighty United States Homeland Security Secretary's many aides de camp?"

"Hello, Abi," the secretary said glumly. "I take it you have already heard about the Atlanta bombing?"

"Of course!" Abi said, "believe it or not, we actually get all the news that's fit to print here in the Negev desert almost as soon as you get it in the all mighty, all powerful, United States of America."

"We need your help," the secretary said.

"You need *my* help?" Abi said, facetiously.

"We don't have time for the usual games, Abi. Too many have died ... too many may yet die."

"And how is your lovely wife, Mr. Secretary?"

"We are divorced, Abi, but of course you know that."

"So I do, so I do," came the two packs of cigarettes a day gravel voice on the other end of the line.

"This was a mistake; I was already sorry about placing this call as soon as I began dialing your number, now I am more than certain it was a mistake. Goodbye, Abi." The secretary began to move the phone from his ear to disconnect the signal when he heard, "Wait. You never did have much appreciation for subtlety, did you Fritz?"

The secretary returned the phone to his ear and, as calmly as he could he said, "No games, Abi, subtle or otherwise."

"Okay, Fritz, what do you want?" Abi said.

"I need to establish a state of the art field hospital outside of Atlanta. The best we can hope for if we use the sources available to us here would be a day or two, we do not have days, we have hours – and not very many hours. After the last tsunami in Sri Lanka your guys had a working field hospital up and running 12 hours from the moment you reached the area."

"Eleven hours and 43 minutes, but who keeps count?" Abi said.

"I told you, no games, Abi," the secretary yelled into the phone.

"Of course I will help, but I'm afraid the request must come from your president, directly," the Israeli said.

"Go to hell!" the secretary yelled into the phone and hung up.

Within seconds, the cell phone came to life. The secretary looked at the caller ID, it read Abimelech Böhmer. He accepted the call.

"You're a real dummkopf Fritz. Of course, I will help, even you couldn't possibly have thought that I would not do all that I could, given the circumstances. All I was doing was tweaking that bulbous nose of yours. Am I not entitled to at least that after all that has gone on between us over the years?"

"Were you or your sources aware of any chatter leading up to this?" the secretary asked, ignoring the Israeli's comments.

"None! If we had we would have alerted your government, you should know that as well," Abi said.

"Yeh, sure," the secretary said.

"You have a specific location in mind for this field hospital?" Abi asked.

"Yes, we want to set it up in an out of the way section of the Atlanta Airport."

"Good, that will cut down on travel after we land and make set up easier because we can taxi right to the actual location. So now that I agreed to help you ..."

The secretary interrupted, "As long as you remember who you are helping, Abi — it isn't me it, is the most important and supportive ally your country has."

"Stop making speeches," Abi broke in, "it will take me a couple of hours to assemble a team, the equipment, and load the necessary supplies ..."

"We can supply you with whatever you need ..." the secretary broke in.

"I prefer to bring who and what I need, Fritz. Nothing nationalistic about it, just works quicker and better if we come fully manned and equipped to hit the road running. Is the final site cleared and ready to build on or will we need to clear the area first?"

"The site is part of an old race track. We will prepare the area before you arrive so that you can taxi right up to the site and begin building the moment you unload," the secretary said.

"Good," Abi said, thinking aloud, "very good. Okay, let's see, it is about 3:30 in the morning in Atlanta now ... it will take two, maybe three hours to get it all together here and loaded onto a plane, or planes... 10,317.29 kilometers... what's that 6,410, 6,411 land miles... maybe 12 or 13 hours flight time ... two, maybe three hours to unload and begin the work as soon as we land ... 10 or 11 hours to do the work ... I will have your field hospital up and ready to turn over to our medical test team by 10 a.m. your time tomorrow morning ... maybe sooner with a little bit of luck."

"We have our own medical staff," the secretary said, indignantly.

"Don't get your panties in a twist, you should know that we never turn over a project until we know it is ready, according to the conditions on the ground," Abi shot back, "We may live in a desert but we are not the *San*."

There was an uncomfortable silence, then Abi said, "The San, or Bushmen, or Basarwa, are indigenous hunter-gatherer people of Southern Africa."

"Now who is making speeches, I know who the San are, you pompous ass," the secretary said.

"I just thought ..."

"You just thought what you always think, that you are the smartest person in the room. Well, here's a tip for you, no one likes someone who always thinks they are the smartest person in the room. Nothing has really changed Abi, has it?"

"Hey, you called me for help, I didn't call you."

"You wouldn't be anything without the backing of this country," the secretary said.

"Ever the bully, here is a little tip for you Mr. Divorced Secretary of Homeland Security, no one likes their rich uncle, either."

"I am not sure that very many people like ungrateful jerks who stoop down to help a friend in need while mocking them. Is there anything you want us to have waiting for you?" the secretary asked.

"Now that the Carnegie Deli closed down, you can have a couple trays of Katz's corned beef and pastrami sandwiches, fresh soft and springy rye bread, plenty of real deli mustard to cover both sides of the bread, of course! Oh yes, plenty of their french fries, or are you people still calling them American fries? See if you can find some real Heinz Ketchup, not the watered-down stuff they now put in their new plastic bottles. A few cases of Dr. Brown's soda – mix the flavors but make sure you include plenty of Cel-Ray and lots and lots of half sour pickles, sour tomatoes, and health salad for us to dive into when we are done. Oh, yeh, while you are on East Houston Street, maybe you can also pick up a few dozen Yonah Schimmel Knishes; just the good stuff, none of the yippy dippy blueberry or chocolate crap?"

"You knew the mileage down to the second decimal point?" the secretary mused.

"I had some time to prepare. You know, CNN has a bureau here too! I knew you would call; I was only surprised at how long it took you to make the call. 'Pride goeth before destruction,' isn't that what your bible says, Mr. Secretary?"

The secretary began to respond but heard a click on the other end of the line.

As so many times before during their turbulent relationship, Abimelech Böhmer had the last word.

Chapter 7

Tuesday, December 25, 2018 – 8:04 a.m.
42nd floor penthouse apartment, the Crystal Palace, Collins Avenue, Miami Beach, Florida

Grinning from ear to ear, Sister Joan tossed the Miami Herald on top of the other morning papers which were scattered across the floor. Each had a banner headline about the previous night's explosion in Atlanta and claimed to have exclusive insight into the search for the perpetrators. Sister Joan scanned a few of the articles ... read every word of others ... at one point, she threw up her hands and howled with anger to no one in particular, "typical sob story drivel ... senseless, idiotic hogwash. They have it all wrong, as usual. They cry their crocodile tears for a few forgettable John and Mary Smiths — the useless nobodies — when they *should* be weeping for the inherent wrongs in their system. No problem ... soon they will get the message. Fools, every one of them, merely empty headed fools ... simply ... clueless. Well, if it takes blood and guts in the streets to get your attention, I am happy to accommodate."

She picked up the remote control, turned on the television, quickly switching from station to station. *The hair spray brigade isn't any better than their print clown cousins*, she thought. She listened as the CNN anchor, Dan something or other, was speaking in front of what had been the front of the movie theater but now was a holiday mural on a wall of 4 x 8 plywood boards quickly erected and painted during the night.

"Sources close to the investigation," the talking head said excitedly, "told this reporter that this Christmas Eve Massacre was clearly a terrorist attack, absolutely no question about it. Quote: 'We will make them pay for this evil example of fanatical slaughter and mindless carnage,' unquote. What now remains to be learned is exactly which foreign terrorist group will be claiming credit and when their next attack will come our way."

"You will not have to wait very long," Sister Joan said as she lowered the sound to a barely audible hum. "You don't know what slaughter and carnage is yet. This little appetizer generated just a hundred or so deaths, the next one will be thousands of deaths – maybe tens of thousands of deaths. You have just had a Christmas Eve to remember ... next I will give you a memorable New Year's Day as well. Then first you will know what real slaughter and carnage is. And even that will be but a small example of what still lies ahead. Before I am through you will look upon last night's little event as the calm before the storm."

She pushed her breakfast plate aside and reached for the next newspaper on the stack.

Scully walked into the room and began reaching for the newspapers on the floor.

"Don't take them away," the woman said, "I like looking at them. Last night I breathed fire on them, Scully. I want to enjoy every little bit of the afterglow."

"What do you think they will do next?" Scully asked.

"Who cares?" Sister Joan shot back, "Whatever they do I will be many steps ahead."

"Aren't you concerned that they will come after us with everything they have?" Scully persisted.

"Oh, Scully, ye of little faith; they will do what they always do when something beyond their wildest imagination comes upon them. They will collectively wring their little hands ... shed enormous crocodile tears ... surround the area with piles of flowers and candles and teddy bears and tear stained notes — even though they had absolutely no interest in these so-called victims a day earlier. Sure, they will talk tough and threaten to get even, but first they will pile on the cuddly teddy bears and quickly wilting flowers and sob sister notes." she laughed, "tear-stained stupid little messages that no one will ever read, and candles, plenty of candles that will light nothing and just pollute the air. It will be another good day for local florists, toy stores, candle and greeting card merchants. Eventually all of that will be bulldozed away so that the huddled masses can return to their thoughtless, hopeless little lives.

Scully motioned to the television set, "They seem to have sanitized the scene overnight."

"Same difference, Scully, their *so-called* crime scene experts must have already found the clues that I left for them. They will continue to pore over all of the surveillance camera footage and scratch their little heads wondering how many people were involved. They will run in little circles until I give them some more to consider." She stretched out on a long couch and added, "Seven plagues, I promised them seven plagues. The Lord she is angry and she will make that anger felt. Last night's little lesson — my small disruption in their otherwise meaningless little lives — demonstrated just a small fraction of what is in store for them after *they* tried to sully my name; soon they will realize that they serve at my pleasure. I will give them a few more days to profile me and then I will give them even more little tidbits to confuse and rattle them again before the next episode. Their pain is my gratification. Soon, very soon, they will see that last night was only the beginning."

Scully stared at the petite, fashionably dressed woman. He knew better than to press the issue but that did not stop him from thinking that last night's attack most certainly woke a tiger from a sound sleep, and now that it was awake it could not possibly rest until it discovered and destroyed the source of its pain. The powers that be will now move heaven and earth to stop the one or ones responsible for the horror Sister Joan had just left on the streets of Atlanta. Scully knew it and couldn't understand how Sister Joan didn't or wouldn't or seemingly refused to acknowledge the possibility. *They will find us all right*, Scully thought, *may take them a while, but they will find us and get their revenge for the dead and injured. It couldn't possibly end any other way.*

"How are you doing on hacking into the Las Vegas power grid for our next bit of excitement? I promised them another plague and it will be fun to see how they handle total darkness."

"I'll be ready well before next month Sister Joan."

"Oh, did I tell you next month? I meant to say next Tuesday, New Year's Day."

"That's impossible," Scully stuttered.

"Now, Scully, you certainly know that nothing is impossible. Not if you believe. You do believe, don't you?" She stared at him, "Just make certain we are ready and in place for the *next* example of what death and destruction *they* have brought onto themselves. That wretched fisher woman hasn't seen the last of me, not by a long shot. I'll show her what losing a battle with me *really* means. Meanwhile, make sure I am not disturbed. I need my rest."

Scully spoke barely above a whisper, "Can't we wait a little until we see how they respond to last night?"

She glared at him, "The decision has been made, Scully. I can't go back on my commitment. 'Seven plagues'; I promised them seven plagues. You aren't getting cold feet are you?"

"I thought the next one was the last one for at least a little while," he said meekly.

"I had a change of mind," she said, still glaring at him.

"Have you chosen the locations for the last five plagues?" he asked.

"In time, Scully, you will learn all you need to know in good time. Now, run along won't you? I need my rest, we have a lot of the Lord's work ahead of us."

Scully stood motionless, then flashed a broad smile and quietly picked up and carried away the breakfast dishes. *It can't possibly end any other way*, Scully kept thinking as he walked out of the room.

*****

Although Sister Joan shared more with Scully than any other human being, there were things that she kept to herself for she was the only person she really ever trusted completely. She waited for him to leave the room, and then she walked toward the door, locked it, and went to her custom made French Antique Style Carved Writing Desk. She removed her gold choker and using the end of the clasp as a key she unlocked the top right side draw and gently removed it from the desk.

The drawer was made with a three-quarter inch high false bottom. She emptied the drawer, turned it upside down, and again using the specially designed end clasp of the gold choker, she released the false bottom. Inside was a cloth bag, rimmed with black fringes and a huge plastic daisy attached to its zipper pull. It contained a few flat documents ... assorted photographs ... 72 crisp new $100 bills ... nineteen D level diamonds classified as to Color, Clarity, Cut, and Carat Weight and to be internally and externally flawless by the Gemological Institute of America. There were also several perfectly counterfeited passports. This was her emergency survival kit. When she was away from the apartment — even if was for just a few hours — the bag went with her, strapped to a leg or arm, depending upon the outfit of the day. If need be, the emergency survival kit could fund most any escape of her choice and be more than enough to keep her in the manner to which she had become accustomed for the rest of her life. Unfortunately, she had been forced to sell off a couple of the stones over the last year or so, first to pay for the lawyers who defended her so well in the murder case and then to live on because fewer donations were coming in since her murder trial and she refused to reduce her living expenses accordingly. She expected that by the second or third step of her *Doomsday Schedule*, enough people would return to her ministry because of the fears such acts will create, enabling her to stop withdrawing anymore from the survival fund. *Time will tell*, she thought.

Also in the bag was a legal sized envelope. She removed eight 3 by 5 index cards, from the envelope, put them to her lips and then made the sign of the cross with them, and finally placed them on top of the desk. Along the top of each card were the words, "In the name of the Lord - My Doomsday Manifesto," followed by a different Roman numeral on each card.

The top card had a huge "X" written across it. The words "to do" were crossed out and replaced with the word, "failed."

> *I — Thanksgiving Day, November 22nd, 2018 — Take back the prize given to the one who manipulated the innocent minded into confessing to a crime he may not have committed. Partial payback for the years of shame and humiliation I have endured because of an ancestor I never knew anything about except how he died.* ***It is mine to avenge, I will repay, sayeth the Lord — Romans 12:19***
> ***Place: Pueblo, Colorado — Remedy: Take back the Devil's Spoils***

To do: speak to Arturo to arrange for the liberation of the ceremonial handgun
Budget: $5,000, travel and incidental

The next card she held up and kissed, and then she crossed out the words, "To do," and replaced them with, "DONE TO PERFECTION."

II — Christmas Eve, December 24th 2018 — The world now celebrates the Lord's Birth by further enriching the money lenders & trinket merchants. I will change that forever. ***I will send down a thunderstorm of hail and fire — Exodus 9:13***
Place: Atlanta, Georgia — Remedy: A GREAT BOMB
To do: I will handle personally. (After last month's debacle in Colorado I will make this a success.) Have Arturo supply a ready to ignite explosive
Budget: $160,000 for bomb & incidentals + $50,000 for Arturo *she picked up a pen and in the margins, she wrote, "Warn Arturo that he better not screw this one up."*

She reviewed the remaining cards:

III — New Year's Day, January 1st 2019 — out of the darkness that I can and will create will come a new respect for the light — I am the light! ***Darkness for three days — Exodus 10:21-29***

Place: Las Vegas, Nevada — Remedy: PLAGUE OF DARKNESS
To do: Have Scully hire/supervise disruptors; access power facilities; supply all necessary equipment; install someone in local power authority office
Budget: $250,000 for access, personnel, travel & incidentals + $50,000 for hush money and protection

IV — Super Bowl number 53 — February 3rd 2019 — Football, the new religion, celebrating warlike actions by some while others overindulge, spread out lazily, gorge themselves — eating and drinking to excess until they simply cannot move. ***Water into blood — Exodus 7:14-24***
Place: Atlanta, Georgia — Remedy: POISIN FOOD & DRINK AT GAME
To do: Have Scully hire/supervise necessary personnel; personally scout out area; install someone inside of the stadium food service operation
Budget: $200,000 for access, personnel, travel & incidentals + $150,000 for hush money and protection

V — Valentine's Day — February 14th 2019 — A day set aside for, by, and of the greeting card industry. I choose Las Vegas — a city built to honor Sodom and Gomorrah — for our blessed revenge against power, fame, lust and the

trafficking of human flesh for money. ***Death of the firstborn — Exodus 11:1-12:36***
Place: Las Vegas, Nevada — Remedy: CYONIDE GAS INTO NURSERIES
To do: (Much too important to delegate, I will handle this one personally)
Budget: $250,000 for gas pellets, air duct access, assorted, travel & incidentals + $250,000 for hush money and protection

VI — St. Patrick's Day — March 17th 2019 – What was originally a religious feast day is now a reason to carouse, drink until drunk, shun work & responsibilities — ***whose end is destruction, whose god is their appetite, and whose glory is in their shame, who set their minds on earthly things — Philippians 3:19***
Place: Savannah, Georgia — Remedy: INJECT COMMERCIAL CHICKENS WITH DISEASE
To do: Finalize purchase of Marek's disease serum from Ukrainian; hire German couple to work disease into water tanks; (they cannot be permitted to live after work is completed)
Budget: $25,000 for serum + $100,000 for personnel, travel & incidentals + $150,000 for hush money and protection

VII – Federal Income Tax Day – April 15th 2019, dedicated to the tax collector; greed, like lust and gluttony, sins of excess, made lawful by

government ... theft by decree ... ***They have no sense of shame. They live for lustful pleasure and eagerly practice every kind of impurity – Ephesians 4:19***
Place: Los Angeles, California — Remedy: **NUCLEAR PELLETS IN RESERVOIR**
To do: Make final payment for fusion materials; final payment to Bulgarian, need 1 additional person, (the resulting radiation will probably get them but if it doesn't, they cannot be permitted to live after their work is completed)
Budget: $21,000,000 for fusion materials, assorted hardware, travel & incidentals + $2,500,000 for hush money and protection

VIII — Easter Sunday — April 21st 2019 — DOOMSDAY CLIMAX — Resurrection Sunday, meant to be a festival and holiday celebrating the resurrection of Jesus from the dead. ***But they did not believe the women, because their words seemed to them like nonsense — Luke 24:11*** *I'll show them nonsense!*
Place: Philadelphia Mint – Remedy: HEAT PRODUCING BOMB — MELT THE COINAGE
To do: Finalize acquisition from Russian military Colonel Chichornyey; (he cannot be permitted to live after delivery)

Budget: $500,000 for device, personnel, travel & incidentals + $500,000 for hush money and protection

*****

"Just six to go," she said proudly as she put the cards back into the envelope.

Chapter 8

Wednesday, December 26, 2018 — 9:22 a.m.
Secluded area at outskirts of the Atlanta Airport

Abimelech Böhmer notified his prime minister that he was about to turn the field hospital over to the local Atlanta medical team more than half an hour ahead of schedule. "Don't gloat, Abi, we still need them more than they need us."

The prime minister hung up and then placed his call to the American president.

"Good morning, Madam President," the prime minister said.

"Boker Tov *Good Morning*," the president said, "Ma Nishma *How are you*?"

"I didn't know you spoke Hebrew," the prime minister said.

She laughed, "I don't, but I did pick up a few snippets during my many visits to your country. I felt that it couldn't hurt to do so."

"No, it couldn't hurt," he repeated. "I wanted to officially inform you that our disaster relief team is ready to turn over the field hospital to your medical team in Atlanta."

"Thank you, Mr. Prime Minister. We appreciate your help in this matter."

"It is the least we could do for our oldest and most supportive ally," he said.

"Have you heard anything to lead you to believe that this is the first of more to come?" she asked.

"We don't think this is something from *the usual suspects*," he said.

"Our people have come to the same conclusion," she said.

"We live in interesting times," he said, "Tzeteh' Leshalom VeShuveh' Leshalom *Go in peace and return in peace*, that's the proper Hebrew expression to a woman."

"Too interesting for me, some days. Tzeth'a Leshalom VeShuvh'a Leshalom *Go in peace and return in peace*. If I'm correct, that is the proper Hebrew expression to a man," she said, and then disconnected the call.

As the prime minister hung up he thought, *phony Arab lover*.

The president clicked off the phone, turned to Mindee Danielle and said, "What a sugary sweet phony ... he works the Jewish lobby and Congress against me like a dyed in the wool Republican, and then is all sweetness and light to my face."

*****

The president picked up her cell phone and scrolled through the list of saved phone numbers. She stopped when she came to Abimelech Böhmer's personal cell number and hit dial.

"Why good morning, Madam President," Abi said sweetly.

"Ever the charmer, Abi," she said, "We go back a very, very long time Abi. We each know enough about the other to sink any, and all future ambitions."

"Now, now, Madam President."

"Don't now, now, me, Abi. I know what good you have and can still do; I also know what bad you are capable of. I also know that you have the need to *play* cat and mouse with those you feel have hurt you in some way."

"I would never hurt you, Madam President."

"I am not talking about me and you know it. I am talking about Fritz. Whatever you may think he has done to you or not done for you he is my Secretary of Homeland Security and this is *not* the time for you to add to his pain. Do we understand each other?"

"Fritz is a big boy, Madam President. Don't you think he can fight his own battles?"

"He is fighting a different battle right now and I need him to be fully, totally, entirely focused on this current battle. Do we understand each other?"

"Now ..."

She interrupted him, “I seem to remember a warm night in the Aria Hotel in Budapest. There was an almost empty bottle of Pálinka on the table. We were having a long and heated argument about the coming election in Israel and you ...”

“I will not add to your secretary’s anguish ... at this time,” he quickly said.

“Look Abi, if there aren’t statutes of limitations for such things there should be. Enough is enough. Let it rest. I want your word of honor that you will give Fritz your very best now and in the future.”

“You know Madam President, you are one tough broad.”

“Pass it on. I need all the positive advertising I can get.”

She hung up and smiled. “If he could cook I might have married him.”

“In that case I would imagine that you would have been the elected leader of Israel instead of the United States,” her chief of staff said.

“That would have been too much power even for me,” the president said.

They both laughed.

Chapter 9

Wednesday, December 26, 2018 — 9:29 a.m.
New emergency complex on the outskirts of the Atlanta Airport

Abimelech Böhmer was packing up to return to Israel when the secretary walked over to him.

"Good job, Abi. Thank you." He held out his hand to the Israeli, but the other man just continued to pack.

"Are you going to eat anything from the deli? Your people have been enjoying it."

Abi turned to face the secretary. "There is a lot of *stuff* between us, Fritz. I am committed to put it all aside, but that doesn't make small talk with you easy for me."

"Don't be a jerk all your life, Abi. I can't walk away from all of that baggage so easily either — but can't you call a short truce for one meal?"

Without any emotion on his face, Abi said, "Maybe for one meal."

"See, that didn't hurt, did it," the secretary said, "Or is it just the thought of a good corned beef sandwich?"

"The corned beef in Israel is pretty good as well. Actually, it was the thought of a real Yonah Schimmel knish," Abi said.

*****

Abi ate quickly and stood to leave. The secretary motioned for the Israeli to sit back at the makeshift table. "I'd like you to stay a bit longer."

"Okay, another few minutes," Abi said.

"No, I was thinking a few days, maybe a week or two. I'd like you to take part in the investigation."

The Israeli did not expect this and it showed on his face. "I really have to get back, Fritz."

"I think you can help. This isn't an easy request for me to make Abi, but I think you could help, and that is why I am asking. If the situation were reversed, you must know that I would put the past aside and do whatever I could."

"I'm flattered," Abi finally said, "But ..."

"But nothing, stop thinking about revenge and put on your national security hat," the secretary said, "we both know that this isn't the act of a traditional terrorist – we have a very dangerous criminal or group of criminals on our hands and need to think out of the box. You can help."

They were both quiet now, waiting for the other to break the silence. Each of these war-weary men were experienced enough to know that the next one to speak, loses.

Ivy Chan walked by and sat down. "Nothing like a deli sandwich to attract old friends," she said. They both stared at her, "So maybe not old friends," she said.

"This is a private discussion, Miss," Abi said, dismissively.

"Allow me to introduce you to someone who is far wiser than you and I put together," the secretary said, "This is Ivy Chan."

"And this is *still* a private conversation," Abi said.

Ivy smiled, "With all due respect Tat aluf Böhmer, there are no private discussions in this complex. Allow me to remind you that as of the latest count, 62 people have died, 19 of these were between the ages of 4 months and 14 years of age. Many people are rushing to this complex, putting everything on hold in order to concentrate on identifying – and catching – the fiend behind all of this mayhem before he or she or they can generate even more misery. I respectfully suggest that you do the same."

"Have you been eavesdropping?" the secretary asked.

She smiled, "If you haven't yet or do not plan to ask the Brigadier General to join the investigation, I will have to wonder who is appearing today claiming to be the Secretary of Homeland Security that I know and respect."

Abi stared at the diminutive woman. "And who are you?" he asked dismissively.

"I don't matter," Ivy said. "What does matter right now, with all due respect, is that both of you get to work; there is a small army of professionals waiting to be led."

“You may think that you have been up against powerful forces before but until you go a round or two with this woman, you ain’t seen nothin’ yet,” the secretary said.

“And I have nothing to say about this?” Abi asked, indignantly.

“You certainly should have as much to say about this as those poor victims in the theater did,” Ivy said.

The Israeli stood slowly and said, “I guess I can stay for a day or two.”

Chapter 10

Wednesday, December 26, 2018 — 9:53 a.m.
42nd floor penthouse apartment,
the Crystal Palace, Collins Avenue,
Miami Beach, Florida

A very nervous Scully and a jubilant Sister Joan were sitting around a small café table on her terrace.

"Just five more days of planning and then *poof*, there go the lights over Las Vegas," she said triumphantly.

"Please consider waiting just a couple of weeks, what do we have to lose?"

She put her hands on his shoulders and pressed down, hard, "We have been over this too many times, Scully, do I have to question your commitment?"

"Of course, I am committed. I am committed to you and always have been, but this is different. This could put us both in a high security prison for the rest of our lives. I'm not all that concerned about my life, I'm an old man, I have already lived my life, maybe a few times over, but you, you are still in the prime of your life. You have accomplished so much ... you have acquired so much ... you are loved by so many ... you have so much to lose. Why would you risk all of this?"

"The Metcalf sniper attackers still haven't been caught, and that was more than five years ago. They showed how easy it is to play havoc with the power grid. What makes you think we aren't at least as good as they were? When they shot out the transformers, that system was down for 27 days — *27 days*! I realize that there are more safeguards today than there were in those more innocent days, but even if we put them in darkness for a few hours, we will create enough havoc to make them fear our next move. Can you not see the fear we will inspire? Can you not visualize how our collections will jump if a major city loses its electricity for an hour or two or maybe even a few days?"

"First of all, that was Silicon Valley — this would be Las Vegas — there is still plenty of mob muscle in Las Vegas. Silicon Valley sent guys in suits and ties to investigate, the Vegas hotels will be sending *made men*."

"Since when did you turn into such an old lady? Nothing ventured, nothing gained." She stood up and leaned against the railing. She always found it soothing to stare down at the people walking along Collins Avenue. They looked so small from this high up. *No worries little specs,* she thought, *I, the Lord, am watching over you.*

The pains in her head were beginning to come back. That always meant that the voices would soon return. *I don't want to disappoint the voices.*

She turned back to face Scully, "I expect you to do as you are told," she said sternly. She picked up her Kahlua and Cream. Her hand was shaking, she quickly returned the glass to the table and some of her drink spilled. Scully quickly moved to wipe the spill. "No, do not touch it," she yelled. "It is there for a purpose. Everything is there for a purpose."

Then, in an instant, her tone completely changed, "You know, Scully, you used to be more fun." She picked up her drink again, this time her hand was steady. She reached over and playfully pressed the glass against his bald spot and then calmly walked inside, leaving him to think about what she was expecting him to do.

She has become certifiable, he thought.

Chapter 11

Sunday, December 30, 2018 — 7:43 p.m.
ICE Field Office, Ted Turner Dr. SW, Atlanta

It was now almost a week since the bombing and each of the ones in charge of the investigation knew that they had hit a wall. Still unanswered was who — or why?

The Homeland Security Secretary initially chose the Atlanta U.S. Immigration & Customs Enforcement Agency office to be the official nerve center and his primary headquarters during the investigation into what had quickly become known as the "Christmas Eve Bombing." However, he spent most of the last week, a series of 18 to 20 hour days, at the newly created field hospital/morgue and crime scene reconstruction site on the outskirts of the Atlanta airport.

It was almost eight o'clock, less than an hour since his last conversation with the president. She was not happy with the lack of progress and told him so. But what could he or any of the seasoned professional investigators do that they had not done? It didn't help that the original crime scene was trampled beyond belief by the National Guard, but they all knew that it wasn't a lack of clues that was holding them back as much as the lack of determining the *who* and understanding the *why* of this manmade disaster. What could possibly be the reason for this human and physical destruction?

He walked into the Atlanta ICE office in hopes that he could quietly review the latest updates and see something he had missed during the many previous reviews.

Sitting alone at one of the desks was Ivy Chan.

He walked up to her and slumped into a guest chair by her desk.

Ivy was his first and only choice to be his emergency chief of staff for the Atlanta investigation. Ivy already headed up the Georgia Department of Human Services and had been the long-standing liaison between local and state law enforcement departments and the U.S. Department of Homeland Security. She was well respected within the law enforcement community, and had built a solid reputation for calmly and effectively handling whatever was tossed her way; somehow, she always came through.

When she reached the age at which retirement was mandatory, the secretary of Homeland Security at the time said that even though she more than earned the right to retire, he considered her to be far too valuable to be permitted to leave. A special bi-partisan bill was quickly passed by the state legislature and was just as quickly signed by the governor, exempting her from mandatory retirement until further notice or until *she* decided that she no longer could adequately fill the position. When the current secretary took over, one of his first official acts was to call Ivy to tell her that he didn't agree with much of what his predecessor had done while in charge of the department, with one glaring exception — his having fought to keep her on the job. The new secretary told Ivy that he was looking forward to working with her in the challenging weeks and months ahead. Neither realized at the time *just* how challenging those days were going to be.

Tired and weary, slumped in the side chair, he said, "We are missing something, I feel it in my bones. I don't know what it is but I do know that when we finally see whatever *it* is, we are all going to slap our foreheads and ask how we could have been so stupid to miss the underlining reason for all of this. But as much as I keep thinking about this mess on our hands, nothing seems to stick out."

"You're not alone, Fritz. None of us can see it either," she said.

"Let's start from the beginning," he said, "a call to a Richmond, Virginia, based radio talk show. Why didn't he call an Atlanta show? There certainly are plenty of them; he could have had the ear of Atlanta from the start; and then an even bigger question, why Atlanta at all?"

"Maybe he didn't want our ear from the start," she said.

"So he calls Norfolk, Virginia, of all the places he could have chosen ... and on Christmas Eve? Why here and now?"

*****

By 10 p.m., the two decided to break for dinner. "Maybe the fresh air will spark something new," he said.

One of the few eating places within walking distance still open on a Sunday night was a dingy little diner. Although they were the only customers, they opted to take seats at a back table by the window. They told the waitress to bring whatever could be put together in the shortest amount of time. She suggested grilled cheese sandwiches and they each said okay. He ordered a large Diet Coke and she asked for a cup of tea.

"Let's begin again," he said after the waitress walked away, "A call to a Richmond, Virginia, based radio talk show; a lot of meaningless small talk and then he drops the ax. Why?"

"No," Ivy broke in, "this time, let's start from the end and work backwards."

"Okay," he said, "a bomb goes off in a packed movie theater on Christmas Eve, now what?"

"I would like to make a suggestion," she said, "I would like to bring in someone who I have been following for quite some time."

"Sure, at this point I'm open for anyone or anything."

"It's a really unorthodox suggestion," she said.

"Orthodox hasn't gotten us very far up to this point. I am open to anything."

"I would have made this suggestion several days ago, but I held back because I know that it will put you in a difficult light. Wanda will fight it all the way," she said.

"If you think it could help, let's do it. I'll handle the *fisher woman,*" he said.

Chapter 12

66 years earlier ...
Thursday, April 10, 1952 — 11:13 p.m.
Tangshan, People's Republic of China

Ivy Chan was born Man-Yee Chan, in the city of Tangshan, in Northeast Hebei province, China, a little more than 90 miles east by southeast of Beijing. Her parents and four brothers worked a small parcel of land just outside of town where they planted wheat and raised chickens. In addition, her father and her oldest brother were active in the town's local governing board and even though they never tried to benefit from their political connections, they did enjoy a somewhat higher status and standard of living than their relatives and neighbors.

Man-Yee was their fifth child and only daughter. The Chans held out little promise for their new offspring: "After all," her father insisted, "she was just a girl. We can't count on her to ever be able to take over the farming and unless she marries well, she'll never be able to support us in our old age."

No one in Ivy's immediate family had ever been more than 15 miles away from the place of their birth. Her father and mother — almost 30 years apart in age — shared a respectful and caring relationship almost from the moment they were first introduced to each other, which was the Sunday before they were to be wed.

Ivy's mother was a devoted Catholic and when time permitted, counseled others in her faith. Ivy's father was what their minister referred to as a "reluctant Sunday visitor" with four passions — his family, his farm, his work with the local council, and American movie star, Steve McQueen ... but not always in that order.

From well before dawn until the sun set, every day but Sunday, the family worked their fields, served their community, and seemed to live each moment to love God and care about and for each other.

Both her father and her brother worked tirelessly to bring the community's problems to the attention of the other town leaders which made them somewhat of an irritant for the other members of the council and super heroes to their neighbors.

The name they chose for their baby girl was *Man-Yee,* meaning intelligent child — "She was intelligent enough to be born *after* four brothers, who would help tend the fields and someday care for us and maybe even her," her father said when her mother suggested the name for their new baby. Her mother also gave her the anglicized name *Ivy* because she thought it would be easier to pronounce and remember when her daughter attended Catholic grade and high schools.

They might not have expected very much from Man-Yee, but soon they had reason to change their minds. From the moment she could walk and talk, she could also reason. Man-Yee Chan became the "go to" for friends and relatives alike when they needed judgment free, common sense advice. Somehow, just voicing their problems to her enhanced their ability to better understand what they needed to do next. She was definitely a more mature and thoughtful person than anyone of her contemporaries, and often seemed to have more intellectual curiosity than some of the other adults in the community.

Just two and a half years after the Chinese Communist leader Mao Zedong declared the creation of the People's Republic of China, the local governing boards that quickly moved to support Mao's forces enjoyed slightly more independence. Man-Yee's parents and brother were among the local holdovers during the early rounds of internal power struggles. As long as the national leaders were emphasizing local self-sufficiency, the Chan family had whatever it needed; but eventually the family was also caught up in the country's political skirmishes. Unlike some of their counterparts who were either killed or sent away to labor camps when the national party leaders decided to bring all decision-making powers to the central committee, Man-Yee's family was encouraged to just return to their farm.

The *Great Famine* which began in the late 1950s, nearly decimated their region. When the family crops could no longer support all of them, seven-year old Man-Yee was sent to live with an aunt in the United States. Her work ethics and natural abilities helped her enormously in her newly adopted country.

At the root of her approach to most any challenge was her deep and unshakable religious faith and love of God. While never doubting the existence of God, she did question the sincerity of those who profited most from organized religion. Growing up in China, she watched her mother and grandmother worship idols made by men; she thought that was sheer foolishness and told them so. Religious training in school encouraged her to look deeper into most of the world's religions, hers as well. Eventually, the prophets, the martyrs, the saints of the early Christian church, became her mentors. She found comfort in the bible and its basic teachings. She did not preach or judge – she merely lived her life in such a way as to set a positive example for those around her.

Being an immigrant in the U.S., new to the culture and language, effectively made her a tougher competitor within the workplace; she saw mediocrity and chose a different path. At first, she worked in the kitchen of her aunt's restaurant; as she grew older she moved out of the kitchen and into the restaurant as a waitress while simultaneously earning a B.A. in Social Sciences with a major in Sociology and minor in Psychology. She moved through a series of additional jobs – often working more than one job at a time – while hunting for more permanent work that could make the best use of her training and abilities. Eventually, she was hired by the Georgia State Department of Social Services. A supervisor recommended her for a pilot program where she would be the liaison between the local community leaders and the Atlanta Police Commissioner. She proved to be an efficient and capable negotiator which led to her current position as head of the Georgia Department of Human Services and liaison between local and state law enforcement departments and the U.S. Department of Homeland Security. This position helped to hone her natural communication and investigative skills. She impressed most everyone who came in contact with her, first because of her Old World work ethic and then by her natural abilities and willingness to contribute fully as a team player.

Life in her new country wasn't easy, and became even more challenging along the way. She married a childhood sweetheart; much of their first years as a married couple were spent apart — she in America, her new husband still in China. Eventually, her husband was able to immigrate to America.

Soon after the birth of their first child, she became a full-time working mom, constantly juggling between domestic responsibilities and work. The challenges forced her to organize, prioritize, and work through tough situations efficiently — typical of Ivy, neither complaining nor failure were ever acceptable options for her.

Shortly after her second child was born, she was diagnosed with cancer. Once again, rather than bring her down, her struggles with the disease and treatments resulted in cherishing life and those around her even more than before. Somehow, what might have destroyed others merely moved her toward an even more positive outlook.

Eventually, the treatment halted the growth of the cancer and the doctors advised her that she might, just might, have beaten it. They then told her to reduce her work load and enjoy the extra time on Earth she had been given.

She considered their advice but as she told her husband and children, "What good is having more time to live my life if I do not live my life to its fullest?"

Chapter 13

Sunday, December 30, 2018 — 10:10 p.m.
700 Block, Royal Street, New Orleans

Will James' eyes were locked onto the entrance to the Green Parrot Gallery D'art in the 700 block of Royal Street in New Orleans' *seamier* part of the city's art district.

As usual, before the start of a stakeout in a city other than his home base, James did two things. First, he paid a courtesy call to the local police commander to avoid the possibility of getting tripped up later by a local beat cop just doing his or her job. The Green Parrot Gallery was in the Fifth Police District. He walked into the station house on North Claiborne Avenue, commanded by Billy Greer, a 23-year veteran of the force and commander of the Fifth District since 2015.

James advised Commander Greer that he would probably be the only one on this surveillance assignment, and that there would only be one surveillance vehicle involved. He gave the commander the make, model, and color of the car, as well as the license plate number. He assured the commander that he and his associates, if more were later assigned here, would honor all local laws and regulations.

The commander asked to see James' identification.

James removed his driver's license from his wallet and placed it on the desk in front of the commander.

"You're from Washington, D.C.," the commander said, "Good; I understand their laws concerning concealed gun carry permits. May I see your permit?"

"I don't have a permit, concealed or otherwise," James said, "I don't own a gun."

"Okay, then let me see your private detective license."

James' face reddened a little. He smiled, and said, "I don't have a private detective license. As you probably know, in Washington, D.C., among other restrictions, you can't have any felony convictions if you apply for a Private Investigation License. I was convicted of a felony, hacking government computer systems."

"Whew," the commander said, "that's a crime all right. If my memory is correct, it is classified as fraud, under the United States Code 18 Section 1030."

James slowly nodded, "Your memory is correct."

"So," the commander said, "Let's start all over. Hi! How are you? Now, who are you and why should I let you stalk one or more of our citizens?"

James smiled.

"You think this is funny?" the commander asked as he reached for the phone.

James took a tattered business card out of his shirt pocket, placed it on the desk in front of the commander and then put his hands up, in mock surrender. “Before you call anyone else, please call the number on this card.”

“What is it,” the commander asked, “a get out of jail card?”

“Something like that.”

“I should tell you that I have a very low tolerance for people who think something like this is a joke.”

“It’s an ‘800’ number, please, just call the number on the card.”

The commander picked up the card; it read “Federal Judge Theo McSimmons.”

“And what will I hear when I dial this number, that I just won the Publisher’s Clearing House Million Dollar prize?” the commander asked, facetiously.

“Commander Greer,” James said, “You’re a serious man, I’m a serious man. Please call the number, he will vouch for me.”

“How does he know you?”

“Before Theo McSimmons was a federal judge — before he was the National Chairman of the Republican Party — he was a lawyer. He was the court-appointed defense lawyer assigned to represent me in the federal computer hacking case.”

"The case you lost resulting in being convicted as a felon?"

"Yes."

"And he will vouch for you?"

"Yes."

"And it should matter to me that he can vouch for you?"

"Yes."

"Why should that matter to me?"

"Because he is a federal judge, and they too have a very low tolerance for people who think something like this is a joke."

About 10 minutes later, Commander Greer shook James' hand and welcomed him to the Fifth District.

Once cleared of any suspicion, a general claim of client confidentiality usually allowed James to keep the specific purpose of his stakeout to himself. This was especially true with local law enforcement officials who sought personal cover so that if anything went wrong, they could always claim that they knew nothing about it. Will James knew all too well that "Ignorance of the Law is No Excuse" only holds true for those without a badge. Because of his rocky start here, James considered telling Commander Greer more about why he was in New Orleans, but then thought better of it and left.

*****

James routinely ran a full scan on all known home or work addresses for the person he was about to shadow, in order to determine how best to hack into any and all computer signals the targeted individuals might be using. What is usually a simple task for James was proving to be surprisingly difficult in this assignment. There seemed to be an impenetrable fire wall surrounding the upper third of the art gallery building. It was as if the bottom two-thirds of the building was separate and distinct from a self-contained upper third.

The last time James ran into such a high degree of obstacles was when he tried to hack into the Department of Defense's system. He was only 16 years old then, but eventually found several back doors into the department's deepest secrets. It cost him six months in prison and made him a hero of the underground hacker community.

When he tried to hack into the Defense Department's system those years before, he eventually found a link which opened it up completely. This was proving to be very different. This time, there was a lack of what he would call a planned sequence. The barriers he encountered here seemed to have been placed at random and were not connected in any way that he could see to the ones before or after. It was a challenge, but eventually he found a way through and into the maze. This process made him wonder if his current target was more than *just* a scamming art dealer. This Arturo Hornedo was becoming more and more interesting to him.

Several weeks earlier, James met with a group of independent artists who told him that they had been cheated by Arturo Hornedo, the owner of the Green Parrot Gallery

D'art. James later confirmed that Hornedo had built a profitable business by scooping up the works of promising young artists. Some of the artworks he accepted on consignment — payment to be made after a sale was finalized, or whenever the mood struck him — which varied from a few weeks to a few months after he had been paid by his clients; occasionally he would dole out small advances of cash or supplies to the few artists who no longer accepted his promise of "I'll make it up to you, later." What he never told the artists, was that he only *purchased* works that were already pre-sold. He had a Rolodex filled with potential buyers willing and able to snap up his new discoveries. Many of his repeat customers were the new generation of American pop entertainers, sport stars, television and movie heartthrobs, so called *personalities* and Chinese, Japanese, and Russian millionaires and billionaires who decorated their offices, mansions, vacation retreats, and mistress's apartments with artifacts that were more interesting because of their over-the-top price tags, than any artistic appeal or possible future resale value. In fact, most of his clients paid little or no attention to the subject matter of the paintings — they sought paintings that met specific measurements or furniture color swatches. He then commissioned young artists to create pictures that met those unique specs. He had learned how to say, "You want red, I will give you red; you want purple, I'll give you purple, you want two feet by 37 inches and I will provide a framed treasure down to the centimeter," in almost a dozen languages and dialects.

Hornedo evaluated each piece and carefully set the price to these buyers and then authenticated the price to be *a steal* compared to the open market value. He was in a unique position where he could both under pay the artists and over charge the buyers. If that was not enough, he also extracted an additional 20 percent *finder's fee* from the buyer as well as his *standard* 27 percent commission from the artist on each transaction.

Generally, beyond the artist and buyer of any given painting, all transactions stayed off the radar. Most sales were consummated over the phone, paid in full by wire transfers to one of his Swiss accounts and the pieces found their way out of the country within hours of the purchase request. Although taxes were collected, they rarely made it back to the local or state or federal agencies in this or the landed country; tax became just another profit center for Hornedo.

Unfortunately for Hornedo, one of the paintings he sold was stolen from the buyer's hotel room the same day it was picked up from his showroom. The Washington Post broke the story as part of its *Traveler's beware* series. The story ran under a three-column headline above the fold on the first page of the Metro section, "Valuable artwork stolen from visiting Japanese businessman," at the top right of the story was a photo of the stolen item. The businessman had snapped a photo of his new *bargain buy* when he was in the showroom, and was able to turn the photo over to the police when he filled out their crime report.

It must have been a slow news week, because within days the story made most of the wire services and eventually was picked up by many local newspapers across the country.

Seymour Maxx's mother cut out the article from her morning newspaper and sent it to her son along with a hand-written note saying that the painting pictured in the news clip looked an awful lot like the one she saw him working on the last time she visited his loft. Maxx realized instantly that it was one of the pieces he gave to Hornedo just a few weeks earlier and which he had been told could *possibly* sell for as much as $75, less of course, Hornedo's commission. When Maxx read that the work had been insured for $4,000, the amount shown on the receipt Hornedo gave to the Japanese businessman, Maxx called Hornedo. Hornedo denied that the piece in the news story was the same one he purchased from Maxx. After an angry back and forth, Hornedo angrily hung up on Maxx.

Maxx talked it over with others in his local artist's community who now believed that they too had been short changed by Hornedo and since none of them — individually or collectively — could put together enough money to hire a lawyer, they decided to try to get the Metro section editor at the Washington Post to help them. Eventually, the story was passed along to Henry Sweet, the Washington Post senior editor who reached out to Will James. Sweet knew James well enough to believe that he might want to help the artists fight for their artistic and commercial rights. He offered James a fee to dig into the matter, "You could help a group of starving artists and this paper at the same time," Sweet told James, "As for me, all I want out of this is to get an interesting story — if there is one to be had."

*****

As always, James began his investigation with a broad web search, touching upon all generally unsecured public, criminal, and financial records on the internet. He quickly identified numerous small scams over the years linked to Hornedo, some going back as far as when Hornedo was only nine years old, although he was never prosecuted for any of them.

There was also a series of unexplained dead bodies along the way, among which were those of his parents and twin sister. Authorities questioned Hornedo, seeming to believe that he might know more about these deaths than he shared with them or might even have been involved in some way with these and other serious crimes over the years, but there was never enough evidence to charge him criminally.

The most meaningful asset that showed up on this search was a co-ownership in a bail bonding business in Puerto Rico with a Mr. and Mrs. Isaiah and Isabella Maravega. The documents showed that Hornedo owned only 2.5 percent of the business but had 100 percent authority to make purchases or expenditures in the business's name. When James then went looking for more information about the Maravegas, the trail hit a brick wall. Both Isaiah and Isabella seemed to begin and end with the bail bond business; *strange*, James thought, *very, very strange, could this have been just a Hornedo alias?*

James could now account for almost every day of Hornedo's life from his birth until July 4, 2000. On that day, the trail stopped, picking up again about 16 months later when he showed up in the art gallery in New Orleans.

Then James began a second series of deeper searches, hacking into confidential banking files and sealed court records, as well as "works in progress" and "dead case files" from local, state, and federal law enforcement agencies and military computer systems across the country. He also trolled through the highly secretive and generally thought to be hacker-proof computerized case files maintained by various foreign law enforcement agencies. These files almost always led to a treasure trove of additional data and could be counted on to fill in gaps and timelines.

James hit pay dirt almost immediately — not with Hornedo's name but under the names Isaiah and Isabella Maravega. Here again, the 2.5 percent ownership/100 percent control arrangement surfaced around a single-level commercial building, coincidentally at the same address as the art gallery in New Orleans and a 99-year lease of a small island off the coast of Bermuda. Both real estate transactions were settled in cash, and totaled just shy of $47 million. James dug as deeply as he could, but could not account for either the source of the money or for the days between July 4, 2000 and October 29, 2001 — about a 16-month period.

After what looked like another dead end, James came across a disgruntled former employee of the art gallery who quickly told James that Hornedo had a secret area built into the top floor of the art gallery. The employee thought it was where Hornedo stored really valuable pieces. He told James that the word among long-time employees was that Hornedo might even have a fully furnished apartment in the upper space so that he could effectively disappear from time to time.

James scouted the area. The sales floor for the gallery was a wide-open space; all public architectural drawings showed the building to be a single level commercially zoned structure — no additional living or working space above or basement below. However, the building's outer height was at least 40 feet taller than the gallery's internal floor to ceiling dimensions suggested. Whether there was a finished or unfinished space above the gallery was not clear but what *was* clear, was that there was more space above the gallery's space, enough to support at least two, possibly three additional levels of livable space.

James tracked down a series of newspaper photos of the street over the years. In the earlier photos Hornedo's building appeared to be dwarfed by nearby buildings. A more recent photo/article about a small manufacturing plant next door to the gallery showed Hornedo's building to be equal in height to the three-story building to its right. James went back into town records to look for construction or renovation permits or any official documents to help explain the sudden height gains of the structure but found nothing.

The employee also told James that Hornedo liked to walk the streets of New Orleans late at night to peek into apartment windows. "Frankly," the former employee said, "he's a real piece of work, that guy. Hey, it ain't no skin off my nose if people fall for his phony charm but the rotten bastard still owes me a couple month's pay."

Hornedo went missing soon after Maxx confronted him on the telephone; that was several weeks ago. Believing that it was only a matter of time before Hornedo surfaced again at the gallery, James began his stakeout about half a block up the street with a clear view of what he believed to be the structure's only way in or out.

*****

Spending days on end shadowing a suspect was not new to James; he actually enjoyed the solitude of an extended stakeout. Usually, during a potentially long drawn-out surveillance such as this promised to be, the back of his car quickly filled up with a collection of empty Diet Coke cans, violently crushed coffee cups and sandwich wrappers, countless empty packages of M&M peanut and double stuff Oreos, and an assortment of empty or almost empty Chinese takeout food containers.

This time was different. He was on a diet of sorts. No calorie counting — just smaller portions and healthier choices. On the first day of the stakeout, James bought a wide variety of health bars and several huge bags of fresh and canned fruit. At least once a year he put himself on a diet, some of the diets showed progress, some didn't, but none so far helped him keep the extra pounds or inches off for more than a few weeks. This time the diet seemed to be working. He had already reduced his waist by a belt buckle hole and was halfway into a second one. Whatever the good it was doing to improve his waistline was more than matched by a worsening of his disposition. Never much of a charmer, his current behavior, especially with those working the closest with him, was making him even more difficult to be around than usual. Both Schless, the one who helped him start the business and Elizabeth, his newest team member, each of whom were always able to reason with him, were now batting zero. The last time they spoke Elizabeth said, "If you don't get off of that diet and soon, I may have to get out my garden shears — and you won't like what I do with my garden shares."

His phone broke the silence; he answered it on the second ring, "Yeh?"

"Hi, Will," said a soft voice on the other end of the line.

"Who is this?" he yelled into the phone, impatiently.

"It's Angela, Will. Have you been watching the news out of Atlanta?"

"I'm on a stakeout, Angela," he barked, "unless you know something that I don't, they don't deliver newspapers to parked cars these days."

"71 people died," she said, ignoring his last response, "27 of these were children."

"I'm sorry, no, I didn't hear about it. I'm also sorry that I bit your head off. Really I am."

"There are also more than 200 people in various nearby hospitals," she continued, "a fair percentage of these are not expected to live through the week." She began to weep, "Not that there could ever be a *good* time for such a tragedy, but it all started on Christmas Eve — Christmas Eve, Will."

He heard her blow her nose, "Oh Will, it just seems to be doubly perverse to have taken place on Christmas Eve." She was sobbing uncontrollably now.

James noticed movement near the Green Parrot but couldn't get himself to break off with his friend in the midst of her obvious pain.

"Please get involved, Will. Please," Angela pressed.

"First of all, I'm nowhere near Atlanta right now; I'm in New Orleans, on a stakeout. You know I would never refuse you or Frank anything ... but this is a really bad time."

"It can't possibly be half as bad a time for you as it is for the many people who have lost their loved ones or for the many others, still fighting for their lives." With that the line went dead.

*****

James compared the photo on his visor with the man sneaking out of the Green Parrot — it was a definite match.

He speed-dialed Angela. She picked up on the first ring. "Okay," he said softly, "give me a few hours and I will give you my full attention. I'll call you back later tonight. Send as much factual data as you can to my care of the 24-hour Western Union office we use here in New Orleans; I will review it all before I call you back." He hung up and stepped out of his car.

The suspect stepped into the powder blue vintage Cadillac sedan. James had pushed a raw baked potato into the Cadillac's exhaust pipe, and attached a small magnetic surveillance device to the inside of the rear bumper on the passenger side to make certain the suspect couldn't jump right in and drive away without allowing him sufficient time to react.

He slowly got out of his car and circled around so that he was close by when the Cadillac backfired. He then continued to walk past the car as he heard a huge popping noise, followed by grinding engine sounds.

He slowly turned back and walked directly towards the driver's window. He gently tapped on the driver's side window, stepped back to reduce any perceived threat by the driver, and then motioned for the driver to roll his window down. The driver just stared ahead.

Speaking loudly enough to be heard through the closed window James said, “I know a little bit about cars, want me to give a quick look under the hood?”

The man continued to ignore James. “Suit yourself,” James said as he began to walk away. The car door opened and the man yelled out, “Sure, that would be great.”

James slowly walked back towards the car, “Release the hood lock and I’ll take a look,” he said, nonchalantly. The man released the hood. James lifted it up and pulled a series of wires towards him, eventually yanking two out – exposing the ends. He said, “Quick, get out of the car, I think it is going to explode.”

As the suspect jumped out of the car James touched the two exposed wires creating a series of sparks.

“You got a phone?” he yelled to the driver, “Quick, call 911 and get to the other side of the street. You are one lucky guy! I think that there might have been some kind of a bomb in that engine – I tried to pull the wires ...”

“You saved my life,” the man yelled back.

“I’m no expert on such things,” James responded, “and it could be nothing at all, but it sure looked like a homemade bomb to me; you must have really pissed someone off, big time.”

The man ran to the other side of the street, breathing heavily, he leaned against a car.

James said, “You’re in no condition to call anyone — I’ll get 911 on the line.” He turned and walked several yards to the left while appearing to dial a number into his phone.

“It’s okay,” the driver shouted to James as he reached for his wallet. “Let me give you a reward for saving my life.” He handed James a $20 bill, then almost as an afterthought, took all of the bills out of his wallet and thrust them into James’ hand. “Here, take this and please, not a word to anyone about this. I don’t want any trouble here.”

“It’s your funeral, man,” James said as he shoved the money into his pocket and started to walk back to his car. He waved to the suspect as he pulled out of the parking space, keeping an eye on the Cadillac from his rearview mirror. He smiled as he watched the suspect rush back into the gallery.

*****

James drove towards the Western Union office to wait for Angela’s wire to come through. On his way, he stopped at an all-night news stand and purchased a few local and out of town newspapers. Returning to the car he skimmed through the headlines, all of which were about the latest news from Atlanta. He cut out the lead story with a Washington Post byline, and then called Henry Sweet at his home. As the phone began to ring, he pulled out his small pad and made a few notes.

Chapter 14

Sunday, December 30, 2018 — 11:13 p.m.
Outside the Crowder Blvd. Western Union office, New Orleans

James called Angela on her secure line. "I scanned some of the latest newspapers and quickly reviewed the information you sent to the Western Union office for me. It's been a week since the bombing — surely, they have zeroed in on some likely suspects by now. What more is known since you and I last spoke?"

"My cousin, Ivy, works for the Atlanta Police Department and is their liaison with the Department of Homeland Security," Angela said, still shaky but more composed than before. "She called me last week, as soon as the news first went public. She arranged for the on-scene investigators to send some of the evidence to our lab by special messenger. As you know, Frank, I, and our senior staff all have Top Secret personal security clearance, and our lab — as a separate business unit — has the very highest level facility clearance from Homeland Security, the Department of Defense, and the CIA. The Homeland Security Secretary quickly gave Ivy his official approval to get our lab involved. We spent the better part of last Monday running a series of tests. Whoever did this is no rank amateur, Will. We were able to identify traces of the primary explosive used, and it is a favorite of the Teehalpen branch of the Chechnya guerillas. They have been at the center of violent separatist uprisings and bloody bomb-related killings for decades. Interpol has identified the trigger mechanism from this bomb as having first surfaced during a series of house arrests involving former KGB operatives from the Ukraine."

"But mainstream Chechnya mujahedin have not traditionally been a direct threat to the United States," James said.

"The lead investigators tend to agree because they don't think this is a foreign terrorist attack. The Chechnyan's might be broadening their interest ... working as independent agents ... I don't know — neither do the teams of professionals who have been working on this for a week now, but what we do know is that the telltale signs of their handiwork was all over this device and *coincidence* is never a comfortable conclusion. Having said that, there hasn't been a second attack since last Sunday night even though both the Atlanta police and Homeland Security fear that this is only the beginning."

"I know what I do well and what others do better, Angela," James said hesitantly, "There can't be very much that I can do to help in something like this. The big boys will be all over this, if they aren't already. They have the muscle and manpower and funding as well as legal and counter terrorist authority to do whatever is necessary. What makes you think they need or would even accept *my* help?"

"Oh, Will, you should know better than most, that those with ultimate power often trample all over the obvious. From what Ivy has told me, the number one concern from the minute the — what did you call them ... *the big boys* ... yes, *the big boys*, from the moment the big boys got involved, their primary concern was how best to prepare their interview poses and public statements. The state's concerns about negatively affecting the holiday tourist season may already have contaminated the crime scene. It's a full week later and there is so much political infighting that they haven't even gotten to the nuts and bolts of the investigation yet. Ivy fears that by the time they do, the trail will be ice cold; hey, a week has come and gone, the trail may already be stone cold," Angela said.

"Tell me what you think I can do?" James said.

"Ivy isn't a political bureaucrat – she is dedicated and honest and has zero confidence in those currently in charge of the investigation. From what she told me, the one heading up the investigation is a strong headed woman with the governor's mansion on her mind. She sees this as her key to becoming the next governor if not senator from Georgia."

"So maybe her ambition will spur her on to getting the job done," he said.

"If only that were true," Angela said, "But this person has a long history of headline seeking over team building, and Ivy is convinced that it will take a cohesive team effort to solve this one."

"Who is heading up the investigation, locally?" James asked.

"It's Wanda Parent ..."

"The *fisher woman*?" James asked.

"The one and only," Angela said, "That woman is all show and no go; which is the key to certain failure in this investigation."

"You may or may not know," James broke in, "but I am *not* a stranger to the *fisher woman.*"

"No, I didn't know that," Angela said.

"Yeh, she had just joined the Washington, D.C., police force when she arrested a homeless couple and accused them of breaking into a supermarket one night. Although I never knew for sure, it certainly looked like she may have known that they were innocent, but went gung-ho against the couple anyway. I helped prove that they were innocent. Instead of taking her losses and moving on, she then came after me."

"So she is braver than I thought," Angela said.

"Brave or not, we tangled back and forth until the Washington Post did a series of editorials against her about what they called "out of control citizen harassment." It created such a public furor, that she was asked to turn in her resignation in exchange for a guarantee that they would take no disciplinary action against her. They threw in a promise to give her a positive letter of recommendation," James said.

"Well, that was then and this is now. If you can help in any way to solve this, you would almost certainly be saving lives. In the interest of time and to insure the up to-the-minute accuracy of the information, let me put you directly in touch with Ivy."

"Okay," he responded, hesitantly, "but how do I introduce myself to her?"

Angela laughed, "That won't be necessary, she already knows more about you than I do."

"Excuse me?" James responded.

"Think back to when you first met Frank and me, when U.S. Immigration wanted to deport me back to China when I had remained in the country illegally after my visa expired all of those years before. Ivy was the first person I went to for advice. Ivy has been the first one I and my sisters have always gone to whenever we were faced with a problem we couldn't resolve on our own. She was the one who suggested that I seek *you* out when I faced deportation."

"But I don't think I know her," James said in amazement.

"Well, she definitely knew you, and I thank the Lord each and every day that she did," Angela said.

"You know that local police rarely permit an outsider to just waltz in and poke around in one of their cases," James said.

"This was never a local police matter," she said, "The entire Homeland Security apparatus has been in control of the investigation since the blast."

"Even worse," he shot back, "the Feds generally like me being involved in one of their investigations less than the locals do."

"You would be working with Ivy. She reports directly to the Secretary of Homeland Security on this."

"And the Secretary of Homeland Security is okay with my coming in?" he asked.

"If he weren't, we would not be having this conversation right now," she said.

"Okay," he said, shaking his head, "give me your cousin's contact information and I'll call her, but first I will have to arrange for someone to replace me here."

*****

As soon as he disconnected from Angela, James called Schless, who picked up on the third ring. "Hi, how are things in 'The Big Easy'?" Schless asked.

"A little complicated, I need you out here as soon as you can break free," James said.

"Want to share what's going on with the rest of the class?" Schless asked.

"I got an emotional call from Angela and I think I am going to have to change horses and get to Atlanta."

"'Menlo Park' Angela?" Schless asked, in amazement.

"The same," James said.

"Angela, who with her husband Frank, runs the CIA's favorite research lab?" Schless persisted.

"Hey," James quickly broke in, "we are on an unsecure public phone line here – stick to *happy talk*."

"Secure or unsecure, 'Menlo Park' Angela may be the calmest person I've ever met; I didn't think she got emotional about anything," Schless said.

"Well, I agree that she is one of the more stable human beings around, but I tell you that she did get emotional tonight – very emotional – and that is why I chose to check it out as soon as I could. Look, you know me well enough to be able to accept as a given that I wouldn't just switch screens and run off without a very good reason. Angela asked me to go to Atlanta; I told her I was on an assignment and she said that this thing in Atlanta couldn't wait. Pick up a current newspaper or turn on the radio or TV and you will see what she wants me to get involved in."

"Stop it you two," Schless said.

"Who are you talking to?" James asked.

"I have my two neighbor kids in the back seat and they are picking at each other *again*," Schless said, annoyed.

"What are they doing in the back of your car?" James asked.

"I told you, they're acting like siblings."

"I got that, what I didn't get is why they are in the back seat of your car at this very moment."

"Oh, we share this love for country music and I promised them I would let them see the Grand Ole Opry for themselves. But leave that alone right now. You called for a purpose, tell me the purpose."

"Take me off of speaker."

Schless pulled along the side of the road and stopped the car. "I need the two of you to be very quiet and respectful to each other, at least until I finish this call. Okay?"

"Okay," Stella said.

"I need to hear two distinct 'okays,'" Schless said.

"Okay from me too," Mason said.

Schless picked up the phone and said, "Okay, you are off of speaker."

"Have you been following the Christmas Eve bombing in the news?" James asked.

"Are you talking about last week's bombing of the movie theater in Atlanta?" Schless asked.

"The very same — and remember we are not on a secure line," he cautioned, "It is in all of the newspapers, a lot of deaths and injuries and the ones in charge of the investigation are saying that it could just be an example of what is yet to come."

"I have been following it in the papers here, terrible stuff," Schless said.

"This tragic event in Atlanta is clearly a game changer," James said.

"It is mine, give it back."

"What was that?" James asked.

"Stop it or I will turn this car around," Schless said, "It is two young people about to miss out on an event of their lifetime if they don't settle down. Now, back to you; what about the art dealer in New Orleans?"

"As far as this case here in New Orleans, I don't think the suspect is going anywhere soon," James said.

"I don't know, it really isn't like you to leave an assignment in mid-stream. Promise me that you will end this diet you are on! I think you have got to stop that fruits and roots nonsense of yours and get back to real food. It's changing you in all kinds of strange ways."

"Does everything have to be connected to food with you?" James said.

"I'm just saying that you haven't been the same since you swore off M&M peanuts, double stuff Oreos, and shrimp with lobster sauce; jumping from one assignment to the next on a minute's notice is definitely not like you."

"Are you listening to yourself?" James yelled, "There is one or possibly even more bombers terrorizing a major American city. As we speak I really don't know that I can do anything to help, *but* on the tiny chance that I might, I have to make the effort; you would do the same if you weren't so preoccupied with what I choose to eat or not to eat."

"So let me get this straight, the Feds, your bosom buddies, *not,* are going to love having you work on one of their cases, *not,* because only you can solve it for them? *Maybe, not*! And your diet has nothing to do with this rash of temporary insanity," Schless shot back.

"Hey cut me some slack here," James yelled, "And as far as my diet is concerned, it seems to be working quite well, thank you very much. I'm already down a belt notch and a half. Maybe you should try it."

"Well it hasn't done very much for your *usual* sparkling personality. Frankly, right now we all think that it is your disposition that needs more help than your waistline," Schless said.

"New subject," James said sharply, "I just had a brief conversation with the art dealer here in New Orleans. Actually, I almost blew his car up in front of him. I would guess that will keep him close to home at least for a few days — if not longer."

"You did what?" Schless screamed into the phone.

"Well. Maybe 'blew it up' is a little strong; I created a small fireworks display in his car's engine. The engine wiring harness — that bundle of wires that distributes electricity throughout the car's engine — is now probably a useless melted mass and will have to be completely removed and replaced. There may also be some front-end repair and refinishing work too," James quickly added.

"Oh boy, well, so much for 'Undercover Surveillance 101,'" Schless said, half under his breath.

"Oh, stop it – he'll probably never see me again. Hopefully, you will successfully close this all down quick and clean while I am in Atlanta," James said, and then he went on to describe the events in front of the art gallery.

"You don't think you might have spooked him, and as a result he might just skedaddle out of sight for good?" Schless asked.

"He has too much invested here to just walk away," James said, then thought for a moment, "Maybe, maybe not, but I did slap a bug under his passenger side rear bumper. You shouldn't have very much trouble catching up with him if he does bolt – at least not for the time being. And if he leaves this car for another or moves on to public transportation we know where his bank accounts are and can tie him up in knots financially. All in all, this assignment is under control and the end is within sight."

"If he is spooked and connects you to the artists what are the chances he will now go after them with a new passion?" Schless persisted.

"Sure, he is capable of looking for revenge, which would be true of anyone, but I watched him run back to his gallery; I shook him up really good and I think he will feel much safer in his gallery than out in the open for a while. Right now, I think that he is concentrating on his own survival; revenge is almost certainly on a back burner," James said.

"Well, if he does retreat for the moment, he could still send some muscle to get even with the artists," Schless persisted.

"From everything I now know about him, he is a loner. I have not found traces of a support team; it certainly doesn't look like he has surrounded himself with any muscle with which to fight back. The kinds of crimes the police have actually tied to him are simple cons. Yes, they *think* he has done worse, but they have never been able to pin anything stronger than *bunko squad* stuff on him, nor have they come up with any fellow travelers we need to be concerned about. He also has a history of not being able to trust anyone but himself. For the moment, that is what I'm counting on."

"While I'm listing concerns, let me add one more," Schless said, "it is also not like you to create a lapse in surveillance; it would have been more like you to wait the few hours until I or someone else could get there?"

"C'mon Schless, give me more credit than that. We both know that you could be here in a matter of hours; the subject is covered for at least that lapse in in time. The big question is if you are ready to come back to work from your long vacation?" James asked.

"Give me a break," Shless shouted back, "I drove 13 hours, on my time, to witness history with two of my favorite people in the world, to be present for a once-in-a-lifetime blue grass event ... crazy happens — and you call that a vacation — worse yet, a *long* vacation?"

"First of all, there isn't anything such as my time vs. your time vs. company time in our business. We don't punch time cards; we solve people's problems and when they need us we must be there. Second of all, it wasn't a few hours, it has been the better part of two days – which you clearly deserved – and crazy isn't happening here, it has happened in Atlanta. Now, just let me know if you can get your well-rested tush down here so that you can pick up the pieces."

"You're asking a whole lot of me. Plus, I have Stella and Mason with me, I can't very well bring them to a field assignment," Schless groaned.

"You can't be too far from one of our field operatives, just get them to take the kids back to their home. I'm only asking if you can break free and get out here or not," James persisted.

"You know how hard it was to get a backstage pass for this Bill Monroe and the Bluegrass Boys tribute at the Grand Ole Opry?" Schless groaned, "Alison Krauss will be there, and Del McCoury and Ricky Skaggs ..."

"Is that a yes or a no?" James asked.

"I promised Stella, specifically, that I would take her here. All of these years I couldn't get my own kids to listen to blue grass, but here she is, a 10-year old blue grass addict."

"Just give me an answer, yes or no?"

"Let me think about this, a backstage pass at what is likely to be a once-in-a-lifetime event and a chance to create a memory that Stella and Mason will remember for the rest of their lives or the cold reality of rushing off to New Orleans so that I can sit in a drafty car all day and all night freeing you up to traipse off to Atlanta for a really cool assignment."

"Calm down, you know I wouldn't ask you to do this if I had any other option — now, for the last time, can you break free and get here or not? Come on Schless, just answer the damn question."

There was a short pause, and then Schless said, "Sure, I'll head down to lovely New Orleans. Lucky you, I'm in Nashville. I'll call Fender and ask him to take my place here. He hates blue grass, but he loves kids and I know he will take good care of Stella and Mason and get them safely back home after they enjoy what I will only dream about for the rest of my days on this earth. I made the trip once some years ago from Nashville to New Orleans in exactly seven hours and 34 minutes — of course that was to meet up with a real cutie with whom a much younger me backpacked in Europe — but that's another story for another day. I'm older now and my kidney does require more frequent stops today than it did when I was younger, but I probably could still make it in less than eight hours; I will just have to settle for some of that gumbo and crawfish."

"Again with the food connections; you just have to get your mind out of the kitchen, Schless, it's making *you* crazy. Please get here as quickly as you can. I'll leave the Hornedo file in the trunk of the car. It will be parked in the lot just down the street from the 24-hour Western Union office; the key to the car will be in an envelope left at the office in your name."

"And how, exactly will I know which car you have waiting for me down the street from the 24-hour Western Union office?" Schless mocked.

"What, are you regressing on me? You will have the key, you will press the car alarm, you will hear the horn and see the blinking lights."

"I just can't wrap my arms around this whole conversation. It isn't like you to drop an assignment in mid-stream, nor is it at all like you to expose yourself to a target so early on in an assignment," Schless said.

"You have already said that," James said, "Now, any questions before I hang up?"

"Yeh, I'd like to know when you will be saying goodbye to this diet."

"Calm down, Schless. The diet didn't make me do anything I didn't want to do. Please, don't analyze me. Sometimes a carrot is just a carrot. Now, get your well rested persona down here and pick up the pieces. If I didn't spook the suspect, there will be an easy transition if I did spook him, I will need you to step up the pressure and quickly."

"You never listen to me."

James hung up.

About 15 minutes later the phone buzzed again, James looked at the caller ID screen, Elizabeth was calling.

James clicked the on button and said, "Yeh."

"We are really worried about you," she said.

"You just spoke to Schless, right?" he said.

"I just spoke to Schless, yes," she said.

James hung up and put his phone in his pocket as he moved out into the street and hailed a taxi.

Chapter 15

Monday, December 31, 2018 — 1:13 a.m.
In a taxi on the way to the airport, New Orleans

James would have been willing to make arrangements to go to Atlanta based upon the news reports and Angela's insistence, but he wasn't prepared to actually board a plane until he spoke directly with Ivy. He dialed the private cell number Angela had given him.

Ivy looked up from her computer to the telephone screen, quickly lifted the receiver and said, "Good morning Mr. James."

"Good morning to you," James responded, "although I would guess it has been anything *but* a good morning for either you or Atlanta if I am to believe what has been in all of the news reports."

"That is the height of understatement, Mr. James," she said with a heavy sigh, "unfortunately, the news reports have only just begun to touch upon all that we are dealing with here."

"I apologize for waking you up at this late hour," he said.

"Sleep is for another time with all that we are facing here at the moment, Mr. James, I was actually staring at a computer screen when your call came in."

"First of all, please call me Will or James, everybody calls me one or the other."

"All right, Will," she said.

"Let's begin with basics," he said, "you seem to have me at a disadvantage, according to Angela, you know me even though I am certain we have never met. Can you put me on a more even ground?"

"Yes, Will — I do know quite a bit about you and yes, you are correct, we have never met," she said, "But I can't believe that there are many people in law enforcement who have not heard about you or your adventures."

"My adventures?" he asked.

"Come now, Will, you *were* the first juvenile ever to be tried and convicted for computer hacking."

"It was so long ago; I was just a little more inquisitive than those around me. I'm surprised it is still of interest to you or anyone else," he said.

"Let's be real here," she laughed, "you successfully broke into the Department of Defense's computer system, Will," she paused for a moment and then emphasized each word, "the ... United ... States ... of ... America's ... Department ... of ... Defense ... computer ... system; surely you can understand why *that* would not soon be forgotten."

"I was just an inquisitive teenager at the time," he said.

"All the more amazing," she quickly responded, "do you think such a *success story* would or even could be easily forgotten?"

"If I remember clearly, it wasn't considered a *success story* at the time," he said.

"Yes, I guess the Department of Defense was a bit short on a sense of humor back then," she said, "as well as the necessary vision to realize how valuable you *could* have been toward helping the so-called grownups develop a more forward thinking internet defense system."

"And you would want my help on this bombing even though you know about the so-called *success story* past?" he asked.

"Actually, from the moment I was briefed on this horrendous event, I knew that we were facing something the likes of which none of us had ever dealt with before."

"Bombings aren't new — unfortunately," he said.

"Sure, we have had bombings, and every day there is a new wrinkle to deal with from terrorists and wannabe trouble makers all over the world, but this bombing seems to be breaking new ground — literally and emotionally. I thought that getting on top of this would take a high level of *out of box thinking* that you seem to have in abundance. I thought of you at that moment, and was able to convince the Secretary of Homeland Security that you could add value to the investigation."

"Angela told me that you have the ear of the Secretary of Homeland Security, which of course got my attention. But, I must ask you very specifically, what do you think I can do that the *all-knowing* Homeland Security team cannot do? Aren't these the best and the brightest?"

"*The best and the brightest* indeed," she laughed, "yes, actually they are very good and extremely bright – in most instances. Unfortunately, they have been trained to think in straight lines; *your* past shows an ability to think in curves. Clearly, we are facing a foe that, at least for the moment, seems to be more effective at making trouble for us than we seem to be able to make trouble for them. I, for one, think they have out-thought us because, unlike us, they are not thinking in straight lines, *they* are thinking in curves. That makes you exactly what we need right now." She paused, sighed deeply and then said, "I hope that I have given you enough to make you want to come to Atlanta. If not, we definitely may have a problem because I cannot share any more information over an open phone line."

"And neither the secretary, nor anyone around him had concerns about bringing me in?" James asked.

"Let's just say that the secretary voted yes, and so the 'yeses' won the day."

"Angela said that you were also the one who suggested she get in touch with me when she had that little spat with the immigration people." He said, trying to change the subject.

"Spat?" she asked with a chuckle, "I still haven't figured out exactly how you did it but she is still in this country and we are all better for it – thanks to you."

"It wasn't much."

"You are being modest, Will. Suffice it to say, that I and everyone I could get involved on her behalf tried our best and failed. You succeeded, and that level of success is what is most needed now. Frankly, everyone here is stumped beyond belief."

"Well, let's get to it then," he said, "What can you add to what I was able to read in the newspapers?"

"You're slick, okay," she said, "slight change of subject then a quick backtrack. My compliments – Now, as I have already said, there isn't very much more that I can share with you over an open and unsecured phone line. Are you willing and able to come here to Atlanta right away?"

"Yes, in fact I am in a taxi on the way to the airport now. But I would feel a lot more positive about dropping everything to join you if I knew at least something more about what you are facing."

She was quiet for a while, he wondered if they were still connected. "Are you still there?" he asked.

"Yes, Will, I am still here. I just don't know what I can share with you over the phone."

"Come on, any clues to who did this?" he persisted. "It has been a week since the bombing – surely some clues have surfaced in a week.

"Clues," she repeated, "Oh yes, we have *clues*, in fact we have plenty of *clues*. If we choose to follow the clues, which we will *not* do, we would have a solid case against one specific person. No question about it, zero doubt."

"Soooo," he prodded.

After another long pause, she said, "Let me list some of the *evidence* we now have for you. We have closed circuit television footage from various positions at the crime scene – although his face was hidden by a wide brimmed hat, we have clear footage of the doer's movements prior to the explosion because most of the footage survived the blast. We have a recording of his voice, we have physical evidence left at the scene, we have DNA, and it did not take us very long to match the DNA to a known murderer in the national data base. There were items still in storage from an earlier arrest, so we were able to isolate his DNA. In the getaway cab, we found a cross pen with his full name engraved on the barrel and even partial prints – and if that wasn't enough, he left a hair comb with hairs that matched his DNA."

"Soooo," he repeated, "social media alone should make it relatively easy to quickly find and arrest him, regardless of where he might be hiding."

"Oh, he isn't hiding. We know exactly where he is. In fact, we put him there."

"What am I missing?" he asked, "Then all you have to do is put out an all-points bulletin. He can't escape your net forever; please tell me what I am missing here? With prints and DNA, it is a slam dunk," James said.

There was another long silence and then she said, “Neither the prints nor the DNA can help us in this situation.”

“I may sound a bit dense here, but, as long as you can place the suspect’s prints and DNA at a crime scene, you don’t need any other clues,” he said, “Why wouldn’t the prints and DNA be enough to begin building a solid case?”

“Will, the prints, as well as the DNA belong to Joe Arridy.”

“I don’t recognize the name, but now that you have a clear identity, all you have to do is pick him up,” he said, “You can even let him sign his confession with his own cross pen, and comb his hair before you snap a new mug shot.”

“Not so easy,” she said.

“What could possibly be easier?”

“Joe Arridy died on January 6, 1939, in the Cañon City, Colorado, gas chamber.”

Now the long silence was on James’ side of the phone. “That was almost 80 years ago,” he finally said.

“Exactly six days shy of 80 years ago.”

“How can that be?” he asked.

“That is exactly what I am hoping you will help us find out,” she said.

"I will be on the next plane out. I have checked schedules and the next plane to Atlanta leaves here shortly after six in the morning. When I get to the airport I will ..."

She interrupted him in mid-sentence, "I am happy that you are on the way to the airport – the secretary has requested a Cessna 680 be sent to pick you up, it has already taken off and is due there shortly, it should be fueled and waiting to bring you back here to Atlanta by the time you get to the airport."

"Excuse me?" he said.

"I apologize for just assuming you would come; I just didn't think you could pass up taking part in the type of mystery facing us here!" she added.

"I guess you *do* know me," he said.

"Oh, one more thing," she said, "Please tell your driver to go to the old Lakefront Airport, *not* the Louis Armstrong New Orleans International Airport. They are both only about 15 minutes from downtown New Orleans, but in opposite directions. This time of day there should be little or no traffic, but I assume you are on your way to the big commercial airport by now so it will add a bit to your taxi fare."

James could hear someone calling Ivy in the background, "Sorry," she said briskly, "I must go now; I will be on the tarmac to meet your plane when you arrive."

The line went dead.

Chapter 16

Monday, December 31, 2018 — 3:19 a.m.
Hartsfield-Jackson Atlanta International Airport

The Cessna 680 Sovereign was cleared for landing and as instructed, taxied to a small secluded grassy area several miles from the primary runways.

James was asked to remain on the plane and was advised that the Secretary of Homeland Security was on his way and would board as soon as he arrives. About 15 minutes later, the aircraft door opened and an armed guard, two women and a huge man in a wrinkled business suit entered the plane.

The three crew members deplaned, and as the last crew member walked onto the tarmac, the armed guard that had just entered the cabin reached up and engaged the door latch, then took a seat by the door. James noticed that the guard never took his eyes off of him.

The huge man walked forward and extended his hand to James, "Good morning Mr. James, I'm Homeland Security Secretary Willis," he pointed to a diminutive Asian woman and said, "this is Ivy Chan, the Atlanta Police Department's liaison to Homeland Security, and currently my special assistant in this investigation. I believe you have already spoken with her, and," pointing to the other woman, "this is State Attorney General Wanda Parent. Frankly, Attorney General Parent is the reason we are meeting here on the plane instead of a more comfortable space in the main terminal."

“Thank you for the show of support, Fritz,” Wanda said with a grimace, “so much for ‘we are all in this together.’”

James smiled at the woman and extended his hand. There was a noticeable delay but eventually she reached out to accept his hand. “Ms. Parent and I are old friends,” James said, with a warm smile.

“Maybe *friends* is a bit of a stretch,” she said.

“Come on Wanda,” the secretary chided, “What faces us here is far more important than any past misunderstandings.”

“There isn’t a misunderstanding on my part,” Wanda said, glaring directly at James, “I never framed anyone – never would, never did, not once, not ever!”

“That couple was innocent,” James said softly.

“I never framed anyone,” Wanda repeated, her voice slightly more elevated than before.

“Can we agree to deal with that *after* we catch the fiends responsible for this act of terror?” Ivy said, sternly.

Wanda’s face flushed. “Sure,” she whispered.

“Of course,” James quickly added.

*****

Wanda Parent, applied to the United States Navy after leaving the Washington, D.C., Police Department. She eventually joined the Navy’s Judge Advocate General’s Corps and proved to be an effective trial lawyer. Upon her honorable discharge from the service and with the help of her former boss at JAG, she was hired to be an assistant district attorney in Atlanta. While still a relatively new member of the department, she was credited with a series of highly publicized convictions. But it was her only major loss that propelled her onto the national scene. Her impassioned closing remarks against a television evangelist, who had been charged with the murder of a New Orleans businessman, made her the darling of talk radio, cable news, and the supermarket tabloids. Almost overnight, she became a household name.

Several years later, it helped her to win a close election as district attorney against the same man who had first hired her as his assistant. A series of other high profile cases led to her holding on to that office through two more hard fought elections. She became one of the most talked about district attorneys in the nation, a regular on the Sunday morning news shows, which led to even higher ambitions. Currently her eyes were fixed upon the governor's mansion and she didn't care who knew it.

Her love of fishing became well known during the height of her prosecution against the television evangelist. One day, her office received a very large and heavy package sent anonymously to Parent. A strong odor radiated from the package and since it did not have a return address, they called the police to check it out.

The first ones to arrive were the beat cops, followed quickly by several Atlanta Police Department's Tactical Field Officers. This was not the first time they were called to the State Attorney General's office about a bomb, especially since the beginning of the evangelist trial. The lead officer quickly had the building cleared and then inspected the package for switches or conductors. He used a robot to carefully move the package out to a bomb containment van in the parking lot.

When the package was unwrapped, they found about a hundred pounds of ground up decaying fish wrapped inside newspapers with articles about the evangelist's trial, a scenic post card of Acapulco Bay, and a copy of a page from the bible: "Again, the kingdom of heaven is like a net that was thrown into the sea and gathered fish of every kind. — Matthew 13:47" was circled and highlighted.

The officer asked Parent if the contents of the package could have any specific meaning to her. She told them that earlier in the year, while vacationing in Acapulco, she caught a sailfish that was 10-feet long and weighed just under a 110 pounds.

"Who would have known that," the lead officer asked.

"Everyone," she said, "I had a public relations person get it into every newspaper in the state."

Within hours, the governor assigned six state troopers to provide around the clock security for her; this security force remained in place until an innocent verdict was handed down in the case.

*****

As they left the plane, Wanda whispered, "Break into any top-secret computers lately, *Spider*."

"Please call me Will or James," James said, "I tend to ignore people who can't or won't do that."

"I don't think you will be able to ignore *me*, Mr. James. I intend to be on you like white on rice until you leave my state, preferable in chains, but I would gladly accept a less dramatic exit if it would get you removed from here quicker."

"Let's not fence, Ms. Parent. I came to help; if I can't be of help then I am perfectly happy to get on the next plane back," James said.

"Fine with me," Wanda barked.

"Wait one minute here," the secretary said, "I have something to say about this and I suggest we all back up a few miles."

Wanda turned and glared at the secretary, "Your Mr. James, here, is a convicted felon. He has done time in a federal prison. I wonder what the newspapers would do with an anonymous tip that a convicted felon was being asked to help in this matter," she said.

"I don't do well with threats, Wanda, but while we are wondering ... I wonder what those same newspapers would do with a quote from a sitting Secretary of Homeland Security commenting on a *would-be* governor who walked away from *someone* who might be able to help in this matter because of a personal vendetta?" the secretary said.

"The *Fisher Woman* doesn't take lightly to threats either, Mr. Secretary," Wanda said.

"Hey folks," James broke in, "I'm here to help. If my presence here will take away from you guys harmoniously working together, I'm just as happy to leave. No problem for me either way."

"And how exactly do you think you can help Mr. James," Wanda asked.

"I'm not sure that I can. But the good news is that it shouldn't take very long to find out. Meanwhile, whoever was responsible for all that happened here in Atlanta is free to repeat the mayhem somewhere else while we just pick at each other."

"Just let Mr. James try to help in any way he can; damn it, what damage do you think he can do?" the secretary barked.

"Probably none," Wanda smiled, "I'll see to that. I just don't like felons to be on the inside of an investigation, especially one as close to home as this one."

"So you want him out, before he begins, and I want him in. How about you, Ivy, break the tie for us," the secretary said, facetiously.

"I'm far from impartial Mr. Secretary; after all, I am the one who asked for Will to come here in the first place. What I can say is that I have followed his work over the years and I can't think of a single instance where his presence did not add value in one way or another."

"Clearly," Wanda moaned, "I am outnumbered here."

"As far as I am concerned, that does it," the secretary said firmly. "Now, Wanda, what do you say we go on our way and let Ivy bring Will up to date?"

"Hell no," Wanda said, sternly, "clearly I can't keep him out — at least not for the time being — but I plan to go wherever he goes until I feel more comfortable about his presence here. Just for the record, I am against employing this felon or any felon in this volatile case."

"Done," the secretary said, "you have the 'I told you so' card. Use it well, Wanda, because *if* he proves to be helpful in the search for the animal or animals that did this fiendish act, I plan to rub your stuck up little nose in it until hell freezes over."

Wanda sneered, "Likewise I'm sure."

Chapter 17

Monday, December 31, 2018 — 4:09 a.m.
Atlanta Airport — secluded general aviation hangar

They were all on the tarmac now. The secretary pointed to a car next to his and told James that it will take him, Ivy, and Wanda to the evidence staging area. He shook James' hand and told him again how much he appreciated his having dropped everything in order to join the investigation. The secretary then walked over to Wanda and whispered something into her ear. She leaned back and glared at him. She quickly responded, loudly enough for James to hear, "I won't soon forget or ever forgive you for this, Fritz," then she walked stiffly towards the waiting car. James followed quickly behind her, opened the rear passenger door and held her huge bag while she settled into the passenger seat. When she was seated, James handed the bag back to her and said, "What do you have in there, rocks?" She grabbed the bag, gave him a dismissive wave of her hand, and grabbed the door handle, slamming it closed.

Ivy had already settled into her seat and noticed James helping Wanda into the car. *That's odd*, she thought, under normal circumstances and for normal people, this was little more than an example of common courtesy. However, this was not a normal set of circumstances and both Wanda and James had been at war with each other for such a long time that it seemed to Ivy to be a strange move on James' part. He was far too smart to think that such a simple act of kindness would create even a slight thaw in their relationship; and Wanda had expressed such deep distrust towards James that it was all but certain that she would think he had some ulterior motive for his action. She made a mental note to ask James about it later.

The driver nodded to each of them and then eased the car away from the landing strip. James quickly opened his laptop, inserted an ear piece into the jack on the side and stared attentively at the computer screen while Wanda and Ivy, each sitting stiffly in the back seat, stared out of their respective side windows. They passed a series of no trespassing warning signs along the way. Finally, they came to a high security barbed wire fence with a series of military vehicles blocking access to the entrance. James estimated the fence to be at least 20 feet tall; he read the sign on the fence aloud:

WARNING: THIS IS A TOP SECRET AREA
X1400 **—"Q" LEVEL**
RESTRICTED ENTRY
ALL OTHERS WILL BE ARRESTED
ON SIGHT
United States Department of Homeland Security

Four armed military policemen, guns out and pointing down, began to encircle their vehicle. James was becoming annoyed by what he was beginning to see as overreacting by the authorities, mumbled to himself, “If the movie theater had been this well protected, no one would have died last week.”

“This isn’t a joke Mr. James,” Wanda said, “None of us, not a single man or woman currently working in this area, has a sense of humor tonight. Do not provoke!”

The car rolled to a stop. An armed guard appeared out of the shadows and motioned for the driver to open his window. The guard aimed a flashlight into the car; even though he seemed to know the driver, he asked for his identification and then for the identification from everyone else in the car, starting with James. Ivy removed a laminated card from around her neck and while handing it to the guard, advised him that they were here at the request of the Secretary of Homeland Security. Wanda gave the guard her laminated card as did the driver. The guard held onto their IDs and asked the driver and all passengers to slowly exit the car. Several more guards appeared. One had a mirror attached to a long pole and began checking the underside of the car while another walked around the car with a bomb sniffing dog. As soon as the passengers were out, a dog jumped into the front seat, sniffed around and then leaped into the back seat, jumping out of the opposite side passenger door. One of the guards got into the car and released the hood and the trunk lid.

Finally, after the engine and trunk had been inspected, the three passengers and their driver were permitted to get back into the car and drive through the gate. A military vehicle followed them as they slowly made their way towards a huge structure. The accompanying military vehicle was waived off and as it returned to the front gate, the car with James, Wanda, and Ivy was again surrounded by a group of armed guards.

"Why is there such a high level of security?" James asked.

"Are you suggesting that there be *no* security?" Wanda asked.

"There is a wide range between no security and what seems to be going on here," James said, "Do you really think anyone attached to last week's bombing is still in the area?"

"I really don't know," she barked, "Do you?"

"No, I don't know for a fact, but I just don't think it is very likely that the bomber is still in the area," James said. "If I was running such an operation, I would either have tried a follow up attack on the first defenders last Sunday night and would have been in deep hiding since – or at the very least, I would be far away from here before dawn the next day, much less today, a week later."

"I'm sure we will all take your well thought out evaluation under advisement," Wanda said, dismissively.

"Come on you two, we are now on sacred ground; let's be a little more respectful of the victims," Ivy said.

The guard motioned for them to all exit the car. As she got out of the car, Wanda handed James a surgical facemask. "I think you'd better prepare yourself for something that no one should ever experience," she said sternly.

"I've been to crash sites and field morgues before," James said.

"I would hope you have never been to anything *exactly* like this one," Wanda said, "please, take the mask and secure it tightly when you put it on."

James took the mask and put it in his pocket.

They were approached by another guard. Ivy and James followed Wanda who had already removed the laminated card from around her neck and handed it to the guard. The guard aimed his flashlight at Wanda's card, then her face, then back again to the card as he compared it to the photo on his laptop. He then asked her to place her right thumb on a device attached to his clipboard. They heard a high-pitched beep.

"May I see your credentials as well," he said to Ivy. She took a similarly laminated card from around her neck and handed it to the guard. She then placed her right thumb onto the device and again they heard a beep. He nodded approval and then turned to James. Ivy stepped between them, "This is Mr. Will James, he has been approved for access to the site by the Secretary of Homeland Security," she said as she pulled an envelope out of her pocket and handed it to the guard. The guard carefully removed a document from the envelope and read it; he asked for James' driver's license and then asked James to roll up his left pants leg and push down his sock. He centered his flashlight on a small tattoo of a Jefferson head nickel just above James' ankle bone.

The guard told them all to wait where they were standing, then motioned to several other armed guards and they moved closer while the first guard walked into a small booth about 50 yards from them. A guard on either side of them stood at attention, each with one hand loosely around his gun holster.

James whispered to Ivy, "I don't understand why he checked you and Wanda before he got around to me. I have to believe that he's seen each of you multiple times during the past week; he's never seen me before. The earlier checkpoint checked me out first, as any well-trained guard would. I wonder why this guard didn't."

"I wouldn't attach any special meaning to that, Will," Ivy said, "he knows that by the time any visitor gets to this checkpoint they have been quite thoroughly vetted. I expect that he was sent a complete dossier on you the minute your plane landed." She smiled, then added, "He seemed to know where to look for that tattoo, didn't he?"

After a few minutes the first guard returned with a camera. He ran a cable from the camera to his clipboard and then took two photos of James, one full face and one profile. He asked James to put his right thumb on a device attached to his clipboard and typed in James' name and a security control number. He went back to the small booth and minutes later returned with a laminated card attached to a long chain. He handed the license, laminated card and chain to James and said, "Do not separate the card from this chain; it has been specially coded so we can monitor your physical location anywhere within 100 miles of our electronic readers — which tonight are positioned throughout greater Atlanta. Please keep both the chain and the laminated ID card in clear sight anytime you are in this area. You will be asked repeatedly to show it. Should you delay in responding or refuse such a request, you will be escorted out of the area and not permitted to return, under *any* circumstances, do you understand what I have just said?"

James nodded affirmatively.

"I need to hear you say it," the guard said sternly.

James said he fully understood and would follow the order.

The guard moved closer to James, "Possible family members and friends of victims are inside the hangar. They are trying to identify missing loved ones," he said solemnly, "we ask you to give them their space and privacy; under no circumstance are you to attempt to speak to any of them. Do you understand?"

"I understand and will not communicate with anyone inside this complex except with my minders," he pointed to Ivy and Wanda, "Or to anyone with whom they introduce me."

"Thank you, Mr. James," the guard said.

They walked the few yards to the main entrance of the structure. Two armed guards were at the entrance, one approached the trio. One by one, he passed a security wand across and around their bodies and then moved it up and down from head to toe. He then opened the door and ushered them into the huge hangar.

James instantly realized that Wanda was right, this was like nothing he had ever seen before. He was instantly aware of a nauseating combination of odors which could only be described as aircraft fuel heavily mixed with disinfectants barely covering the stench of burned and decayed human flesh.

He reached into his pocket, pulled out the mask and quickly put it on. Parent watched, not trying too hard to hide her pleasure at his sudden discomfort.

The first things that hit James as he entered the space were the blinding bright lights and icy cold temperature coming from the interior of the hangar. It took a while for his eyes to adjust to the bright lights. He looked around the space, surprised by its sheer size; it now appeared to be far larger than he thought it to be from the outside. He estimated that several thousand people were milling around within the structure. There were two enormous walled off sections to the left of the hangar entrance with a series of smaller open areas, possibly set aside for one-on-one meetings. Groups of people, James assumed to be family and friends of those still missing, some walking as if in a trance like state, were being led from the smaller areas into the walled off structures by people in hospital greens, while a larger group slowly walked in single file along a series of rolling racks loosely filled with articles of clothing, and tables with orderly rows upon rows of shoes and what he thought were probably personal belongings of the still to be identified victims.

In spite of the many grief-stricken people milling around, and the various teams of investigators working inside the huge hangar, the overall noise level was barely measurable.

A uniformed guard approached them and asked to see their credentials. Each promptly removed the cards from around their necks and handed them to the guard who carefully inspected each one and then passed the credentials back.

As Ivy walked, James noticed that her eyes were fixed upon a table on the far left with shoes neatly lined up; some in pairs, most just single shoes. He followed her gaze to a specific section made up entirely of children's shoes. She later told him that even though she had entered this hangar many times in the past week, each time her eyes just automatically locked onto the row of children's shoes. She told him that for her, this particular sight brought the enormity of the disaster home to her in ways that pulled at her very being. "Those could be my children's shoes in that neat little row." She wiped tears from her eyes, "The horror of what happened in this city on Christmas Eve will haunt me to my last day. How could anyone do this to other human beings? How? How? How?"

James reached for her elbow, "Are you all right?" he asked, gently.

She gave him a weak smile and nodded, yes.

Wanda was also watching Ivy. She turned to James and said, "Welcome to our world, Spider, *this* is the real world."

Ivy gave Wanda a dirty look and gently led the way towards the center right of the hangar. They were now entering a roped off section about the size of a football field.

A uniformed guard approached them and asked to see their credentials. Each removed the cards from around their necks and handed them to the guard. The guard carefully inspected each card, held it close to their face, stared back and forth from card, to face, to card, and then passed the cards back to them.

The area to their right was filled with huge pieces of twisted metal, bits of theater furnishings, some with broken and charred glass still attached. "The night shift manager died trying to save some of the theatergoers," Wanda said. "The day shift manager and several other theater employees helped us to stage the remains of the lobby and the auditorium so that we could get a sense of where and how the bomb was placed."

"A week later and we still have so many unidentified victims," Ivy said, with a deep sigh. "We know how many tickets were sold and who was working that shift but we may never have a final count of all who died that night merely because they tried to take in a movie." Ivy shuddered, as if hit by a sudden chill.

"This is all that is left of The Plaza Theatre?" James asked.

"No, there is more," Wanda said.

"Why was all of this moved from the crime scene?" James asked.

"We decided that we would be better off taking all of this away from glaring eyes," Wanda said.

"The governor was concerned about souvenir collectors and an inquisitive press, as well as any disruption in downtown Atlanta during the holiday tourist shopping season," Ivy added.

Wanda glared at Ivy disapprovingly.

"Did you take photos before these items were moved?" James asked.

"Of course, we did," Wanda said, now clearly annoyed by both Ivy and James.

"May I see the photos," James asked, then pointing at the distorted pieces of metal and furnishings he again asked, "What else were you able to salvage?"

"There is more evidence, lots more," Wanda said. "Some are in a separate facility undergoing further examination by teams of forensic scientists. I will answer *some* of your other questions about the evidence and the crime scene photos in due time."

"We will answer your questions, all of your questions," Ivy interrupted.

"Hey, first I have to be completely certain that his presence here can be of value to the investigation," Wanda said, then moving closer to James she added, "I never framed anyone — I never would frame anyone, I never did frame anyone, not once, not ever!"

"That couple was innocent," James said.

"I never framed anyone," Wanda repeated, her voice slightly more elevated.

Ivy pointed towards a small construction shed by the far wall. "We have excellent quality surveillance tapes. We also have the actual sound tape from the radio station."

As James and Ivy followed Wanda into the shed, a guard moved quickly behind them. He entered the room and positioned himself by the door.

James said, "I understand you have clear fingerprints, may I see the file on the person linked to those fingerprints?"

"In time, in time," Wanda said, "first, let's all sit down and establish a few rules of the road." She led them to a long table and sat down.

"Do we really have time for this?" Ivy asked.

"We do this my way or we don't do it at all," Wanda said.

"Then let's get to it," James said, as he sat down.

Ivy remained standing.

Chapter 18

Monday, December 31, 2018 — 4:26 a.m.
Atlanta Airport — secluded general aviation hangar

"Our job is to pick away at the physical evidence, uncover and document the perpetrator's mistakes, and finally, identify the bad guys and either send them to their waiting place in hell or bring them to justice," Wanda said.

James looked at Ivy and smiled. Then he turned to face Wanda and said, "I have a fair understanding of your many successes as a trial lawyer; however, I am not aware that you have been in charge of many investigations like this in the past."

"Well," Wanda said, "The fact is that I *am* in charge ... so to speak. This is my jurisdiction, and prosecuting those whom we arrest will be my responsibility if the Feds don't grab it for themselves. But you do have a point; we haven't gotten many terrorist bombing cases since I came here and I haven't been exposed to many like this in the past."

"How many *would* you say you have been exposed to?" James persisted.

Ivy slowly shook her head as she glared at James.

After an uncomfortably long silence Wanda said, "Actually ... none, personally. And you, how many terrorist attacks have you worked on?"

"A few," he said.

"A few terrorist attacks?" Wanda said.

"Yes," he said.

"Well," Wanda said, "A few, in the kind of *loosy goosy*, mixed bag career you have had may give you *some* small bragging rights."

"A few within the last couple of years or so," he corrected, "Many more over my *loosy goosy* career – so far."

He took a small pad out of his pocket, thumbed past a series of pages and then said, "Based on *my* experience, I don't think this is a terrorist attack at all – international or domestic. In fact, I wouldn't use the word terrorist to describe the person or persons who planned and executed this crime."

"I don't know about what may or may not be in that little notepad of yours but in my book," Wanda broke in, "anyone who wanders into a public building packed with families on Christmas Eve and then proceeds to set off a bomb are nothing less than terrorists, plain and simple."

"I understand," James said, "but in the currently accepted definition of the term, this does not seem to be a terrorist act. It is a horrendous crime, yes. It is unspeakably evil, yes. But I do not think we will later discover it to be fanatical or revolutionary inspired as a terrorist act usually is."

"Semantics, mere semantics, there are so many dead and dying people, and you are playing linguistic games? What is wrong with you," Wanda asked.

"Okay, let me rephrase," James said. "I understand how insensitive my comments may sound, but there is a method to this madness. Unless we correctly define the kind of crime we are trying to solve, we risk overlooking the more likely perpetrators we need to capture. I also don't think we will be helped very much by looking for mistakes made by this particular criminal."

Wanda shook her head in obvious disgust, "They always make mistakes."

"Generally, you are right; however, if we focus on this specific case, I don't think there will be many, if any," James said.

"What arrogance — and you know this, *how*?" Wanda yelled back.

"Since you seem to be reluctant to share what you know with me, please allow me to share what I know with you," James said.

"What could you possibly know that we do not?" Wanda laughed. "Even if you peeked over the shoulders of the teams of professionals who dissected each and every inch of the crime scene during the past week, or as is your customary *modus operandi* — illegally hacked into their confidential files — I don't understand how you could have *any* theories yet. Do I have to remind you that you *just* got here?"

"Did you really think I would drop everything and rush onto a plane headed to Atlanta or anywhere else, without doing at least some initial leg work?" James asked, smugly.

“Then please, enlighten me,” Wanda said.

“When I spoke with Ivy, she told me that the DNA found at the scene and in the getaway taxi belonged to a Joe Arridy. I didn’t know who Joe Arridy was, so I looked him up.”

“So, you think Joe Arridy hovered in the atmosphere all these years, finally wound up in Atlanta just so that his ghost could blow up a theater full of people?” Wanda mocked.

“No, I don’t think that at all, but I *do* think that it would have had to be an awfully big stretch to think that it was just a coincidence that his prints were found at the crime scene, much less the getaway taxi,” James said, “so I looked him up.”

“You mean you hacked into confidential police files,” Wanda said, with obvious contempt.

“I could have ... I might have ... but as it turned out, I didn’t have to hack into anything because everything I needed to know was already out there for anyone to see.”

“Stop it, both of you,” Ivy said.

“Please, let him continue,” Wanda said, “I look forward to learning at the feet of the master.”

James thumbed back and forth among the pages in his pad, “I learned that Joe Arridy was a 23-year old male who was charged and convicted for the rape and murder of a 15-year old school girl in Pueblo, Colorado.”

"We knew that," Wanda said, beginning to drum her fingers against the table top.

"And he was murdered in the gas chamber by the state of Colorado on Friday, January, 6, 1939."

"We also knew that."

"Then you also should know that he was mentally disabled and – given today's more humane justice system – probably never would have been charged with this crime or any crime ... much less tried and convicted ... and much, much less likely to be murdered in the gas chamber for this or any other crime," James said, anger building with each word.

"Yes," Wanda responded, "We knew all of that as well."

"And you also must know that just seven years ago, almost exactly 72 years from the day he was murdered in that gas chamber ..."

"Joe Arridy was officially pardoned," Wanda broke in, "yes, we knew it all. Maybe that was the kind of mistake you said they wouldn't or couldn't make. Maybe, just maybe, they thought it would push us off track for just enough time to allow them to get away."

"No, I think that anyone who has ever seen even one of the many television crime shows or movies would know that given today's super computers, DNA can be almost instantly identified," James said.

"So what?" she shouted, "None of what you have in that little note pad of yours helps us one little bit."

James closed his pad, slowly put it into his shirt pocket, and almost as an afterthought said, "Then I guess it really doesn't matter that you, personally, have been so closely associated with one of Joe Arridy's descendants."

"What in God's name are you babbling about?" Wanda said.

"Wanda," James said, "could you possibly have already forgotten the Atlanta trial that made you the darling of the supermarket tabloids; the case that actually replaced all other celebrity gossip and alien visitor stories and even Elvis sightings on the trash filled pages of the informative ... *not* ... supermarket checkout tabloids? You were the cover girl of those yellow rags; it was your comings and goings as 'Atlanta's spirited legal eagle' that captured those readers week after week after week. That is what they called you wasn't it, 'Atlanta's spirited legal eagle?'"

"Have you completely lost your mind?" Wanda asked, "please, come to the point. What *are* you talking about?"

"I am talking about your case against Sister Joan, the television evangelist; surely you remember bringing charges against her for killing her lover."

Wanda stared at James, slammed both palms against the table and howled, "What does that phony evangelist have to do with Joe Arridy?"

While still staring directly at Wanda, James reached into his pocket and again pulled out his pad. He made a point of flipping through the pages, back and forth, again and again until she screamed, "Tell me already."

"Now, let me see here — Sister Joan was born Jessie Mae Fontaine on February 27, 1985 to Scolai and Bessy Fontaine of Sarasota, Florida. Her father, Scolai Fontaine was born on July 17, 1967 to Fred and Ada Jo Fontaine of Roanoke, Virginia. Ada Jo Fontaine was born Ada Jo Arridy on October 29, 1944 to Henry and Mary Arridy, immigrants who came from Syria to Pueblo, Colorado some years earlier. Henry and Mary Arridy were the parents of Joe Arridy, who died in the Pueblo, Colorado, gas chamber slightly more than five years earlier. The very same Joe Arridy whose fingerprints and DNA were found at the bomb scene, so, if I am correct here, *that* would make Jessie Mae Fontaine, or as you know her better, Sister Joan, the great niece of Joe Arridy; one of Joe Arridy's descendants several generations removed, but an actual blood descendant none the less."

Wanda sat staring at James; her face was now beet red.

"Cat got your tongue, *fisher woman*?" James finally said. "I can't believe that you did not know that."

Slowly, Wanda shook her head from side to side. "No, I did not know that," she said followed by a very deep sigh. "I assume you are entirely correct, though. You would be a fool to make all of that up. You are a lot of things but I do not think a fool is one of them. Please, tell me, *how* do you know that?"

"When I learned that you were involved here I was certain you would do whatever you could to make my days a living hell, for certain I expected you would try to limit my participation in the investigation and I really wanted to help in any way that I could. I consider what happened here last week to be a national disaster. I'm ashamed to have to tell you, but I quickly went looking for anything that I might be able to use against you. I dug as deeply as I could and it became clear to me that your career while at JAG was flawless. When I read that you lost a major case – the one and only major case that you personally lost while assistant district attorney ..."

"The only case of any kind I have ever lost," Wanda said.

"The only case you ever lost in *Atlaaanta*," he repeated, emphasizing and stretching out the word, "there was that little case in Washington, D.C., that is at the route of your problem with me."

Wanda half saluted and said "Got me!"

"The only case you lost while here in Atlanta was the tele-evangelist case," he said. "Once again, I dug in to see what could have ended such a *near perfect* winning streak. That was when I found out that Sister Joan had a convicted murderer in her family. Putting one and one together, I had to assume that you knew this as well and did the noble thing, opting to leave it out of your case – as well as your closing argument – even though it might have swayed the jurors in your favor. I have to admit that I was impressed that you took the high road by holding that information back, and I was and am still ashamed that I only learned about it because I was just looking for dirt to use against you."

"Now it is my turn to be ashamed," Wanda said, slowly, "I did not know about the convicted murderer in her family tree."

"You needn't be ashamed that you missed something that took place almost a century ago," Ivy said.

"That isn't what I am ashamed of," Wanda said, "I am ashamed that I probably *would have* used it if I had known about it, even if I thought that it would have sent an innocent person to jail."

"Actually, she wasn't innocent," James said.

"But her lawyer was able to prove that she was at a revival meeting in front of almost 10,000 people, and live television cameras at the same time the murder took place – she couldn't have been in two places at the same time," Wanda said.

"Maybe she didn't kill him with her own hands, but she did hire someone to do it which would make her an accessory."

"How can you possibly know that?" Wanda asked.

"Does it really matter?" James asked. "A jury of her peers declared her innocent. She can never be tried for that crime again."

"Please, tell me," Wanda said.

James thought for a few seconds and then said, "I have a very special young friend whose grandfather has become a sometimes source for such information. He was willing to fill in the details for me."

"Excuse me?" Wanda said.

"You are going to persist until I tell you, aren't you?" James said.

"Wouldn't you if the positions were reversed?" Wanda said.

"I guess so," James laughed. "Well, here it is. This particular grandfather has access to a lot of information that is available to very few others."

"What is he, another *private investigator*?" Wanda asked dismissively.

James laughed, "A *private investigator*," he repeated. "No, he isn't a private investigator. Actually, he is the current head of the New York Gambino crime family, or at least what is left of the New York Gambino crime family."

"Are you serious?" Wanda asked.

James held his hands up in mock surrender, "It is what it is."

"And he told you what, exactly?"

"He told me that Sister Joan paid a hit man $120,000 in small diamonds to kill her former lover."

Wanda sat up straight and again began nervously tapping her fingers on the table, “Would he say that in open court?” she finally asked.

“You’re kidding, right?” James said.

“Do you know who the hit man was?” Wanda said.

“Yes, he told me that as well,” James said.

“And his name is?”

“It won’t help you.”

“Humor me.”

“It will not help you!” James insisted.

“You started this stream of conversation, just finish it, okay?”

“Okay, it was Dmitri Donskoy, a former KGB hired gun from Donetsk, a mining town in the Ukraine, and now a freelance hit man here in the states.”

“She couldn’t find any homegrown talent?” Wanda laughed.

“Look, you asked me so I am telling you. Don’t shoot the messenger,” James said.

“And you believe everything this ... this ... *‘grandfather of some anonymous friend of yours’* told you?” Wanda asked.

"If Carmine DeStefano says it is so, it is so," James said. "He neither has the need, nor the temperament to string me along. If he didn't want to share that information with me he would just have told me to get lost. Now, what do you say we get to work *here*?"

"Just one more thing, tell me why you think this bomber didn't make any mistakes," Wanda said.

"I didn't say that the bomber didn't make any mistakes, I can't say that for certain yet, I haven't seen all of the evidence. What I did say was that I don't think we will find that she made any mistakes that will help us with our investigation."

"Did you say she?" both Ivy and Wanda said, almost simultaneously.

James tried to hide his embarrassment, "I really shouldn't have let that slip because I can't prove it quite yet, but yes, I do believe the bomber was a woman."

"Wow!" Ivy said.

"As far as thinking that he, she, it slipped up in some way ... I just don't think we are going to get very much help from it even if there is some screw-up that eventually surfaces," he said. "Pardon me for rubbing it in, but you seem to be intentionally standing between me and the rest of the evidence. I am not a clairvoyant, in fact I am fairly confident that I have only seen the smallest possible fraction of the evidence that you and your associates have culled through during the past week. However, from what I *have* seen, I believe the person on the closed-circuit television surveillance tape was a woman and this is a well thought out ... extremely well executed performance."

"A performance," Wanda asked.

"Yes, this has all the markings of a carefully staged, methodically rehearsed performance by a seasoned performer. I believe that each word spoken was carefully chosen, rehearsed and delivered; I believe the timing was carefully worked out, so as to make any advance notice we might have gotten from the initial radio telephone call virtually worthless *prior* to the blast. There was probably no chance that we could have caught the doer either before the bomb went off, or immediately after." James said.

Ivy slowly sat down at the other end of the table and said, "You don't seem to have any doubt about what you are saying, could you walk us through your thought process?"

James turned back to his pad, then looked at Wanda and said, "I have to admit I did hack into your laptop, Wanda."

"When ... how?" Wanda roared.

"In the car driving from the landing strip to this complex," he said.

"Wait just one minute, Will James. I know that there are all kinds of protective software and alarms imbedded into my laptop, you couldn't have hacked into it."

"Actually, you are right, and I stand corrected — in this instance — hacking is not the correct word; it would be more accurate to say that I simply used your computer without your knowledge. To be even more truthful, I switched laptops as you got into the car at the landing strip."

Wanda quickly reached for her bag and pulled out her laptop, "Here it is," she said clearly relieved, "It is right here."

"I switched it back while we were waiting to clear security outside of the hangar," he said.

Wanda stood up and slammed her hands on the table, "You no good son of a ..."

"Wanda, stop!" Ivy said, giving her a stern look, and then turning her glare towards James she said, "There will be no more of that, Will James. Trust is a very perishable commodity. Once it is lost it can rarely be reclaimed."

"I'm sorry, Ivy," James said.

"It is Wanda you need to apologize to, before anyone else." Ivy interrupted.

Wanda looked like she was going to say something but instead just threw up her hands, and said, "Just tell us what you are going to tell us."

"I can show you how to protect your laptop from such an invasion in the future," he said apologetically.

Wanda was clearly annoyed and did not try to hide it; she waved him off, staring up at the ceiling as she said, "Please, just tell us what you are going to tell us."

He looked closely at his pad for a little while and then said, "You had a copy of at least one of the closed-circuit television tapes saved on your hard disk. I was able to play it over, and over again while we were driving here."

Wanda was getting angrier, "Get to the point, some point, any point, just get to it a lot quicker? This is like listening to paint dry," Wanda said.

"Let him present it in his way," Ivy said. "We know how our investigators evaluated the very same data resulting in embarrassingly little for us to act upon. We are now into week number two, still asking ourselves *who* and *why*; maybe he can see something we missed, after all, that *is* why he was invited here. I would also like to understand his thought process. Please continue, Will."

"Okay," James said. "I found the tape to be very revealing. First of all, it was quickly apparent that we were not dealing with some foreign terrorist. The person on the screen was an American speaker, confident and calm especially given what was about to take place; this person was in complete control of all emotions, exhibited none of the anxiety that would have been natural for someone about to be responsible — possibly even a victim — of so much destruction, be they foreign or homegrown. There was absolutely no sign that he, she, or it, felt fear of the unknown or fear of anything, for that matter. There was also a lack of propaganda in view — no signs, no banners — that plus the thing with the 80-year old fingerprints convinced me we were watching a staged play and a pretty good stage player. I also noticed that the *so-called* man on the bench had buttoned *his* coat from the left side. Women's clothing buttons on the left side, men's clothing buttons on the right side. The combination of the small screen and fearing that you could reach for your laptop at any moment and learn that I had done a quick switch made it hard to dig deeply enough to be able to see if the person was left handed which might have explained the way the coat was buttoned.

"Then there is the precise number, 'eight minutes and 43 seconds,' given to the radio host as a warning. Nowhere near enough time to figure out where the caller was, or to stop the explosion or, for that matter to get anyone to the scene in time to capture the doer before he, she, or it, could escape. I am still confused about why there was such a tediously detailed description of the snack or why Orwell's *1984* was brought into the conversation. Of course, that could have been just a selection of red herrings, but I believe these are real clues and eventually we will work through the haze to get some useful meaning from them."

"You did not address the reference to the Quran," Ivy said.

"No actual quotes were used from the Quran," he said. "That leads me to believe that it might have been thrown in to confuse. However, at this point in time, especially since I have not seen most of the evidence, I am not prepared to throw anything out."

He opened his computer and pulled up the closed circuit recording he had earlier sent to himself from Wanda's computer.

Wanda slowly moved her glare from the ceiling to James's computer screen.

Ivy stood up and walked over to James, standing just behind him.

Ivy thought back to when she first entered the car at the landing strip and saw what she thought to be James trying to help Wanda into the car. *So much for gallantry,* she thought. She was impressed with his split-second timing. Now that she knew his ulterior motive she understood that had he reached for Wanda's bag a moment sooner, while she was still completely out of the car, Wanda would have instinctively and probably quite violently pulled the bag away from him. Had he moved a moment later, after Wanda was fully seated inside the car, the bag would have been out of his reach. Yes, he had acted at *just* the right moment and he made good use of the time between the airstrip and the new complex to carefully dissect the tape. Maybe he picked up valuable clues from the tape. If so, the end result would be a win for the investigation. But it still troubled her; *should the end ever really justify the means?* She thought, *Should it?* This was not a gray area, it was black or white, the moral answer was clear to her — no, the ends *never* justify the means. She was learning more about this very multifaceted man and couldn't help but think that she might have made a mistake recommending him so strongly.

James started running the images from his computer.

"Wait," Wanda interrupted, standing up, "If we are going to do this, let's do it right. We'll work from the original closed-circuit television recording."

Chapter 19

Monday, December 31, 2018 — 4:41 a.m.
Atlanta Airport — secluded general aviation hangar

Wanda walked over to a playback machine on a far shelf and pressed the start button; simultaneously she linked in the sound from the radio call-in show.

She directed James' attention to the huge screen on the opposite wall. The image blinked on and off — seconds later, the image that filled the screen was of an old man sitting on a bench, with his back severely bent forward, possibly in his late 70s to early 80s. A wide brimmed hat covered much of his face. The sound from the radio call in show and the images from the closed-circuit recording were not completely in sync, but they were close enough for them to piece the events together.

As the man pictured on the screen hobbled towards the exit, Wanda tapped the stop button. "There, now you have it. That is the closest we have to a smoking gun. Now, if there is anything productive you can add or if there is more insight that you can bless us with, please, let's hear it."

James said, "Please run it again for me."

"Okay," Wanda said, "but the chances it will change the second time are rather infinitesimal. This movie only came with one ending!"

When she hit the stop button again, James skipped through a few pages in his pad and said, "Let's go back to the call to the radio station. At first I questioned the various throw away lines which couldn't possibly have anything to do with the impending attack ... the reference to George Orwell's *1984*, the ridiculous offhand remark, 'today is the day we give babies away at 19-84 plus five cents a pound,' the comment about the first blood, that really got my attention, the caller's concern about the high price for popcorn and a drink, it just seemed to come out of left field. Taken as a group, all those comments seemed to lack any rhyme or reason. At first I thought the suspect was just trying to stall until the 8:30 start of the movie when the majority of the seats in the auditorium would be filled, and the potential body count could be at its highest ... but no, that would not jive with my initial assessment of how calculating and very much in control this murderer seemed to be. After I learned that Joe Arridy's prison number was 19845, the reference to Orwell's *1984* began to make sense." He looked at his pad and said, "Here it is, the actual quote, 'I have been thinking about the George Orwell book, *1984*, 5 stars, a must read. The ignorant among you seem to have missed the first few drops of blood.' 1984, 5 stars ... Arridy's prison number was 19845. Then his line, '19-84 plus five cents a pound.' Arridy's prison number was 19845".

"He did use the words, 'animal farm,'" Ivy said, "another George Orwell book."

"This criminal was playing mind games with us," James said, "and although I still cannot explain the bulk of the other remarks, I am convinced that they were not just throw away lines. We were clearly being played with. That is why I wanted to see the full tapes as well as the crime scene photos. I am convinced that the answers are in there, somewhere. Please, play the tape again."

Wanda mumbled something to herself and then replayed the tape.

"Stop the tape!" James said, "Look there."

"Look where?" Ivy asked.

"Look past the bomber's left shoulder; there is a concession stand right behind her."

"So what?" Wanda howled.

"Look there," he said, getting up and pointing to a place on the screen, "There is a small sign taped just below the counter, I missed it the other times around:

SANTA SPECIAL!

A SMALL POPCORN WITH REAL BUTTER
PLUS
A SMALL DRINK OF YOUR CHOICE

ONLY **$8.50, sales tax included**

(Please do not bring food or drink purchased elsewhere into the theater.)

"That ties in the popcorn comment," James said.

Wanda walked over to the screen and smiled, "Cute, but that doesn't help us one little bit."

"It does tie up a loose end," James said, "and it is another tweak of our collective noses. It also speaks to the casual, almost whimsical frame of mind of this criminal."

"Using the word 'whimsical' when the image before us is of the many dead and dying is another sign that you have no clue as to what we are facing here," Wanda said.

"Maybe you're right," James said, "maybe you're right."

He made a note in his pad and then said, "When will the results come back from the lab?"

"All of the results have been back for days already," Ivy said.

"This was a movie theater," James said, "There had to be thousands of prints and probably as much or more examples of DNA all over the place, how did you zero in on Joe Arridy's so quickly?"

"The comb and pen we found in the taxi the perp used to get away from the crime scene had almost a full set of Arridy's prints as well as his DNA. We also found partial prints on the outside of the juice container," Wanda said.

"Did you get DNA from inside the juice container?" James asked.

"No," Wanda said, "the juice container was sealed."

"But we clearly saw the suspect drink from it while sitting on the bench," James said, "May I see the crime scene photographs and the file you have on Joe Arridy?"

Parent started to say something, then in mid-thought nodded towards the guard by the door. He moved to a four-drawer metal filing cabinet, put on a pair of white cloth gloves and then removed a slim box marked "crime scene photos." He also took out a thick file from a lower drawer plus a fresh pair of white cloth gloves. "The Arridy file is almost 80 years old and the pages are quite fragile," the guard said as he handed it all to James.

After putting on the gloves, James carefully separated the various documents from the file – first the photos, then the time-weathered pages and said, "Please play the tape again, don't bother with the sound for now."

Wanda sat with her head in her hands.

Ivy moved towards the machine, rewound the tape and then pressed the play button.

Without moving his gaze from the screen James asked, "Can you do that again?"

Wanda sighed loudly.

Ivy did as he requested.

"Again, please," James requested.

"What is the use," Wanda asked, throwing up her hands in disgust, "some of Georgia's best forensic pathologists, as well as crime scene examiners from the FBI, CIA, and *all* of this country's military branches have looked at each and every inch of that recording — not once — probably dozens of times. There is nothing there."

"As you said before, 'humor me,'" James said, "How much can you magnify the hands without blurring them beyond recognition?"

"I don't know," Ivy said, "Let me get one of the technicians." She poked her head out of the door and signaled for someone to join them.

"This is Sid," Ivy said, as a middle-aged man with a barrel chest entered the room.

"How can I help?" Sid asked.

"I would like to be able to look at the hands, frame by frame. Please magnify the image as large as you can before it goes out of clear focus?" James said, still staring at the screen.

The man made a series of adjustments, "That is probably as large an image as I can get, will it do?" He asked. Then he slowly ran the tape.

Without answering directly James yelled "stop."

"Do you see something?" Ivy asked.

"I'm not entirely sure," he said, "I understand you also have a tape from a second camera. Can you run the other tape to exactly this same moment in time?"

"I sure can try," the man said, beginning to remove the reel of tape from the first machine.

"No, I would like you to leave the first recording queued up exactly where it is and run the other recording on a different machine, I would like to compare both sets of images at the same time?" James said.

The man walked out of the shed and quickly returned with a second machine. When he had the second recording synced to the image on the first screen James said, "that's it!"

Wanda stood up and moved closer, "What do you see?"

James pointed to one of the hands, "Look at that."

"Look at what," Wanda said, sounding slightly defeated but still clearly annoyed, "what are you making such a fuss about now?"

"Look at the hands," he said. He looked over to Sid and asked him if he could freeze one frame while slowly reversing the tape on the second machine. Sid did as he was directed.

"I'm sorry, Will, I don't know what I am supposed to be looking at," Ivy said.

"See there ... it isn't as clear from the first vantage point but it is crystal clear on this second tape. She is palming the apple core and juice container and you can now see how she slips them into her coat pocket; about a dozen frames later when she *seems* to be struggling with the garbage can lid we see that she is actually pulling a different juice container out of her pocket and places it into the garbage can; she doesn't throw it in; she is *placing* it in."

James then asked Sid to slowly run the portion of the tape as the suspect walks out of the building. "Run both tapes over again."

As the tape ran, James slowly tapped his finger on the top of the machine, as if keeping time. "Follow the beat as she moves. That *limp* of hers comes and goes, it is not constant. Watch it again."

Wanda slumped down into one of the chairs and told James to continue.

"Please play the tape again," James said.

Sid rewound both recordings and hit the start button. Some minutes into the recording they watched the person as she dropped a cell phone into her right pants pocket. They watched her hobble over to a garbage can and struggle with the can's lid. Then she seemed to place the apple core and juice container inside the garbage can. She stopped briefly to stare directly into one of the closed-circuit cameras; nodded slightly toward the camera above the candy display and then, apparently walking with great difficulty, exited the building.

Sid hit the stop button.

"Suppose, for just a moment, that I'm right; that this is a carefully staged performance. If you look at this last bit of tape within that scenario, then the nod to the camera becomes a simple attempt at misdirection. Your attention is brought to the seemingly innocent nod but the real activity is the switching of juice containers," he said.

"Okay, the show is over," Wanda said, "no more repeat performances, if I had wings and could fly I could be a bird but I am not a bird so with or without wings I cannot fly."

"Do you have a diagram of the building showing the placement of the closed-circuit cameras in the lobby?" James asked.

"No we don't," Wanda said, harshly, "the lobby went up like a backyard grill with too much lighter fluid. We have the tapes; why would we need the diagram of the cameras as well? You are just wasting our time and I am beginning to resent it."

"Well I have a diagram of the placement of the closed-circuit cameras. Would you like to see it?" James said.

"What are you doing? Do you think this is some kind of a party game? I don't know about you, Ivy, but I have had quite enough of these theatrics."

Ignoring her flare-up, he calmly said, "On the day of the bombing there were four closed circuit security cameras operational in the lobby. One camera was in clear site, and three cameras were carefully hidden away. We just saw the bomber nod at a closed-circuit camera above the candy counter; that camera was one of the three hidden cameras. How do you think she knew it was there?"

"Who cares?" Wanda said.

"How do you know that?" Ivy asked James.

James sat down and said, "They passed the Georgia Historic Preservation Act ..."

"Stop it!" Wanda said. "Maybe it is the lateness of the hour or the accumulation of a week without end but I think you are dragging us through a maze that can never lead to a solution."

"Let him complete his thought," Ivy said.

James looked at Wanda and said, "Please, whatever you may think of me, you can't believe that I only came here to waste time."

Wanda let out a sigh, "Okay, finish your thought."

"They passed the Georgia Historic Preservation Act of 1980 to create a basis for local governments to protect historic resources within their jurisdictions," James said. "It took Atlanta politicians about 25 or 30 years to finally get around to this theater. They received a grant to update the electrical wiring without reducing the historic value as a first step to spruce it up. They hired a contractor who has done a great deal of similar work with some of the most famous museums in the country. She has also worked on a couple of my assignments over the years. She did the initial study here in Atlanta, and then oversaw the actual work. She used the opportunity to include a few security features. While I was still in New Orleans, I called her and she walked me through the work on this theater. She sent the final approved designs to me in an e-mail." He tapped a few keys on his laptop and up came a schematic of the wiring. "As you can see," he said pointing to various areas of the lobby drawing, "There were four cameras; only one was visible to the naked eye. It sure looks to me like the person on the tape sat so that three cameras could catch her every move. Almost anyone who worked in the building for a while would have eventually learned where two of the three hidden cameras were placed. The fourth was what is called an *executive controlled eye*. Only the chief architect, the general manager of the building, and the local police precinct captain would know about the placement of the fourth camera." He pointed to one of the cameras on the diagram, "this is the executive control eye. It is right above the main entry door leading into the theater. My guess is that it was probably lost in the explosion."

The two women stared at him; Ivy finally broke the silence, "So either the bomber worked in the theater in a high management position or used the services of an accomplice from within the theater's crew?"

"I would say that the latter was a very likely possibility," he said.

Ivy opened her laptop and began typing. She then nodded toward Sid who quickly reached for his cell phone and stepped outside of the room.

They were all quiet for a while. Sid returned to the room and nodded towards Ivy.

"Okay, let's get back to the matter at hand; I don't want to rub salt in the wound but the copy I saw on Wanda's laptop showed the person almost tripping over something just before walking out of the lobby. Can I see that part on the big screen?" James said.

Sid hit the start button.

James stood up and walked over to the screen.

"What are you looking for?" Ivy asked.

"I'm not completely certain. Please, run it back once more from the moment the person heads for the door. This time pay attention to the area around the shoes, zero in on the right cuff."

They were each standing close to the screen now. "Yes," he said, "did you see that?"

"See what?" Ivy asked.

"The person almost tripped over something but quickly caught hold of the walking stick and righted him, or her, or itself. Run it again and this time look closely at how the right pant leg lifts enough to show an ankle — *her* ankle?"

"I think you are right, that is a woman's ankle." Ivy said. "But even if it isn't a woman, it is definitely *not* the ankle of an old man; further confirming that, the person moved too quickly to be the old person we first saw on the bench."

"Maybe it is and maybe it isn't," Wanda said, "but I still don't feel comfortable discounting everything else that seems to point to our perp as a man."

"We have the garbage can he, excuse me, she used," Ivy said, pointing out to the open area, "hard to believe it survived the bombing with little or no damage. Thanks to that, some of the remains of his, no make that *her*, snack were saved."

“A lot of good it does us,” Wanda said, under her breath.

“Were you able to retrieve the remains of the apple?” James asked.

“Give us a break,” Wanda screeched, “how could you expect an apple core to survive that blast? We are lucky we have what we have.”

“I don’t think *luck* has anything to do with it. I think we have exactly what she wanted us to have — no more, no less,” James said. “Logic told us that the Arridy fingerprints were planted, but if we had something she had bitten into we would have had valuable DNA to work with and I think this person on the screen knew that.”

“Do you really believe that none of us also knew that?” Wanda said.

Wanda’s phone rang. She looked at the caller ID and answered it, “Yes Sir.”

She listened intently then said, “I didn’t order the theater employees to be picked up and brought in for questioning ...”

“I did,” Ivy said.

“When,” Wanda asked.

“Actually, it was Sid who did it, which was why he left the room before,” Ivy said.

"Why?" Wanda said.

"One of those people might be the one who gave the bomber inside information about the cameras," Ivy said.

"Say that again," Wanda said into the phone.

Her face went white; she ended the call and slowly put the phone back into her pocket. "The head cashier was the victim of a hit and run driver yesterday morning. He is dead."

"Let's do a thorough background check on all employees, those on or off duty during the night of the blast, and pay additional attention to the one killed in the hit and run incident. Maybe something will surface to tie one or more of the employees to other possible suspects," Ivy said, nodding to Sid who was seated by the door.

"From what we have, it's clear that she knew she was being recorded, knew exactly where the cameras were placed and simply positioned herself and the bomb or bombs so as to allow us to see *just* what she wanted us to see," James said. "She couldn't have known where all of the cameras were placed without at least some inside information. Then there was the theatrics that created initial questions in my mind as to who or what we were dealing with — was he/she a young, vibrant person or an aged person, in good health or poor health, a Scottish national, because of the accented speech on the radio call in show or a German national as described by the taxi driver. Was it a man or a woman, tall or short, fat or thin? Every bit of that seemed to me to be choreographed to the smallest degree so as to baffle or at least confuse investigators. This perp was clearly playing with us and seemed to be having a *very* good time while doing so. *That* is not the work of a committed terrorist. To me, *that* says, 'you can try to catch me but it isn't going to be easy.' There is more, but that should support my initial gut feel; now, how about our getting to the *real* work before us. What do you say we just move on to the rest of the evidence?"

Ivy looked at Wanda and said, "I think we need to share that just a few hours after the blast the primary CSI team was satisfied that this had none of the telltale signs of an act of international terrorism."

"They, like you, were 100 percent convinced that it was planned and carried out by one or more homegrown murderers with something other than terrorism on their mind. You have now confirmed all of that," Wanda said.

"So why do all of the newspaper headlines credited to 'sources close to the investigation,' refer to a terrorist plot?" James asked.

Ivy considered her response carefully and then said, "We wanted the criminal or criminals who were responsible for this to feel safe, maybe even feel like we might never figure it out. Our experts believed that it might delay any follow up crime, buying us a bit more time to work it through. Unfortunately, we completely missed much of what you have pointed out to us today."

"If I am right, then by feeding the press this line of copy you might have actually played right into the perp's hands," James said.

"And you say that, *why?*" Wanda asked.

"I think one of the goals of this perp was to let the public think that those in charge are tripping over their own shoelaces — to paint the investigators as bumblers — unable to really protect the public," James said.

"So, I guess you are now going to tell us exactly who the bomber is, where they can be found, and what they ate for breakfast!" Wanda said.

"This early in an investigation, especially in an investigation where evidence has been moved so far from the actual crime scene — without seeing it all, I would be careful about making any 100 percent conclusions; especially about what they ate for breakfast," James said.

Ivy put her hand in front of her face to hide a broad grin.

"Be more specific, will you?" Wanda said, "I am still working out your right to be working here."

Ivy looked at Wanda and said, "Let me get this straight, we — you, I, plus teams of investigators have been working feverishly for a week of 24-hour days to make heads or tails out of this crime. Dozens of professionals have dissected these tapes 40 ways to Sunday. Will James, with no physical access to the crime scene, the witnesses, or the remaining evidence; not to mention any of the funding and investigating tools we had at our beck and call; entered our world and within a few short hours, with absolutely no guidance from us at all ... in fact, the complete opposite ... was able to point out clue after clue after clue, as though he had a secret decoder ring. Do you still believe that he doesn't belong here? Maybe it is *we* who do not belong here!"

Wanda stared up at the ceiling, heaved a giant sigh, and barely above a whisper said, "I think you're right, Ivy." She then stood up, slowly walked towards James, stared at him for a few seconds and then slapped his face, hard. "That's for switching computers."

He put his hand to his cheek and smiled, "Okay, I did deserve that." He rubbed his cheek again, "You know you pack quite a wallop."

Wanda half smiled then extended her hand and said, "Welcome to Atlanta, Mr. James."

Without missing a beat, James said, "Please, call me Will or James."

Without a moment's hesitation Wanda said, "Welcome to Atlanta ... Will."

Chapter 20

Monday, December 31, 2018 — 7:35 a.m.
700 Block, Royal Street, New Orleans

Schless drove through the night, arriving in front of the Green Parrot just past 7:30 a.m. He saw the blue Cadillac still parked in front of the gallery, not a guarantee, but a good sign that Hornedo was more than likely still tucked away in the gallery. Tired and hungry, he drove to Verti Marti, the famous 24/7 deli farther down on the corner of Royal and Governor Nicholls Streets. He freshened up in the men's room, had a double slice of apple pie and coffee, and then, drove his car to the nearest Schwegmann Giant Supermarkets, parked in a far corner of the parking lot, curled up in the back seat, and fell fast asleep.

A little after 9 a.m., he woke and returned to Verti Marti for a huge breakfast, after which he spent 10 or 15 minutes looking at the sheets of plywood hanging on the walls of the restaurant, tagged with love notes and best wishes by the restaurant's many loyal customers. A six-alarm fire closed it down in mid-2010, but it reopened eight months to the day later.

He then drove to the Western Union office, picked up the keys to the stakeout car, parked his own car in the same lot and drove the stakeout car back to the Green Parrot.

As he circled the block, Schless saw that the Cadillac was still in place which should have meant that Hornedo was there as well, but now he had to make sure. He looked up the gallery's phone number and dialed it. A female voice answered on the second ring.

"May I speak to Mr. Hornedo?" Schless asked.

"Who is calling?"

"This is the office of the Fifth District Police Commander. We had a report of a disturbance outside of your gallery late last night and just wanted to follow up."

There were muffled sounds at the other end of the phone and then a male voice spoke, "This is Mr. Hornedo, Owner of the Green Parrot Gallery D'art. I understand that you are checking up on the disturbance here last night. One of my employees had done a little too much holiday celebrating and had to be driven home. No problem at all. Thank you for checking up, but no need to trouble you any further."

"No problem," Schless said, still pretending to be from the local police, "I will make a note and that should satisfactorily allow us to close the report. Thank you." Schless hung up.

Hornedo noticed that the caller ID screen was blank. *Strange,* he thought, *usually the police district number is on the caller ID; the caller did say he was speaking from the commander's office; maybe the commander's office generates a blank screen.*

He checked for the local police district's general telephone number in the local phone book and dialed the number.

"New Orleans Police, District 5, Philamena Charles speaking, what is your emergency?"

"Hi," Hornedo said, "This is Mr. Hornedo, Owner of the Green Parrot Gallery D'art on Royal Street. We have been getting prank calls recently, innocent in nature, just annoying and somewhat disruptive to our business routine. I think I just had one and the man at the other end of the line claimed to be calling from your commander's office; can you tell me if it was really from your office or actually another prank call?"

"I'm the only one at the board so far this morning, Mr. Hornedo, and I assure you that I am definitely *not* a man, however, if you will just give me a moment I will check with the commander."

Several minutes later, the commander came to the phone, "This is Commander Greer, Mr. Hornedo. I have checked and no one from this office placed a call to your gallery today. We have a zero-tolerance policy for anyone falsely representing themselves as police, would you like me to have your line checked to see if we can trace the call back to its origination?"

"No, you have satisfied my question, I'm sure you have far more important things to worry about this holiday season," Hornedo said.

"Okay, but if they call back again please let me know," the commander said.

"Will do, happy holidays to you and the Fifth District's finest," Hornedo said.

*****

Smiling broadly to himself, Schless put the car into gear and began to drive around in search of a parking space with an unobstructed view of the front entrance to the gallery. He noticed a man and a young boy huddled in a doorway. Schless turned to look at all of the food James had left in the car. He pulled along the curb, parked the car and got out. "Excuse me," Schless said to the man, "I wonder if you can help me out."

The man smiled, "In case you haven't noticed, I'm not in much of a position to help myself, much less you or anyone else, but I'd be happy to try. What do you need?"

"I have a quota to fill for today," Schless said, "I need to give away a car full of healthy snacks and fresh fruits and I am at least a half a car behind schedule. Can you suggest a place where all of this will not go to waste?"

"You're kidding, right?" the man said.

"No, I'm perfectly serious. Can you help me?"

The man stood up, tried to brush away the dirt and wrinkles from his clothes, ran his hands through his hair. "If you are serious," the man said, "then I would be happy to help you." The man slowly walked towards Schless with the young boy following closely behind him. "I can direct you to the soup kitchen where my son and I *dine* from time to time. We happen to know the maître d'hôtel, personally."

Schless pointed to the front door of his car and said, "Would you be willing to ride along with me to show me how to get there? I'll bring you both back when we are done."

The boy looked up at the man, "Can we, Dad?" The man seemed to be thinking it over then said, "Sure, it is probably warmer in his car than out here."

The man opened the back door, looked inside, and then moved to the side so that the boy could climb in. There was barely enough room for him among all the bags and boxes of groceries, but soon he was able to wiggle around enough to free up and connect the seat belt. The man pulled at the seat belt closure, then gently but firmly closed the door. He moved to the front passenger side, got inside, and closed the door behind him.

"Hi," he said, sticking out his hand towards Schless, "I'm Greg Poulakis," pointing towards the back seat he added, "That's my son Niko."

"New to New Orleans?" Schless asked.

"No, we're lifers – well I am but Niko was born in Austin, Texas," the man said, mournfully, "now we are bedraggled, disheveled, even a bit unkempt, but still unbeaten natives of *The Big, not always so Easy*."

"We're homeless," Niko said.

"Just for the moment," Greg broke in, "we won't be homeless forever." His voice trailed off, "Nothing is forever ... nothing is forever."

"I'm going to be a zookeeper when I grow up and then I will take care of my mom and dad and sister," Niko said, proudly.

"A zookeeper, huh," Schless said.

"Hey, mister, this is a nice car," Niko said.

"Life was a whole lot different for us before Hurricane Katrina," Greg said. "I had a great job; I was actually a vice president of underwriting for a fairly large insurance and investment management company. We offered all kinds of insurance products to our customers. What do they say? A shoemaker has no shoes? Well we didn't have enough coverage to either rebuild or refurnish. Eventually, like all too many of our neighbors, we lost it all. Before the storm, my family was together ... life was pretty good, we had a great little baby girl," he took a small billfold out of his pocket and pulled out a tattered photo and showed it to Schless, "that's my wife, Kennan, our beautiful two-year old daughter, Riley, and the miraculous baby bump became Niko just four months later. We were the perfect all American family, husband, wife and two children — well almost two children, we had one and 5/9th children," his voice trailed off again as he turned to stare out of the passenger side window.

"You don't have to talk about it if you don't want to," Schless said softly.

"Hey, it is what it is," the man said. "You know how the old Sinatra song goes, 'You're riding high in April, shot down in May ... that's life,' well I wasn't shot down until August ... August 29th to be exact," then sitting up straight, he wiped away the moisture under his eyes and said, "If you continue to drive up this street you will pass Canal. Keep going in the same general direction about half way around route 110 to Claiborne. The place we are going to is at 4526 South Claiborne Avenue. It shouldn't be more than 10 or 12 minutes away by car. My son and I usually walk it in less than an hour. We make a few stops along the way; Niko's legs are a lot shorter than mine."

Schless put the car in gear and began driving according to the directions he had just received.

"You're pretty trusting," the man said to Schless, "Picking up two strangers the way you did."

"Well," Schless said, "I knew I could fight off any advances from you, it was the killer in the backseat I was really worried about."

The man smiled. While they were driving, the man shared that his family was permanently uprooted by the storm. He told how they had been living the American dream. "We had a great little place on Frenchmen Street; nothing there now for us but a whole lot of memories." He went on to tell Schless that at first, they all moved in with an aunt in Austin, Texas. Work was hard to find but you put your ego in moth balls and do what you have to in order to survive. Some months back the tension between Greg and his wife Kennan reached a point where they decided that a separation might be best. He and Niko returned to New Orleans and Kennan stayed in Texas with their daughter, Riley.

About 15 minutes later, Schless pulled up to a building with a modest sign, "The Salvation Army." There was a handmade sign on a wall nearby, "All of God's children are safe here — you are no longer alone and will always be welcomed."

Schless and Greg moved the food from the back seat of the car into the building. The people in the building seemed to know both Greg and Niko quite well.

When they got back into the car, Schless asked Greg if he minded taking a side trip before they returned to the place where he first picked them up. Greg agreed and so Schless drove back to Schwegmann's. The store was stocked to the brim and the aisles were humming with shoppers and full shopping carts for that evening's New Year's Eve festivities. Schless couldn't help but make the mental comparison to the barren soup kitchen he had just left.

Schless began filling his cart with a wide assortment of cookies and crackers, fresh baked goods, various cuts of meat and fish and produce. He asked Greg to get another cart and when Greg returned with it Schless filled it with fresh vegetables, some canned goods, cheeses, all of the freshly roasted chickens they had on display — 14 in all. He drove back to the Salvation Army soup kitchen and gave them all of the items he had just purchased, except for one of the roasted chickens, a few pieces of fruit, a loaf of bread, and a box of cookies.

When the person in charge of the kitchen asked to whom she could make the donation receipt out to, Schless said, "Baby New Year."

Schless walked out of the building feeling really good for the first time since leaving Nashville.

The three got back into the car and drove in silence back towards Royal Street. About a block and a half before the 700 block Greg said they would like to stop here, so they could visit a sick friend. Schless stopped by the curb and they all got out of the car. Schless got out of the car, handed Greg the bag with the still warm roasted chicken and assorted other items that he held back from the Salvation Army. “Share this with your friend,” Schless said. They shook hands.

Schless put his arms around Niko and said he hoped this New Year would bring better times for them and their neighbors. He returned to the car, waved goodbye, and drove off.

Greg Poulakis watched the car fade into the distance, then he looked inside the bag and saw the food along with five crisp new hundred dollar bills. Tears began rolling down his cheeks as he reached down and showed his son what was inside of the bag.

Chapter 21

Monday, December 31, 2018 — 7:48 a.m.
Hartsfield-Jackson Atlanta International Airport,
Security Division, Third Floor,
North Terminal, Blue Side

The Secretary of Homeland Security was going over his notes for his 8 a.m. presidential briefing when Wanda called. He instinctively stopped to see the name on the caller ID, but with very few exceptions had been letting the calls go to voice mail until after what had become his regular morning briefing for the chief executive. However, he was anxious to hear what, if any progress Ivy, Wanda and Will James might have made.

He put the phone on speaker and said, "I am just a few minutes away from my briefing call to the White House, whatever you have to say, say it quickly."

There was silence on the other end of the phone, "Speak," he demanded.

"I would respectfully suggest that you put off your morning briefing call until *after* you hear what we have come up with," Wanda said.

He was putting his notes in order and only half listening to her, "Which means?" he barked toward the phone.

"Which means that I believe we have come up with enough to put us on a path towards a solution," she said.

The secretary grabbed the phone and said, "Talk to me."

"I just did. I think you should hear about the possible progress Will and I have to show for the long and tedious night we just spent together before you speak with anyone — especially POTUS."

"Stay where you are," he said, "I will call you right back."

Seconds later Ivy's phone rang, she looked at the screen and said, "Good morning Mr. Secretary."

Coming right to the point, he said, "*Fisher woman* tells me that she and James may have broken the case. Is she right?"

Ivy smiled, "I wouldn't exactly say that it was a group effort or that the case is solved but, yes, Will seems to have put us on a clearer road toward a possible solution."

"I have a briefing scheduled for the president at 8 this morning and a press conference scheduled for 9, I don't want to wind up with a batch of eggs dripping all over me. Wanda asked me to delay both the POTUS briefing and the news conference, any suggestions?" he said.

"I think you should take her advice. At the very least buy yourself a little time before either event; let us brief you, then make your decision." Ivy said.

"Is this *little time* more like 10 minutes or 10 hours ... or 10 days?" he asked.

Ivy laughed, “Oh Fritz, you know you could never sit still for 10 hours, much less 10 days.”

He hung up and dialed Wanda who answered on the first ring. “How quickly could you all get to the tomb?” he asked.

“It has been a long night Fritz, could we get at least an hour or two sleep, a quick breakfast and some clean clothes first?” she asked, “I don’t think Will has slept in two days. Remember he hit the road running the minute he landed and that was after a full day’s work in New Orleans.”

“Okay,” he said, “set it up for 8:30, in the tomb,” he said.

“8:30 ... *p.m.*?” she asked.

“Very funny, no, that’s 8:30 *a.m.*,” he said sternly.

“Come on Fritz, give us more than a half an hour. You know I don’t complain, but we are all dragging,” she said.

“If you guys have miraculously come up with some good news, I need to brief the president and I need to brief her *now!*”

“Come on, Fritz, it won’t help you at all if we fall asleep during the briefing,” Wanda pleaded.

“Okay, okay! Twelve noon. Sharp. In the tomb, not one minute later,” he hung up.

*****

When the three of them arrived, the secretary pulled Wanda aside. "How did you go from lead-hater to chief-worrier about his lack of sleep in a matter of hours?"

"Let's not spend valuable time on this," Wanda said.

"No, I need to know that this is not a set-up, or even worse, a sign that you have mentally checked out on us. When I last saw you, just a matter of hours ago, I wondered if Ivy would be able to keep you two from killing each other. Now you are his bosom buddy? Fill me in," the secretary said.

"Oh Fritz," Wanda began, "You must already have heard all about it from Ivy."

"I asked Ivy but all she would say was that you put him to the test and he seemed to have passed with flying colors. Then she said that I needed to talk to you. Come on Wanda, open up," he demanded.

"Okay, believe it or not he made a believer out of me," she said.

"In just a matter of hours?" he said.

"Look Fritz, he is really good; he dissected the surveillance tape and inside of minutes came to the same conclusion our lead investigators did ... and he did it without any of the tools they had. Then he pointed out details none of us saw, in more than a week of around the clock days. He definitely convinced me — and believe me, I didn't make it easy for him."

"So, are you suggesting that we send everyone else home?" he teased.

"All I care about now is that you don't send me home. Let us brief you and you be the judge," she said.

*****

The secretary requested that the various agency heads and the lead team of investigators meet in one of the airport's rarely used interrogation areas. Internally referred to as "The Tomb," it was a windowless, poorly ventilated area – the cinder block walls and bare and the cement floors were painted in dull battleship gray. In the center was a massive oblong shaped table surrounded by a series of oversized red leather high backed chairs.

At one end of the room was a white board, at the other end a tall catering cart. On the bottom shelf of the cart was a supply of paper cups and plates, plastic forks and spoons, and a collection of white napkins from various takeout restaurants, and coffee shops around the airport. On the middle shelf, was a supply of bottled water, cans of soda and various fruit juices, and a huge basket overfilled with individually wrapped muffins. On the top shelf was a 30-cup coffee maker, a supply of sugar and sugar substitute packets, a bowl of ice, and another bowl filled to the brim with small non-dairy creamers.

On the table were six, evenly placed water pitchers. Opposite each chair was a printed name card on top of a yellow legal-sized pad, two sharpened pencils, and a tall water glass placed upon a small cork coaster. The water pitchers, coasters, glasses, and pencils all had the seal of the Department of Homeland Security on them.

A group of mismatched metal chairs were set up against each of the remaining two walls.

The secretary took a quick look around and whispered to the head of the FBI, “Say Jeb, where is Abi?”

The FBI director turned toward his aid seated behind him and slyly winked, then turned to face the secretary, shrugged, and said, “Probably having his second or third breakfast of the day. That man has a bottomless pit for a stomach.”

The secretary motioned for everyone to take a seat by their name card and for any support staff in the room to sit on the metal chairs behind their principals. As soon as everyone was settled he introduced James as one of the department’s contract consultants. Brief introductions were made around the table and then the secretary advised the group that State Attorney General Wanda Parent and James had come up with an interesting theory that might move the investigation along a potentially more fruitful direction. Wanda blushed, said that it was mostly James’ hypothesis, but she thinks he is on the right track. She motioned for James to brief the group.

James was convinced that no matter how he presented his findings, the various agencies would begin pointing fingers, first at each other because no one — at least not up to this moment — had been able to make heads or tails out of the chaos since the previous week. Eventually, they would make him their common target and blame him for the lack of a solution.

James stood, picked up his empty glass as well as the one to his left and walked toward the end of the room with the white board. He pointed toward the opposite wall and asked everyone to focus their attention on the bottom layer of the bowl of muffins. There was a bit of grumbling, but within minutes everyone was facing the opposite side of the room. James lifted both hands and let the two glasses drop to the floor. Most of those around the table quickly dived for the floor, pivoted to face the side where they heard the loud crash; others reached for their weapons, while the rest sat in their seats and stared at James.

James held up his hands and asked everyone to take their seats. "Each one of you has been trained to react without thinking. You are programmed to act fast – to see and completely protect those around you."

The secretary interrupted, "You are either the bravest man I know, Will, or the most reckless – more than half the people in this room have a loaded side arm; I'm surprised that you do not have more holes in you right now than a wheel of Swiss cheese."

"It was a simple example of *misdirection*," James said as he returned to his place at the table and sat down. "I asked everyone to concentrate on the basket of muffins – I will bet a good steak dinner, plus a bottle of your favorite wine, that although you all turned your heads in that direction, most of you were thinking how wasteful this meeting now promised to be. Then *crash,* and your thoughts quickly returned to this room and your training took over; you got into a fighting stance, ready for action. But, as you turned toward the sound all you saw was me, with my 'empty' hands in the air ... no apparent threat. The criminal we are chasing did exactly the same thing last week. She ..."

The FBI director interrupted James, "You mean *he*."

"No, I mean *she,"* James corrected.

"We have surveillance tapes to prove that we are dealing with a man," the Atlanta chief of police said.

"I suggest that we have a surveillance tape which was *created* to give us that impression, but at some point — probably not too much into the future — I am convinced that it would have become crystal clear to everyone in this room that your, *'he',* is in fact a *'she.'"*

A woman at the end of the table raised her hand. "You believe that this fiend dressed up as a man to throw us off the track?"

"No, not to throw you off the track; she had to know that it was only a matter of time before the investigators would put the pieces together."

"Then why the charade?" the mayor asked.

"I believe that our criminal wanted the powers that be to issue initial statements which would only have to be reversed shortly thereafter," James said.

A meek looking man, in his mid-30s, with thick horn rimmed glasses spoke up, "Mr. James, you are telling us that so many of our citizens were killed and maimed just so that a few of us could be embarrassed?"

"I am telling you that I believe that this very well planned and executed attack is an act of revenge, and as soon as this criminal gets the revenge she seeks, she might just go back to her life as it was before," James said.

An older man, several seats to the left of James stood up, "Mr. Secretary, we are wasting our time here."

"Let's hear him out, Sam," the secretary said, "It isn't like we are working any other possibilities right now — let's all be honest here, we have hit a brick wall. Will believes there is a light at the end of the tunnel. It shouldn't take us too long to determine if it is daylight or an oncoming train."

Ivy was sitting to the secretary's right. He turned to her, and covering his mouth he leaned in and whispered, "Are you still sure about this guy?"

"He hasn't given me any reason to doubt him so far. Let's not forget, he was able to turn Wanda into a believer — what does *that* say to you?" Ivy whispered back.

"I don't know about that, but I do know you ... and I totally trust your intuitive skills. Frankly, that and that alone is what I am now hanging on to," he said.

He shielded his mouth again and leaned over to the man seated behind him, his chief of staff, Edward Fraser. "Pull the plug on the press conference. Tell the press that of course we are still working on the case, but today belongs to the survivors and family members of those who have died. Put together a prayer service for later today and I will attend."

"The press will roast you over the coals for that," Fraser said.

"I'll worry about that some other time. I just want to hear this Will James out. Right now, all I have for the press is the usual, 'we are working diligently,' you know we are no closer to a suspect this very minute than we were when the blast first went off. Do you really believe the press will be any kinder to that message?"

Fraser nodded, stood up and walked out of the room.

The secretary motioned to James, "Please, continue Will."

James stood and walked back to the white board.

"No more theatrics, okay?" One of the men said, "I'll be picking glass shards out of my pant legs for days".

"No more theatrics," James agreed, "As I was saying before I so rudely interrupted myself, I suggest that the criminal we are chasing here did exactly the same thing last week. She pointed us in one direction while she moved in a completely different direction." He then began to unravel the radio conversation and the closed-circuit television tape as he had for Wanda and Ivy some hours earlier.

Chapter 22

Monday, December 31, 2018 — 9:14 p.m.
Hartsfield-Jackson Atlanta International Airport,
Security Division, Third Floor,
North Terminal, Blue Side

As the last of those attending the briefing filed out of the room, Ivy walked over to James and sat down next to him.

"Do you think they left convinced?" James asked her.

"It is hard to say. These are hard as nails career spooks. They learn early on in their career to mask all but their most basic reactions. However, I can tell you that as the secretary stood to leave, he told me he thought you had broken through the brick wall."

James smiled, thanked her for her support and stood up. "I know one thing for certain," he said, "I need to get some sleep." He stood up, stretched his arms, and then grabbing on to the edge of the table dropped back into his chair.

"Are you all right?" Ivy asked.

James sat, his face ashen white, perspiration beginning to darken areas of his shirt. Ivy spilled some water on a napkin and began patting his face with it.

"What is going on?" she asked.

"I'm not sure," he answered, "maybe just the lack of sleep catching up with me, but all of a sudden, I got this eerie feeling that something terrible has just happened."

Chapter 23

About a half hour earlier...
Monday, December 31, 2018 — 8:42 p.m.
700 block, Royal Street, New Orleans

Schless sat in his car within clear site of the Green Parrot. The powder blue Cadillac sedan, referenced in James' notes, was parked just outside of the entrance to the building. From the position of the car, it seemed like there had been no movement, in or out since he had initially arrived earlier that morning.

A brown UPS truck pulled up to the front entrance of the gallery. Schless considered getting out of his car because the entrance was now completely blocked from his view, *I'll give you exactly two minutes to move that truck*, he thought.

The driver remained in the truck and moved quickly from his seat to the back cargo area. He returned with a small carton, put it on the dashboard, put the truck into gear, and slowly drove away.

The powder blue Cadillac was gone.

What just happened, he wondered.

Schless turned his head quickly to see someone standing on the sidewalk by the passenger side window. In a blur of movement, the figure pointed a long rifle at him and fired two shots through the glass window. Schless fell forward, his head landing hard on the horn.

The assailant quickly ran away.

Niko had been watching, in horror, from a doorway a few buildings down. He was being held back by his father but struggled free and ran toward the car. "He's shot!" he screamed, "Help him, someone help him. My friend has been shot."

*****

Elizabeth was watching the evening news when her company cell phone rang. She looked at the caller ID, it read, "New Orleans 5"; *who could this be,* she thought to herself. She answered on the second ring, "Will James and Crew, Elizabeth speaking."

"Hello, is this Elizabeth Hillsonrat?" the caller asked.

"Yes, it is," she said, hesitantly, "and you are?"

"I am Commander Billy Greer of the New Orleans Fifth Police District. I was asked to call you at this number in case of emergency by a Mr. Will James."

"Is there an emergency?" she asked.

"Mr. James was shot in his car earlier this evening. He has been rushed to the University Medical Center and is currently in critical condition."

"Do you have a local number for the emergency room?" she asked.

"Allow me to patch you into their community information officer's desk," he said, "Chances are they will respond quicker and in more detail to a call from me than to a long-distance call from you."

Minutes later both Commander Greer and Elizabeth were connected to Abby Marcus, head of community relations at the hospital.

The police commander spoke first, "Hi Abby, this is Billy Greer over at NOPD, District 5, also on the line is a Ms. Elizabeth Hillsonrat in New Jersey. Earlier this evening Mr. Will James, an associate of Ms. Hillsonrat, was rushed to your ER. He is a private investigator from up north, and has been on surveillance here. Because he told me that he did not work with a weapon and since he planned to setup his stakeout in a rough part of town, I asked the beat cops on each shift to keep an eye on the vehicle Mr. James said he would be using. A homeless person in a doorway a few yards from the shooting claimed to see the attack and made sure it was called into 911. The *beats* were just a block away when the call came in. They rushed to the scene and found the victim in a pool of blood, unresponsive, with dangerously low vitals."

Elizabeth and Greer could hear the rustling of papers on the other side of the connection, after a brief silence Marcus said, "We have a John Doe who was brought in a short while ago with life threatening gunshot wounds but there was no identification on him. How can we be certain that our John Doe is your Mr. James?"

"He checked in with me when he first came to town and gave me the make, model, color, and plate number for the vehicle he would be using and the attack took place on a white male in that exact vehicle."

"What can you tell me about his condition?" Elizabeth asked.

"He was hit in the chest by what the admitting doctor thought to be a .22 long rifle shot at short range. It resulted in severe internal injuries that miraculously missed his heart and vital arteries. His body must have been in motion which saved him from the worst of a second bullet that entered through his shoulder in a downward trajectory. There are glass shards throughout the right half of his face and upper torso. As your men reported, he had already lost a great deal of blood by the time he was checked in; he is currently in intensive care. Vital signs are unstable and not within normal limits. That is all I have."

Elizabeth said that all costs would be fully covered and gave her cell phone number to Marcus, asking to be notified as soon as they had more information. She asked for and received a cell phone number from Commander Greer, thanked both Commander Greer and Marcus and hung up.

As soon as the connection ended, Elizabeth scrolled down her cell phone contact list and stopped at Vince Margules' number. Vince was a New York industrialist who owned a private plane which he occasionally made available to James' team. As soon as Elizabeth told him what had happened to James, Margules agreed to have his plane fueled and ready to take her to New Orleans. He added that he would also call ahead to arrange for a limo to pick her up at her apartment and take her to Teterboro Airport where his plane was kept, and offered to have a second limo waiting on the tarmac when the plane landed in New Orleans to rush her to the hospital.

"You have enough on your plate now to have to worry about transportation," he said, "I'll take care of everything; just let me know about his condition as soon as you know more." Almost as a second thought he added, "My foundation has made a series of contributions to several medical facilities in New Orleans over the years, especially during and since Katrina, and it might help you to throw my name around. I'll call ahead to ensure that you receive their full cooperation. One last thing, not negotiable, I'll cover all of his costs."

"Thank you for the plane, Vince, but you know he will never let you pay his medical bills; it's the unbreakable law around here — 'no gifts for any of the crew members from clients, former or current,'" Elizabeth said.

"Well, from what you told me, he isn't in any position to complain right now, so let's consider it a done deal, consider it a sincere show of respect and gratitude for all he's done for me."

"I really can't let you do that," she said.

"The subject is closed," he said. "Good luck, Elizabeth; just let me know if I can be of any additional help. You have my private cell phone number, as well as the number at the lodge and the apartment in the city. You will be able to find me at one of those locations — I'm available for you 24 hours a day. If you need something call me. The answer will be yes, *period*. All I ask for in return is to be clued in until you get him home, safe and sound." The line went dead.

Part 2

Chapter 24

Monday, December 31, 2018 — 10:27 p.m.
700 block, Royal Street, New Orleans

Arturo Hornedo owned one of the nine L-32 flip phones believed to exist in the world. It had no other feature beyond the capability of being able to send or receive secure telephone messages. The research and development had been financed by a select group — including six of the most powerful people on earth, plus three revolving members of their exclusive club: a Colombian drug lord, the head of the Russian mafia, and a high-level representative from the Vatican.

When the Colombian drug lord was captured, his brother — also the drug lord's most trusted banker — broke into his brother's underground safe room, and among other key possessions, sold the L-32 to Arturo Hornedo, his longtime money launderer. When the rest of the group learned that the ninth phone was no longer accounted for they kidnapped the banker and everyone in his immediate family. Fortunately for Hornedo, the banker died of a heart attack before he was able to tell his torturers about Hornedo.

Without alerting them to the uniqueness of this phone, Hornedo only shared the knowledge of how to dial into it with three of his largest clients, one of which was the famous tele-evangelist, Sister Joan.

*****

Hornedo and Dmitri were talking about a future assignment when the L-32 made its distinctive chirping sound. Hornedo picked it up and asked Dmitri to excuse him and wait in the other room. As Dmitri began to close the door, Hornedo flipped the phone open.

"I don't know what influence you might have over the lady but I strongly advise you to tell her that if she goes through with her plans to blow up the power grid in Las Vegas tomorrow night she will bring all sorts of bad on top of her, as well as anyone connected to her. It is unlikely that she will care about anyone but herself – but she does care about herself."

"She would never do such a thing," Hornedo said.

"She already has done worse."

"What are you talking about?"

"She is the one who blew up the movie theater in Atlanta on Christmas Eve."

"Sister Joan blew up the movie theater in Atlanta?" There was a long silence. "I don't believe it," Hornedo finally said.

"Why do you think she wanted you to help her get that stupid handgun from that house in Colorado?"

"What does one thing have to do with the other?"

"Please, for your own safety as well as mine, make her stop. She has become certifiable. If she goes through with this thing in Las Vegas the *boys* will find out eventually who did it, and when they do we are all gonna die."

Hornedo disconnected the call. He sat staring at the phone and then taking his cell phone out of his pocket he dialed Sister Joan.

"Well, hello stranger," she said.

"You sound like you are in particularly good spirits," he said to her, "I can always use good news, want to share?"

"Oh, Arturo, I am always in good spirits. The Lord's work is very satisfying."

"Tell me Sister Joan, I heard that you are planning some mischief in Las Vegas tomorrow night. Please tell me that I am wrong."

She stared at the phone, then answered hesitantly, "Whatever are you talking about?"

"If it is true, tell me now."

"Hey," she shouted, "You don't own me, you make a lot of money because of me but make no mistake, I am free to do whatever I want, whenever I want, wherever I want, so sayeth the Lord."

"Now listen to me and listen good. If I know about this, there must be others who also know about this. Eventually, everyone *will* find out, and when they do the kinds of people we know in Las Vegas will cut little pieces out of you until you beg them to finish you off. These are not the kinds of people you want holding a grudge."

"I fear no man."

"Is it true that you also blew up that movie theater in Atlanta that has everyone in my business running for cover?"

"Where are you getting all of this nonsense?"

"If it isn't true just tell me that it isn't true."

She slammed the phone down and yelled for Scully.

Scully walked into the room, "Why must you scream my name at the top of your lungs, you know that I'm never more than a room away. Okay, what is it?"

"How did Arturo know about our New Year's Day plans?"

"First of all, it isn't *our* plans, it is *your* plans, and I have already told you that if it was up to me, you would wait a few weeks instead of prodding the sleeping tiger again so quickly after Atlanta. As far as how he found out or who else might know ... your guess is as good as mine."

She stared at him, and then threw her hands up in disgust, "If Arturo knows I have to assume others do as well. Without the element of surprise, we stand a stronger chance of being caught, so I will push it off for now."

He held back a smile, "You're in charge," he said, then turned and left the room.

*****

With a broad smile, Dmitri moved his ear away from the door and sat down as Hornedo opened the door and invited him back into his office.

“Now,” Hornedo growled, “where were we?”

Chapter 25

Wednesday, January 2, 2019 — 6:09 a.m.
Atlanta Airport Marriott Gateway Hotel

Most of the previous day, James had been shuffled from one meaningless meeting to another; he was thinking of returning home when his cell phone rang. It was Ivy, "Where are you?"

"What do you mean, 'where am I?' I'm in my hotel room watching the news."

"Why aren't you here?" she asked.

"Where is here?" he asked.

"At the briefing room."

"No one told me there was a briefing this morning."

"There is a briefing every morning?" she said.

"How am I supposed to know that?" he said.

"The daily committee chair informs everyone," she said.

"Well no one informed me, or I would have been there," he said.

"Hang on, let me get to the bottom of this," she said.

Chapter 26

Wednesday, January 2, 2019 — 6:32 a.m.
Atlanta Airport Marriott Gateway Hotel

James's phone rang, it was Ivy, "I'm in the breakfast room of your hotel. Please come down and join me as soon as you can.

As James got closer to the table he saw Ivy, the secretary, and a barrel-chested man in a crumpled army fatigue shirt.

The secretary stood and extended his hand to James, "Hello Will," pointing to the other man at the table he said, "Will James, please meet Abimelech Böhmer."

Abi's head was down as he continued eating. He made no move toward James.

The secretary put his hand firmly on Abi's shoulder and in an in-charge voice said, "Shake the man's hand, Abi."

Without looking up Abi said, "Why should I, he is probably one more of your clerks who can't see because his head is so far up his ..."

The secretary looked at James and said, "Abi Böhmer is ..."

James broke in, "A hero of mine!"

The Israeli looked up for the first time, "What makes you think I give two hoots what you think of me?"

"I'm not asking for your autograph," James said, "and I'm definitely not planning to take you home with me for dinner ... I'm just stating a fact. I'm also wondering if my hero's eyes are beginning to fail him. I worked shoulder to shoulder with you and your people in Saint Lucia when your team went there to build a field hospital in the wake of the hurricane."

"You were in Saint Lucia?" Abi asked.

"Among many others who were also there," James said.

"I never saw you before in my life," Abi said, returning to his meal.

"So, it isn't just your eyes that are failing you, but your memory too?" James said.

"How many womans were there, during any part of the months it took to build that hospital," Abi asked.

"It didn't take months — it took less than a day; surely you remember that. And there were no women — you don't allow women on your projects," James said, "You may be a hero of mine, but you are also a sexist and probably a male chauvinist pig to boot."

Abi slammed his fork down on the table, leaned back and roared with laughter. "You are no clerk, you got guts. I like that. Where have they been hiding you?"

Ivy said, "I advised the secretary that you were being frozen out of the deliberations and he shared the fact that the group seemed to be doing the same to his Israeli guest."

"I had to be sure that Wanda wasn't playing both sides against the middle," the secretary said, "And I am convinced that she wasn't even aware of it. So I thought it would be time to form a *second tier of specialists*."

Just then, Wanda walked briskly toward them, when she reached the table she nodded to those already there, grabbed a chair, sat down and as she reached for a breakfast roll she said, "Okay, I'm here, let's get started."

Chapter 27

Wednesday, January 2, 2019 — 2:22 p.m.
University Medical Center, New Orleans

Soon after she learned that Bonnie Schless's plane had landed, Elizabeth settled into one of the side chairs in the hospital lobby. Her eyes kept moving from the door to her wristwatch. *What could be taking so long*, she wondered, *it is only an hour or so from the airport to the hospital*.

At almost 3:30, Bonnie, and her son Mark, rushed into the lobby. Elizabeth stood up and quickly embraced the woman. Before she could reach out to hug Mark he asked, "How is my Dad doing?"

"He is still in critical condition. They put him into a medically induced coma earlier today," Elizabeth said.

"Oh, my God!" Bonnie said, "Oh my God! Can I see him?"

"Not right now, they are working on him," Elizabeth said.

"Why did it take so long for you to contact us," Mark asked.

Elizabeth pointed to the coffee shop off the main entrance and said, "You must be famished, let's sit down in there. We will have a bit more privacy and there isn't likely to be any news from the doctors for at least another hour or two."

“I can’t eat right now,” Bonnie said.

“Then let’s move over there,” Elizabeth said, pointing to a group of chairs in the far corner of the lobby.

As soon as they were settled, Mark asked again, “Why did it take more than a day for you or anyone in your group to contact us?”

“It wasn’t until late last night that I first learned it was your father who had been attacked. When I was initially contacted, the police seemed to think Will James had been the one rushed to the hospital. When I first got here they wouldn’t let me up because of his condition. When they finally did let me in, I realized it was your dad and not Will. That was when I called your mother. “

“Is Will here?” Bonnie asked.

“No, I have not been unable to reach Will — I am assuming he is on assignment because his cell phone is turned off, so he still does not know about the attack on your husband,” Elizabeth said.

“That’s unusual,” Mark said, sarcastically, “I thought you were all in a *mind meld* with each other.”

“Enough,” Bonnie said.

“So one more time, my Dad took the short end of the stick for the famous Will James,” Mark said.

“I told you to stop it,” Bonnie said.

Chapter 28

Wednesday, January 2, 2019 — 8:17 p.m.
Atlanta Airport Marriott Gateway Hotel

Even though they all agreed that it turned out to be a very productive day, it didn't start out that way. After the secretary left, they seemed to be going through the motions, but neither Wanda nor Abi had been accustomed to working without a support team and so each waited for the other to acknowledge their *rightful* place as committee leader.

After an hour or so, patiently watching Abi take call after call from various subordinates in Israel, and Wanda and James pounding away on their respective computers, Ivy began shuttling back and forth between the three. Her message was respectful but firm; each one has a strength — if not multiple strengths — which the others lack or could benefit from. The challenge is to somehow work towards making the whole greater than the sum of the parts. When that approach didn't seem to be working, she decided to gently light a fire under their egos and said, "The so-called professionals have all but dismissed you." Pointing to Abi and James she continued, "They successfully kept you on the bench. With all due respect, they have treated you like damaged goods, *seconds*, not at all worthy of their time or even attention. And you," she said to Wanda, "they don't know what to do with you. They seem to have come to terms with the realization that you are too well plugged in for them to be able to ignore you but they certainly haven't treated you like an equal, have they."

"Wait a minute," Wanda said.

"Excuse me, I'm not taking sides, I am just telling you what I see," Ivy said.

"So what do you suggest," Abi asked.

"I suggest we gather together and prove them wrong. I suggest we prove the little mathematic equation I just offered, that one plus one plus one equals more than the sum of all the others who have come up empty so far. They are walking around like first place winners, while treating each of you as second class citizens."

"Well I am definitely not a *second,"* Abi said, "I can run rings around the rest of them put together."

"Don't tell *me*, show *them*," Ivy said. "The secretary put you all together because he lost faith in the teams of 'so-called' experts who have wasted a week blaming others and playing jurisdictional games. He thought you three were above all of that. Let us not forget what happened on Christmas Eve. If for no other reason, let's work together in the name of the dead and injured as well as the still missing and their friends and family members who may never know the fate of their loved ones."

"You have no right," Wanda started to say.

"I don't claim any right. I don't matter, I am here as support — your support. You are the ones who matter," Ivy kept saying. "If you agree that you are not 'seconds' to anyone, then I would suggest you meet around a common table; do what the 'so-called first team' has shown that they are incapable of doing — check your egos and prejudices and preconceived notions, at the door. That may be a good way to increase the chances for solving this crime especially since the *so-called* very best in their field with unlimited access and funding, have come up so empty so far. You might want to limit your initial focus to a search for who could have been behind the bombing and how best to bring that person or those persons to justice before they can commit any other crimes against innocent people here in Atlanta or anywhere else. I suggest that you each have a turn at playing out the 'who, what, and why', according to your specific areas of expertise."

Ivy pointed to a small round table in the corner, "I suggest we all sit around that table over there. It is round so each of you can be at the head of the table."

"But it is so small," Wanda said.

"That makes it perfect, the tighter the circle, the easier it will be to form a singular force," Ivy said.

Almost meekly, the three moved slowly toward the table and sat down. Ivy pulled up a chair and the others moved a bit closer to each other to make room for her.

"I declare the first meeting of the *Seconds* is now in session," Abi said.

Ivy smiled and lifted her water glass to the others, "Hear, hear. Now that we are eye to eye, I would suggest that we begin with Wanda's legal assessment, then Abi could restate the facts based upon his vast military experience, and finally we can hear from Will and his unique analytical processes and rare ability to be able to find and access the most protected of all data. Probably the best contribution *I* might be able to make will be as a 'recording secretary' of sorts; to be available to each of you so that you can concentrate on the really important aspects of solving this mystery."

Wanda began, she played out the possible state or federal prosecutor's case, touching upon the concerns the ultimate prosecutor might have because evidence was so quickly moved from the crime scene. She also shared what she thought would be the best way to record this group's findings so that any gains they make could be used in a court of law some day in the future. "It is a given that whatever we come up with will be questioned by many others, including those already working on this case. Let's be real here," she said, "No matter what we do, there will be no shortage of conspiracy theories served up. Shelves full of books will be written about this case."

Abi followed by listing the probable means by which the bomb could have been produced and transported to the scene. He then shared a list of possible bomb makers on the Israeli counter terrorist watch list who are known to have made similar weapons in the past.

Finally, it was James's turn. He had written out both sides of the initial radio conversation on a yellow legal pad and passed out copies to Abi, Wanda, and Ivy. Likely clues were highlighted in Day-Glo red. "I have already said that I think this was a well-planned, carefully scripted, and rehearsed operation. I would suggest we begin with that premise, instead of the one shared by most of the lead teams of investigators who seem to be convinced that it was either a jumble of incoherent musings or a creative way to kill time until the caller got up enough nerve to set off the bomb. I am proposing that we take the position that each and every word the caller uttered may have value in solving this crime."

"Why would anyone purposefully create a mishmash like that?" Abi asked.

"To make the powers that be look inept, ineffectual, incompetent, unable to do their primary job, the keeper of the peace."

"Sorry, that doesn't make a lot of sense to me," Abi said.

"And they couldn't make the same argument without spilling all of that innocent blood?" Wanda asked.

"Sure they could have — but I believe we are dealing with the kind of criminal mind that has little, or no conscience. For such a person — or persons — the quantity of deaths and all of that destruction were positives, not negatives," James said.

"Positives?" Wanda asked.

"I think they were counting on the carnage to drive home the message that no one is safe. Fear is a motivator," James said.

James put his papers down and turning towards Abi he said, "Tell me, Abi, why do you think Israel's citizens are regularly being targeted by rocket fire from the Gaza Strip? No one could possibly believe that such activities will actually bring your government down, or make your people leave the land they have fought for — so many have died to protect each and every second during the past 70 years. I suggest that those who are shooting off the rockets are trying to send more than an explosion; they are attempting to send a very specific message — a message that says they can disrupt your citizen's lives. They want average citizens to constantly fear for their safety and the safety of their loved ones; to question the advisability of merely going to a café, or riding a bus, or attending any public event. They also want the general population to question the basic ability of their government to simply protect them. Unfortunately, all they have to do is create the fear of the possibility of harm; they don't even have to hit anything if their primary objective is establishing fear. I think that is what we have here. Only the delivery method used on Christmas Eve in that theater was far more focused and destructive."

Ivy asked, "Do you believe that there is any more to be learned from this transcript?"

"There probably is, however, there is still one reference, which we have already talked about, that troubles me the most. I keep coming back to it because I think it is a key piece of the puzzle," James said, pointing to the line that referred to the already spilled blood, "The first blood lost was mixed in with the turkey dressing; the Lord, she was not at all happy about that."

"You think that there was an earlier bombing we have yet to tie to the theater bomber?" Wanda asked.

"I think that there was some earlier event, more than likely on a much smaller scale than this explosion, but it might have something to do with this bombing. If I'm right about this, the more we know about the earlier event, the better our chances to stop this fiend in their tracks before more innocent blood is spilled," James said.

Wanda finally asked the question that stopped James in mid thought, "Given the conclusions you are making, do you have any specific thoughts about who in particular did this?"

James nodded his head, up and down. "Yes, I do, or at very least I think I know who might be able to lead us to the one, or ones, responsible for this bombing."

"Well," Abi said, "don't keep it a secret from the rest of us; who is it?"

James had been leaning forward in his seat; he settled back, took a deep breath, and said, "Sister Joan."

"The tele-evangelist," Ivy asked, in amazement, "How do you come to that conclusion? Why would she do this? She would have to be insane – mentally deranged – to think that she could get away with something like this."

"She may well be all of that and more, I am not qualified to put such labels on her or anyone else, but I can say that the pieces definitely point in her direction."

"Why would she do this?" Wanda asked.

"For starters, I think she is seeking revenge," James said.

"Revenge?" Wanda repeated, "Revenge for what?"

"Revenge, yes, revenge for what was truly a miscarriage of justice against Joe Arridy, revenge for putting her on trial; this may just be a collective desire to shame and discredit the legal process – maybe even payback for something that has caused her and her family great shame and personal distress," James said, "There are also the biblical references – actual repeats of the ones she herself has used in recent appearances."

Wanda held up her hands, "I am the very last person on earth to want to defend *that* woman against any charge but she has already had her revenge: she was acquitted. She can never again be tried for that crime, and putting a new spotlight on an 80-year old case is really a stretch for me."

James reminded them of the Arridy fingerprints, personal objects, and DNA picked up at the scene, as well as inside the getaway taxi. He acknowledged that this was all circumstantial, but emphasized that they were collectively too consequential to be ignored.

"So why would she bring all of this to Atlanta? Why not Cañon City, Colorado, where Arridy was tried, convicted, and put to death? And why would she call into a radio station that was neither serving Atlanta nor Cañon City?" Ivy asked, "And why now?"

"I don't have all of the answers yet. All I have is a lot of questions of my own," James said.

"But she won the case. Causing all of this mayhem to get even would be overreaching – even for someone like Sister Joan," Wanda said.

"I do believe that revenge is a major factor at play here," James said, "but not the only one. According to some of the data my crew has pulled up, her family — in general, she in particular — have felt shamed and persecuted because of their family's connection to someone who was tried, convicted, and executed for a brutal rape and murder. Monstrous and shocking acts made even more scandalous by 80 years of whispers and whispered gossip. Few, if any of Arridy's descendants have been spared. Sister Joan, in particular, attended four different public schools in her teens because of almost constant harassment by her classmates. Then there is *her* public trial where she herself was charged with murder. She might have avoided prison, but according to public documents, contributions to her crusade began to dwindle during the trial, and never returned to earlier levels. Since the trial ended, even though she was declared innocent, many of the radio and television stations have canceled their contracts with her, causing her to sell off assets in order to carry on her life style. I think we almost have to consider her to be a prime — if not *the* prime — suspect in the Christmas Eve bombing."

"I would love a second bite at that apple," Wanda said, "but I have to tell you, all of this is just a lot of maybes and 'perhapses.' I would need much more to bring charges against her for this bombing. Without a great deal more evidence, she would only play the public against us, claiming a clear case of vindictive harassment on my part in particular, and the justice system in general."

Ivy passed around a list of possible suspects generated by the lead investigators over the previous few days. She suggested that they weigh each of the names on the list along with Sister Joan. Eventually, one by one, the list got shorter until finally, the only name on the list was that of Sister Joan.

*****

The secretary came by as they were planning to break for dinner. They shared their conclusions with him. He thought aloud about possible next steps and then said, "Let's just bring her in for questioning."

They went around the table and when it was his turn James said, "Sometimes the shortest distance between two points is *not* a straight line. At best, all we have is a series of assumptions; I agree with Wanda's initial reaction, we need much more evidence than we currently have.

"What do you suggest?" the secretary asked.

I have a member of my team who could tail Sister Joan and maybe come up with a lead or two. I would suggest that we bring her in for a few days. If all else fails, if my associate comes up empty, we would still have the option to pick up Sister Joan. All my associate will need is a current photo or two of Sister Joan and her address. As of this moment Sister Joan has absolutely no reason to think she is a suspect, let's see what she does and with whom she does it, while she thinks that she has just successfully pulled off the crime of the century."

"Okay, let's do that and see what happens," Wanda said.

They talked about it some more and finally, at a little past 10 p.m., James reached for his cell phone. As he dialed he said, "I'll have Elizabeth Hillsonrat fly to Miami Beach as soon as possible."

James speed dialed Elizabeth's cell phone. She answered on the first ring, "Where are you?" she yelled.

"Excuse me?" James said.

"I asked you where you are."

James stood up and walked towards the exit, "Hey, calm down."

"Schless was shot and he is fighting for his life. Is that calm enough for you?" Elizabeth shot back.

He reached for a chair in the lobby and sat down with a thud, "When ... how ... who?"

"It happened this past Monday night; an unknown gunman opened fire while Schless was sitting in his, no, make that *your* car," she said.

"Who?" James yelled back.

"We don't know yet who the shooter was, Will, we just don't know. Frankly, the only priority has been to watch over Bob Schless. I am here in the hospital with his wife and son ..."

James broke in, "Why wasn't I notified immediately?"

"At first we thought it was *you* in that hospital bed, when I was finally allowed in to see the patient, and realized that it was Bob and not you, I tried to call you, but your phone was turned off. I then tried to leave a message but your mailbox is full."

"You could have sent someone to tell me ..."

"Oh, Will," she broke in, "give me more credit than that; we couldn't have sent someone to you because none of us knew where you were. You hadn't shared your whereabouts with us. You've been off of the grid for days – something you would never have tolerated from any of us. But none of that matters now. What *does* matter is where are you now?"

It was quiet on both sides of the line. Finally, Elizabeth said, "Come on Will, Schless is holding on by a hope and a prayer, *where are you*?"

"Schless knew where I was," he said, almost in a whisper.

"Well Bob Schless has been unable to communicate with us, with anyone, since someone pumped two bullets into him. He is now in a medically induced coma."

James went into fighting mode, "Tell me everything – don't leave anything out no matter how small or meaningless you might think it is."

Chapter 29

Wednesday, January 2, 2019 — 10:27 p.m.
Atlanta Airport Marriott Gateway Hotel

James was still seated in the hotel lobby, deep in his own thoughts, when Ivy walked over to him. He told her what had happened in New Orleans after he left the assignment — *his* assignment.

"Allow me to ask you the same questions you have been asking me since you first arrived here, 'how are you doing' and 'what can I do to help?'"

He looked up at her with a weak smile, "I have lived inside a thick protective wall of my own making, for much of my life. You can count on one hand — actually on just a few fingers of one hand, how many people I have allowed inside that wall. One of the very few human beings who has been in that very confined space with me since we were each in our teens is now fighting for his life, and I can't let go of the guilt I feel because he is only in that position because of me. He took my place because I asked him to take my place; I'm the one who should be in that hospital bed right now, not him. So, 'am I all right?' No, I am definitely *not* all right."

She knelt down beside his chair, "In my opinion, guilt is neither a very useful emotion nor a very constructive one. *You* asked him to take your place because *I* asked you to come here. I too can feel responsible for what happened as a result. I can wish that it never happened to him or anyone else. I can pray that he pulls through. But I have no right to believe for a single moment that I could either have been the cause or could have kept this terrible event from happening and neither can, or should, you."

"You are kind, but I know what I know and I would trade places with him now in a split second if I could."

"Allow yourself the inner peace you will almost certainly need in order to be helpful to him and his loved ones," she patted his arm, "Let me know if there is anything I can do, besides remembering him in my prayers – which I will definitely do." She then stood up and slowly walked back to rejoin the *seconds*.

James finally got up, went to the elevator and pressed the number for his floor; he moved to the back of the empty elevator and leaned heavily against the mirrored wall. The door opened on his floor and closed again, the elevator then moved back to the lobby. Once more he leaned forward and pressed the button for his floor. This time, when the elevator opened he stumbled out.

He let himself into his room and sat down on the side of the bed nearest to the window. He sat quietly for a while and then took out his cell phone and dialed Schless' cell. It went directly to voice mail and he quickly hung up. It was so natural for him to reach out to Schless at a time like this. For almost 50 years, Schless was the one he automatically sought out when he was in need of a comforting ear. Without Schless, there wasn't a soul on Earth he felt he could turn to.

*****

It was past midnight when he returned to the *seconds*. They were still at the back table of the now almost deserted hotel restaurant. Conversation abruptly stopped as he came closer to the table. He sat down and told them all about what had happened in New Orleans.

To the surprise of the others, Wanda was the first to speak, “Go to him; return as soon as you can ... whenever you can.”

*****

He rushed back to his room, quickly packed and as he raced out of the hotel he called Elizabeth.

She was still sitting with Bonnie and Mark when her phone rang.

The ringing broke the silence, abruptly shaking each of them from their thoughts.

All James said was, “I’m coming to the hospital.”

Elizabeth said, “Okay,” and hung up. She put her cell phone into her pocket and rested her head in her hands. *We must be hopeful,* she kept thinking.

Chapter 30

Thursday, January 3, 2019 — 10:13 a.m.
University Medical Center, New Orleans

Mark was going stir crazy; he left the two women sitting in the hospital lobby and took his coffee cup out onto the street. He was leaning against the building when a taxi stopped abruptly by the front door. He was surprised to see John Zimmer exit the taxi with his young son and daughter close behind. Mark yelled out and ran toward them.

"We had to come," John said, "these two wouldn't give me a moment's peace until I agreed to bring them here. How is your dad?"

Mark just wrapped his arms around John Zimmer and whispered in his ear, "I think we are going to lose him."

*****

Mark led them into the hospital lobby and brought them to where Elizabeth and Bonnie were sitting. Bonnie stood and hugged each one.

Conscious of the young ears listening in, Bonnie tried to bring John up to date.

"He has been put into a medically induced coma."

The little girl tugged at Bonnie's sleeve and whispered, "What is a medically induced coma?"

Elizabeth knelt down by the little girl, "As the doctor explained it to us, it is something they believe could help him rest — to relax — so that his body can heal better, quicker," she said, gently.

"Is he going to die?" the little girl asked.

Elizabeth reached over and took the girl's hand, "We must be hopeful." Then she moved closer to the girl, "You know, we haven't even been introduced yet, what is your name?"

Bonnie said, "This is Stella Zimmer, that is her brother Mason, and that is John, their dad. The Zimmer family have been friends and neighbors of ours for a very long time."

Elizabeth gently shook hands with John, and then Stella, and finally Mason, "I'm Elizabeth Hillsonrat, I work with Mr. Schless."

"She's a spook like the rest of them," Mark said.

"What's a spook?" Stella asked.

"We are private investigators," Elizabeth said, glaring up at Mark.

*****

Eleven years earlier ... late Spring 2007

The Zimmer family moved next door to the Schlesses when their son, Mason, was about two years old, and Colleen was just a few weeks away from the anticipated delivery date for their second child.

As the years passed, the two families developed a warm and caring friendship. Both Mason and Stella became regular visitors in the Schless home. With their own three sons all grown and out of the house by the time the Zimmers moved next door, Robert and Bonnie Schless appreciated having young ones around again.

Both Mason and Stella were smart and intuitive, and each showed a level of intellectual curiosity from very early ages which amazed and delighted both Robert and Bonnie.

Robert Schless' work often took him away for days on end, but when he was home he always enjoyed having the two Zimmer children around. He enjoyed playing chess with Mason, who proved to be quite an able competitor, carefully plotting his next moves.

Schless played tic-tac-toe with Stella, "Think of it as a game of strategy — a different form of checkers or chess, or for that matter, life", he told her, "in all games, as well as real life, you always do best when you keep your eyes open and think through a few moves ahead, even before you begin; do just that and you will win more times than not."

One Saturday morning, while rummaging through a carton of old albums at a neighbor's yard sale with Mason and Stella, Schless learned that, like him, both children were fans of the Beatles, Frank Zappa, and the Grateful Dead; it was through their newfound appreciation for Jerry Garcia and the Dead, that Stella and Mason discovered country music, and specifically blue grass. Stella couldn't believe that Schless also liked country music and listening to Taylor Swift.

When the children learned that Schless was in a hospital, fighting for his life, they begged their parents to let them go to New Orleans to visit him. Finally, John and Colleen agreed, fortunately they did; as it turned out, Mason and Stella became reasons for Bonnie to keep from falling apart while waiting for Bob to return to consciousness.

Chapter 31

Friday, January 4, 2019 — 9:07 a.m.
Atlanta Airport Marriott Gateway Hotel

James called Ivy. He told her that the doctors were operating on Robert Schless this morning to try to completely stop the internal bleeding. He said he wanted to remain in New Orleans for just one more day. However, to keep his commitment to the investigation and his obligation to the *Seconds*, he was sending one of his most experienced associates in the area of terrorist type crimes, Elizabeth Hillsonrat. “She left here early this morning on a private plane and is expected to land in Atlanta within minutes.”

Ivy said she would have someone on the tarmac to greet the plane and rush Elizabeth to a secure area in the hotel where the *Seconds* was now meeting.

*****

There seemed to be a heated argument raging between Abi and the secretary when Elizabeth was led into the room by the secretary’s chief of staff. Conversation came to a complete halt. The secretary stood up to greet Elizabeth. She nodded towards him and extended her hand.

The secretary shook Elizabeth’s hand, briefly introduced the rest of those around the table, and asked, “Do you agree with Will James that you are equally qualified to take his place within this group, even for a day?”

After a moment to consider the widest possible implications of such a question Elizabeth said, “I am not Will James, but from everything Will has been able to share with me, I *do* believe that I am qualified to take a seat at this table and be of help for a day, or if need be, longer.”

“Can you be more specific in what experiences and talents you bring to this temporary assignment,” Wanda asked.

“I was raised in the home of the head of one of the KGB’s highest security facilities in the old Soviet Union during the KGB’s most active and subversive period. I was not shielded from the process, in fact I was encouraged to listen, watch, and ask questions. I learned from the very best and most brutal how to subvert and undermine targeted segments of a population, to penetrate and manipulate and yes, overthrow the establishment when it served our purposes to do so. In my adult years, I was both an active KGB operative as well as an independent agent. The lessons learned from those assignments helped to hone my abilities to know what to concentrate on as well as what to ignore.”

“But we have concluded that this is not the act of a terrorist,” Wanda said.

“I didn’t say it was, but whatever label you place upon the person, or persons, responsible for this gruesome bombing, you must admit that the crime itself was an act of terror, perpetrated upon an innocent population. I can be helpful here.”

“*Helpful* isn’t what we need right now, we need *capable*, we need *smart*, we need *answers*,” Abi said, firmly, “Hey, you’re in charge, Fritz, but if it was up to me ...”

"Well, it isn't up to you, Abi," the secretary said, "and furthermore, this person was not sent to us by some temp agency. Will James knows full well how important every minute — much less an entire day — can be to our investigation, and he sent Elizabeth in *his* place. Frankly, that is good enough for me."

Elizabeth looked straight at Abi. "I hear the same ticking clock you hear. I will help you to maintain focus, help you to identify and quickly minimize the amount of time devoted to false clues, potential dead ends, and wasted efforts. It should help that I understand the mindset of those who want to bring terror to average citizens and government leaders, not unlike what happened here in Atlanta on Christmas Eve. I know what to look for, what questions to ask. I have been trained to know how these perpetrators *think*. Yes, I'd say that I am more than qualified to occupy a place at this table until Will returns. And if I may anticipate your natural follow up question, I am objective — and so is Will. If he did not believe that I was capable to fill in, I would not be standing in front of you now."

"Settled," the secretary declared firmly, "Now, let's get to work."

"Any further news from the hospital?" Ivy asked.

"The operation was scheduled to begin at 8:30 this morning. We were advised that it would be some time later in the day before we would know anything. However, they have given Bob Schless a very slim chance to pull through," Elizabeth said.

“Our prayers are with him,” Ivy said.

“My prayers are with the task at hand, here in Atlanta,” Abi said, under his breath, “Lord save us all from weepy-eyed women.”

“It is clear that those who can make a difference are in place at the hospital and firmly dedicated to the task at hand there — so I have come to help in any way I can here,” Elizabeth said.

No one spoke about New Orleans again during the rest of Elizabeth’s stay.

They had all agreed that Wanda would bring James up to date when he arrived, but Abi started the conversation, “Before he left Atlanta, Will James made a strong case for the television evangelist, Sister Joan, being somehow involved in the bombing. This ‘Sister Joan’ is currently in her home in Miami Beach, Florida. She has been trying to get her evangelist show on Israeli television, and so I had a friend of mine at the Keshet Group, who enjoys the largest viewership in Israeli television, to set up a meeting for me on the pretext that passing a field interview was a standard part of the process used to qualify foreign productions for our airways. She knows Wanda and Fritz, but has never seen any of the rest of us so I and Ivy are scheduled to fly to Miami at noon today. I didn’t know when Will James would be back here, but had he been back now I would have suggested that he join us. I thought he could help us to either disqualify her as a suspect or get something to prove her guilt.”

“I can certainly help to do that,” Elizabeth said.

"Okay," Abi said, holding his hands up in mock surrender, "I know when to retreat, so yes, I will not step in the way of you joining Ivy and me when we fly to Florida later today."

Chapter 32

Forty-three years earlier ...
Saturday, October 2, 1976 — 4:17 a.m.
Donetsk, the Ukraine

Natasha Abruski, an indentured slave, was about to give birth.

At 15, she was barely more than a child herself; she had been brutally and repeatedly raped by Dmitri Donskoy, the eldest son of Boris and Svetlana Donskoy. Boris was the powerful administrator of Roscosmos, an important Soviet government facility, hidden deep within a series of abandoned mines in Donetsk, the Ukraine.

When Natasha's section leader learned that she was pregnant, she was immediately scheduled for an abortion. "You will get rid of that thing in your belly or we will get rid of you," he screamed, "I will not let you ruin that young man's life by waving your little mistake at him." However, when Boris Donsky heard about the pregnancy he quickly arranged for the baby — if it was born a girl, healthy and with all its limbs intact — to be raised in his home. "The little slut that carried this baby must be sent off to a labor camp somewhere else, but my son's child will be raised as one of my own."

When the baby was born, she was placed in an insulated tent, a makeshift nursery, set up in a somewhat cleaner — but far from sterile — section in one of the mines. The baby spent the first nine days of her life with a small band around her right ankle with #100-женщины 13A, (#100-female-13A), written on it. She was to be kept there until a

Moscow doctor could come and examine her. When the doctor arrived, and declared the baby girl to be perfectly healthy, with all her limbs intact, she was brought to the home of Boris and Svetlana Donskoy, who raised her as their own. After giving birth to five sons, Svetlana yearned for a daughter and instantly fell in love with this precious little girl. She gave the baby its name, птах любові, Ukrainian for "Lovebird."

The verbal and physical abuse from her five brothers began for Lovebird as early as she could remember. When their parents weren't around, they would call her "mine trash." All five boys contributed to the abusive treatment but the eldest son, Dmitri, was by far the most antagonistic.

*****

When Lovebird turned 16, her adopted mother organized a huge party. After the guests had left, and the rest of the family had gone to bed, Dmitri snuck into her bedroom, something he was now doing fairly regularly. He ripped off the bed cover and was surprised to see several pillows where he expected to find the young girl. Lovebird, having endured other such surprise visits from Dmitri knew that it would just be a matter of time before he came after her again. She made up her mind to be more than ready for him whenever he returned. Waiting in the shadows, she snuck up behind him and with every ounce of strength in her young body swatted him across the head with a heavy cast iron frying pan. He slumped onto the bed, unconscious, blood spurting from the open wound. She turned him over onto his back and with heavy garden shears, cut off his penis.

She threw the garden shears at him, quickly tossed whatever belongings she could fit into a huge cloth sack, took his wallet out of his pants pocket and tossed it into the bag, and then quickly made her way out through the second story window.

She never saw her adopted mother or father alive again.

For all intents and purposes, Lovebird ceased to exist that night; she quickly created an entirely new identity. She would now be known as Elizabeth Hillsonrat. She chose *Elizabeth*, in honor of the poet, Elizabeth Barrett Browning. Her mother, a true romantic, cherished her black market Russian translated copy of *Sonnets from the Portuguese,* and often read passages from it to her adopted baby girl. It was one of the few happy moments the girl had while living in the Donskoy household.

As a tribute to her escape from her tormentors — the brothers Donskoy — she crafted her new last name from the name she had secretly attached to them, "the puke hill rats."

The newly created Elizabeth Hillsonrat initially supported herself through small robberies. She worked her way from the Ukraine into Hungary and then Romania where she was eventually arrested by the secret police.

After several days in prison, she was able to get a message to her adopted mother, Svetlana Donskoy. Svetlana agreed to speak with her daughter directly. She had suspected Dmitri was the cause of her precious Lovebird's growing unhappiness and never believed his story about being attacked for no reason at all by her precious little Lovebird, but only now would face the reality of all that he had done. She pleaded with her husband to help their adopted daughter. He refused, and instead told her that he would see to it that the ungrateful little witch paid a heavy price for what she had done to *their* son, Dmitri.

Svetlana begged him to help *their* one and only daughter. She locked herself in their bedroom and refused to come out. Boris loved his wife, and the constant sobbing coming from their bedroom was ripping him apart. Eventually, he made a call that could change the girl's fate, he contacted the chief of police who had jailed Lovebird and told him to let the girl go. Understanding that to refuse the powerful Boris Donskoy had long and hard potential consequences, the bureaucrat did exactly as he was told.

Boris then arranged safe passage out of Romania for the girl, with the United States as her final destination. Elizabeth Hillsonrat was provided a new German passport, a fresh set of documents, and eventually sailed into New York harbor.

Boris made one more call, to the chargé d'affaires at the Russian embassy in Washington, D.C., and arranged for Elizabeth to get work in her newly adopted country, which led to progressively more responsible assignments for the KGB, and eventually with Vladimir Putin's powerful FSB secret agent network.

At one point, she found religion and joined a small church in northern New Jersey. Given her ties to Boris Donskoy, she was permitted to retire from the FSB without fear of retribution. She sought out odd jobs to cover her few needs which led her to a job in a small antique store, where she met Will James. In due course, James invited her to work with him and his team of investigators. "What would I do for you in this *group* of yours," she asked him.

"You want a job description?"

"That would be a good start," she said.

"Since no two days are ever exactly the same as the day before, or the day after for me or anyone attached to me, it is hard to say exactly what you would be doing," James said. "However, there is no question in my mind that you could add value in many ways. You're smart — you can, and do think on your feet. You understand the value of loyalty, and your work ethic is second to none. I can promise you that you will never be bored. How is that for a job description? And if that doesn't convince you, how about this ... I can also promise you that you will work long hours — won't get rich, but you will feel great about the team you would be joining, as well as the assignments to which you would be assigned."

She thought about it for a couple of days and then called James late, "Good, bad, or indifferent, I'm in."

"What was it from everything I said that finally convinced you to join us?" James asked.

"I think it was the promise of fame and fortune, or maybe the guarantee of short hours and long pay," she said with a chuckle.

"Did I say all of that?" he asked, "Well, am I a charmer or what?"

Chapter 33

Friday, December 10, 1992 — 6:11 a.m.
407th Military Hospital Chernihiv, Ukraine

Dmitri Donskoy was the eldest son of Boris and Svetlana Donskoy.

Boris had been one of the more politically savvy Russian military leaders during World War II. He caught the eye of Joseph Stalin, all powerful dictator of the Soviet Union during and after World War II. It was Stalin who first saw in Boris, a younger, possibly even more effective version of himself. As a result, Boris quickly moved up through the ranks, eventually into the dream job of all dream jobs — the head of the local committee for state security for the Ukraine, or as it was better known, the local office of the KGB — the Soviet Secret Police. Along with this post, Boris was also declared to be the first administrator of the Roscosmos mining facility, hidden deep within a series of abandoned mines in the industrial city of Donetsk, the Ukraine. It was within this facility that Russia began its initial medical and germ warfare studies and later, its space exploration research program. What better place to house these highly secretive operations, than the same complex that was the home to the area's KGB headquarters?

Although there were others who led local KGB units in each of the old Soviet Union's geographic areas, the senior Donskoy had a sharp edge over the rest — he was an actual war hero, not just a relative or friend of some bureaucrat or paper pusher in the Kremlin. In addition, Boris's staunchest supporters were both Josef Stalin *and* Nikita Khrushchev.

That fact alone put Boris in a uniquely safe position during the many shakeups and local purges within the leading councils of the Soviet empire.

Without question, Boris Donskoy was king of his domain, and if it was good to be the king, it was even better to be the first-born son and heir apparent of the king, something that Dmitri Vissarionovich Sergeyevich Donskoy exploited from a very early age. Virtually, from his first breath, Dmitri was guaranteed anything and everything he might possibly desire — and his desires quickly proved to be almost endless in number.

Shortly after he turned 11, he discovered girls. It didn't take him long to conclude that the many young female workers who were brought to the mines in daily caravans could easily be convinced to find time to satisfy his wildest fantasies. These young women learned quickly that their choice when asked to do something by Dmitri was *yes* or *yes, sir*. No one would dare to refuse Dmitri, *no one*.

Dmitri became attracted to one 13-year old mine worker in particular, Natasha Abruski. Natasha was a firebrand who refused his advances and made it quite plain that she didn't care who his father was; she had no interest in him. The more she refused him, the more he wanted her.

He moved on to other girls but only to try to make Natasha jealous. Finally, when he was 13 and Natasha was 15, he convinced the mine supervisor to schedule Natasha to work in a secluded area of the mine. One morning, an hour or so into the shift, he snuck up behind her, pressed a chloroform soaked rag against her nose and when she lost consciousness, he brutally raped her. He followed the attack again and again over the next few weeks. Some months later she began to tell people that she was going to have a baby; few doubted that Dmitri was the father of her soon to be baby.

At his wife's insistence, Boris Donskoy arranged for the baby to be raised in their home.

*****

When Dmitri was in his late 20s, and his adopted sister was 15, his abuse towards her turned from verbal, to physical, and finally, sexual, which led him to this hospital bed, in excruciating pain.

*****

Dmitri stared up at the yellowed ceiling tiles, as he had for most of the past 27 days.

His had father rushed him to Chernihiv, the military hospital of the Ukrainian armed forces, after he was found in Lovebird's bed, screaming in pain. He told his father that Lovebird called him into her room claiming to need his help with a problem and for no reason at all attacked him, stole his wallet and then ran away. He was now in a stiff partial body cast, secured to his bed to keep him from thrashing around — especially while asleep — those very few precious moments of drugged sleep.

The pain was constant, but he refused medication, unless you consider Balkan 176°, the Serbian triple-distilled grain vodka with 88 percent alcohol by volume to be a suitable pain remedy. It helped, but even the Balkan 176° — which had more than a dozen warnings about its potency on its label, including one in Braille, when it was imported into western countries — couldn't completely dull his pain.

Maybe today I will be freed from this place, Dmitri thought to himself, *at least this time the doctor said, 'maybe,' instead of 'definitely not' or 'get real,' as he did every other time I asked him.* Dmitri was wriggling around in his hospital bed. *That damned back itch*, he thought, *Does it ever stop?*

His youngest brother, Josef, casually strolled into the room. "Hey, Demi, how you doin' today?"

"How do you think I am doing? That crazy mine trash cut me up real bad. You got another bottle of 176 for me?"

Josef poked his head out into the corridor, winked at a nurse walking past the room, closed the door, took a bottle out of his inside coat pocket and handed it to Dmitri, "Some great lookers around here. How do you keep it in your pants with these distractions?" he said with a grin.

Dmitri gave him a long, hard look.

"Oh, yeh," Josef said, apologetically, "I almost forgot, you ain't got nuttin' in your pants no more."

"I'm telling you, Josef — I will get even with that rotten piece of mine trash if it is the last thing I do."

*****

Now, as he lay in the hospital bed, in constant agony, he promised himself that he would find a way to make her pay for this — however long it might take — she *would* pay for this brutal act. *I will make her beg to die,* he kept promising himself, *but before she dies she will be made to feel the pain I am now feeling. She will beg for mercy and the more she begs, the more I will make her suffer.*

He would have his revenge; it was just a matter of time.

*****

Dmitri learned that Lovebird had changed her name to Elizabeth Hillsonrat and had successfully moved to America. With his father's help and having already established a reputation as a dependable contract killer for the old KGB, it was easy for him to get placed into the United States to continue his search for her. One of his assignments required a currency launderer. That was how he first met Arturo Hornedo. The brash young man made it plain that he would accept any assignment, as long as it paid well. Hornedo had many such assignments for him, and soon Donskoy worked solely for him.

Chapter 34

Friday, January 4, 2019 — 1:37 p.m.
the Crystal Palace, Collins Avenue,
Miami Beach, Florida

Sister Joan was moping around the apartment as she had since the disturbing call from Hornedo. Every now and again, Scully heard the sound of breaking glass and things being thrown against the walls.

"I know he is plugged in, but how would he have possibly known about the next item on my manifesto? Even Scully doesn't know everything about the manifesto."

She had questioned Scully, but he seemed to know nothing about how Arturo knew — or why he had called just hours before the planned time of attack on the power grid.

She wondered if her apartment had been bugged. That triggered her pulling things out of drawers, and pulling things off of shelves and away from walls as she searched for listening devices ... but she found none.

"Scully," she screamed at the top of her lungs, "get in here."

"Your door is locked," he said from the other side of the door.

She was on the floor digging through the bottom bureau drawer. She stood up, brushed away the dust on her knees, and unlocked the door, stepping to the side as Scully walked in.

"I need to know who tipped Arturo off about Las Vegas," she said.

"Did you ask him?" Scully said, as he looked around the room in disgust.

"Of course not – if I did, you don't think he would actually tell me, do you?"

"Well, I don't know."

"It better not have been you, Scully."

"Oh, Sister Joan, why would I do such a thing? You know how angry he makes me every time he calls here. Why would I ever share anything with him?"

She picked up a glass snow globe and threw it against the wall.

"Feel better now?" he asked her as he picked up one of the larger pieces of broken glass.

"Not particularly," she said, "I'm really broken up about this."

"So is the snow ball."

"Well he isn't going to spoil my special ending for the Super Bowl," she said.

"The Super Bowl?" Scully asked.

"Never mind, never mind."

Chapter 35

Friday, January 4, 2019 — 5:32 p.m.
the Crystal Palace, Collins Avenue,
Miami Beach, Florida

The Crystal Palace was just one of a series of high rise buildings on Collins Avenue in Miami Beach, Florida. With small differences on the outside, it was hard to tell one bright and shiny tower from another.

Ivy and Elizabeth showed their driver's licenses, and Abi his Israeli passport upon the request of the building security guard. Then they each signed the building's registry. A security guard made a copy of their credentials and then took the three up to the penthouse in a private elevator. It opened into a brightly lit reception area. A tall, thin man was waiting for the doors to open, "I'm Scully, Sister Joan's personal assistant." He led them into a small sitting room, "Sister Joan is on a long-distance phone call. She apologizes for the delay, but will be with you as soon as possible. I would say it will be no more than five or 10 minutes. Would you like coffee or tea while you are waiting?"

Ivy and Abi said they were fine; Elizabeth looked around the small room and asked to use the bathroom.

A few minutes later, Sister Joan walked into the room. Looking around she said, "I was told that there were three of you."

"Yes," Ivy said, "there are three of us. Our associate is using your rest room."

"Would you like to begin, or do we need to wait for your associate?" Sister Joan asked.

Just then, Elizabeth returned and seeing Sister Joan, said, "That's quite an art collection hanging on your walls."

"The Lord likes me to be surrounded by pretty things," Sister Joan said.

Abi moved forward ready to speak when Elizabeth cut in, "I'm not familiar with some of the artists whose work is on your walls, I know that you travel all over the world, are they local or foreign talent?"

"I like to support new young artists from many places," Sister Joan said.

Abi moved forward again, but Elizabeth persisted, "Any local artists?"

"Some," Sister Joan said

"From what I have heard you live such a busy life, when do you find time to seek out new artists?" Elizabeth asked.

"A very old and dear friend of mine is an art dealer and he finds these artists for me," Sister Joan said.

Clearly annoyed, Abi broke in, "I am here," he stared at Elizabeth, "*we* are here to talk about your desire to bring your productions to Israel, perhaps we should ..."

Sister Joan turned to Elizabeth and said, “So he is here to talk about my wanting to bring my show to Israel, are you here just to talk about what is hanging on my walls?”

“I’m so sorry,” Elizabeth said, “I seem to be annoying everyone, that isn’t my purpose for being here at all.”

“Excuse our associate,” Ivy said, “Clearly she is only complementing your taste in art. I would say that we could learn a great deal about the quality of your productions by better understanding that which you surround yourself.”

“I guess so,” Sister Joan said, “well, her purpose or not, she is definitely breaking my train of thought, and yes, becoming quite annoying as well,” then turning her attention and glare to Abi, she said, “If there are no further questions about my wall hangings, let’s talk about the subject at hand. I would very much like to bring my preaching of the Gospel to viewers of all denominations in your part of the world. I am a woman of means, and more than willing to make it worth your while for me to have what I want in this matter. What will it take to make that happen? I understood that you are the gate keepers who can enable me to reach Israel’s television viewers. Are you, or aren’t you?”

There was a bit more conversation, but the mood had definitely cooled down and so a few minutes later, Sister Joan stood, said a frigid goodbye to Abi and Ivy, but barely nodded toward Elizabeth. She then walked them to the front door.

As they reached the door Elizabeth said, “Just one more question, I like your dealer’s taste in art, may I have the contact information so that I can purchase some pieces for my own apartment?”

“I’ll have Scully send you his contact information,” Sister Joan said.

*****

As soon as they were out of the building, Abi grabbed hold of Elizabeth’s shoulders and yelled, “What were you doing up there? I had been in meetings with Will James that lasted entire days and never, not once, did he get up to eat or drink or stretch his legs *or go to the bathroom*. All of a sudden, he sends us you, a woman with sudden urges to empty her bladder at the very worst of times; delaying a meeting we flew more than 600 miles for. But that wasn’t enough; you then further compromise our objective with all of that ridiculous art talk. I repeat, what were you doing up there?”

Elizabeth shook free of Abi’s grasp.

“I have to admit, Elizabeth, it really took away from our primary objective and we never did recover from it,” Ivy said.

Elizabeth led them towards the curb and away from those trying to pass by them.

“When we first entered the apartment, I noticed a huge painting on the wall signed by a very new artist, Seymour Maxx. In the waiting room, there was another painting by Maxx. Maxx is a very new artist. I asked to use the bathroom in order to give me a chance to see more of the apartment. As it turned out, there was one more Maxx painting on a wall just outside of the bathroom.”

"So you thought that was more important than our clearly defined mission, to see if we could connect her to the bombing," Abi asked with contempt.

"Seymour Maxx is a struggling artist who may have sold a dozen paintings in his entire career; some of the other artists with works on her walls were introduced to me and Will by Maxx – combined, *they* have sold even fewer paintings during their careers than Maxx has, *and* they only ... sold ... paintings ... to ... the ... same ... dealer ... Will was tracking in New Orleans, when you asked him to help with the Atlanta bombing investigation."

"So, it was a coincidence," Abi said, "It happens".

"Maybe so," Elizabeth said, "but I can't help questioning *coincidences* like this; more often than not, when so called coincidences are closely examined they rarely turn out to be a coincidence at all. I thought it was worthwhile to dig a little deeper."

"Then dig on your own time, we had a clear objective for our time up there and you blew it up," Abi yelled.

"You think your suspect in New Orleans may have something to do with the Atlanta movie theater bombing?" Ivy asked.

"I don't know. It is more likely that Abi is right; Sister Joan may just be one of the New Orleans dealer's clients. But I needed to know. At the very least, this dealer may know who shot Robert Schless, or even worse, he might have been the one who actually shot Robert Schless."

"I learned a long time ago that you can't dance at two weddings at the same time," Abi said. "The investigation in Atlanta has to be the one and only concern for each of us. As heartless as this might sound to you, our major concern — no, make that our *only* concern — is not your Mr. Schless, it is catching the Atlanta bomber *period*." Walking away from the two women, Abi stepped off the sidewalk to hail a taxi.

"What would *you* like to be our next move," Ivy asked.

"We could have Sister Joan followed," Elizabeth said.

Responding from just past the curb, Abi yelled over his shoulder, "I don't think that would work. Sister Joan is very smart and would more than likely pick up on a tail."

"We could return to 'plan A' and pick her up for questioning," Ivy said.

"I would suggest that we see what we can learn about that assistant of hers, Scully." Elizabeth said, as she reached for her cell phone.

*****

When Scully informed Sister Joan that the guests had left the building, she reached for her private cell phone and began dialing.

"I asked you never to call me on this line unless it was a life or death situation," the voice on the other end of the line said.

"I just had three visitors," she said.

"I am happy to know that you are so popular. Now, why are you using this line?"

"One of my visitors seemed to be overly curious about the paintings on my walls."

"So your guest has questionable taste in art – I repeat, why are you using this line?"

"Something tells me that they are trouble for me, and I want to make it quite clear that if they are trouble for me, they will be trouble for you, as well," she said.

"Give me their names and I'll have Dmitri check them out.

"Hold on and I'll get that information from Scully."

"Call me back when you have the information, I don't like keeping this line open for idle chit chat," he said, gruffly and hung up.

Sister Joan called out to Scully and asked him to quickly call down to the front desk and get the names and contact information for the three visitors. Several minutes later Scully handed Sister Joan a piece of paper.

Sister Joan dialed out again. After the first ring a menacing voice said, "What do you not understand about 'do not use this line unless it is for a life or death reason,' the voice said.

Ignoring the comment, Sister Joan said, "There were three visitors, a pompous ass who called himself Abimelech Böhmer with an Israeli address, an Asian woman, who seemed to have very little to say, Ivy Chan of Atlanta, and the one who was so interested in my wall ornaments, Elizabeth Hillsonrat, with a New Jersey address."

"None of these names have any meaning for me," the voice at the other end of the line said, "It shouldn't be too hard for Dmitri to check them out. Now, hang up and don't use this line again unless it is life or death."

*****

Less than half an hour later, Sister Joan's private cell phone rang, "Yes," she said, hesitantly.

"The second I mentioned the name Elizabeth Hillsonrat to Dmitri, he exploded," said the voice at the end of the line.

"So he knows her, which should make it easier for him to find out who she really is and what she really wants," Sister Joan said.

"Dmitri is an experienced KGB agent, he is trained to keep his emotions to himself, but he didn't, he didn't keep his emotions to himself. He practically melted the phone lines by telling me what he wanted to do to that Elizabeth Hillsonrat person of yours *before* he kills her."

"He wants to kill her? Good, so let him kill her," Sister Joan said.

"Listen to me now," the voice shouted, "If Dmitri has concerns, I have concerns and if I have concerns, so should you. You can't possibly be so foolish as to have allowed such a person to be touring your home."

"She wasn't *touring my home*; she was in my apartment for a matter of minutes. I don't see why you or Dmitri are reacting like this. I already told you, if he wants to kill her, let him kill her." She hung up, abruptly cutting off the speaker on the other end of the phone.

Chapter 36

Friday, January 4, 2019 — 6:07 p.m.
University Medical Center, New Orleans

James felt his phone vibrate. He had turned off the sound earlier that day when Schless was moved into the operating room and he, Bonnie, Mark, Zimmer and his two children were moved into the family waiting area.

James excused himself and accepted the call as he walked out into the corridor.

"Any news," Elizabeth asked.

"Not a lot," James responded with a heavy sigh.

"It's been almost 10 hours," Elizabeth said.

"Believe me; I know that all too well. Just before they moved him into the operating room, a doctor gave us what she referred to as her realistic expectation. We were told that Schless had lost a lot of blood and was not responding well to less aggressive treatment, which pushed them into scheduling today's operation. However, the operation promised risks of its own. He told us that the success rates in an operation to stop internal bleeding depended upon which part of the body was involved or what organ system had been damaged. In Schless's case, he had a ruptured abdominal aortic aneurysm; one of the most fatal surgical emergencies, with an overall mortality rate of 90 percent. The doctor also said that although Schless was in better than average physical shape for a man of his age, the loss of so much blood and weak vital signs were not going to help the odds. She made it quite clear that it would take some kind of a miracle for all of this to end well; she asked us not to give up all hope, because neither she nor her team had given up. She also asked us to stay close to the hospital, anticipating that they should know much more in a matter of hours. That was about 8 this morning. We have heard nothing since," James said, and then he asked, "What is happening with the investigation in Atlanta?"

"The Seconds decided to send Abi, Ivy, and me — in your absence — to Miami to see if we could either clear Sister Joan, or get some incriminating evidence against her, so we met with her earlier today."

"I think that might have been a mistake, before I called for you to join the assignment, I was pushing them to agree to have you just tail her for a few days or a week. I didn't want to alert her that she might be under threat of being nailed for the Atlanta bombing. I figured that if she is the bomber and did begin to think that she was under investigation so soon after the bombing, it might push her to do more mischief, sooner rather than later," James said.

"Well, it is done now so whatever is going to happen, is going to happen," Elizabeth said, "but I have more to tell you."

"More?" he asked.

"While I was in Sister Joan's apartment I noticed a series of paintings hanging on her walls, three were signed by Seymour Maxx."

"Holy cow," James said, "now that *is* really interesting."

"Could it just be a coincidence?" she asked.

"Hey, coincidence or not," James said, "it is what it is, and we both heard Seymour Maxx say that he has sold less than a dozen paintings in his entire career — and every one of those sales went through Arturo Hornedo."

"I took photos of most of the paintings I saw hanging in various parts of her apartment. Some are only partials, I did my best given the fact that there were others close by while I was on the prowl. I just sent them to you," she said.

"I'll forward them on to Maxx to get his input and then I will get back to you. Good work, you may have made a tasty lemon meringue pie out of some over ripe lemons."

He hung up and then checked his e-mails. He opened the ones sent to him by Elizabeth and forwarded them on to Seymour Maxx with a short note asking if Maxx could identify any of them."

Minutes later, his phone vibrated again, James looked at the caller ID and it was Seymour Maxx.

Maxx said that three of the paintings were definitely his — and all but one of the others were painted by two artists who Maxx knew, and also worked with Hornedo. "Where did you find these?" Maxx asked.

"In the Miami Beach apartment of a well-known personality," James said.

"That's strange," Maxx said, "I asked Hornedo about one of the paintings in this grouping just a month or so ago.

He said the painting was still hanging in his gallery and if it didn't move soon he wanted to cut the price to stimulate some interest. Are you getting any closer to putting this guy in jail?"

"Let's not jump to any conclusions," James said, "I'll keep you posted."

James hung up and redialed Elizabeth. "Did it look like these paintings were newly hung?"

"Hard to say," Elizabeth said.

"Okay, just tell the Seconds that I strongly suggest that now that we have poked the bee's nest, we might want to keep our distance for a while."

"You hung up before I could tell you one more thing. Even though I had to go through a metal detector and our belongings were visually inspected when we first entered the building, they did not make out the Entico 76 signal tracking device that I sewed inside the lining of my purse. I turned it on as soon as we entered the apartment. It picked up all of the active cell phone lines within 250 yards of my position inside the apartment. I have stricken all duplicates and the numbers for my phone as well as the ones belonging to Abi and Ivy. That left 19 different numbers for phones in the apartment at the time I was there. I will send the 19 numbers to you as soon as we hang up. Maybe one or more of them can lead us to possible co-conspirators," she said.

"Once again, good work!" he said.

"Hey, that's why I get the *big bucks*," she said.

Chapter 37

Saturday, January 5, 2019 — 11:03 p.m.
Atlanta Airport

James returned to Atlanta late Saturday evening and arranged to meet with Elizabeth before her scheduled return flight to New Orleans. "How is he?" Elizabeth asked as James walked toward her.

"He is hanging in," James said, "the doctors relieved the bleeding but decided against removing him from the induced coma. Bonnie, all three of their sons and the Zimmers are keeping hope alive as best they can. The doctors are giving her very little hope to hang on to. It's bad, and not getting better quickly enough for them to be more hopeful. Bonnie and Bob have been married a very long time, and she knows all about the risks of the job; but it's never easy for the spouse, and nothing can ever prepare them for when an assignment goes wrong, as it did for him in New Orleans."

Elizabeth said, "I don't think I ever heard you refer to him by his first name before. It has always been 'Schless this ...' or 'Schless that ...'"

James smiled, "Over the years we have called each other a lot of things. But, he *is* my best friend and I am *his* best friend — neither of us ever doubted that for a second."

After an uncomfortable silence, he walked closer to her and whispered, "What is the latest from the investigation here?"

"I called in Simpson for the surveillance of Sister Joan's assistant," she said.

"Anything come out of it yet?" he asked.

"Not a thing. All we know about the assistant is one name, Scully. I still don't know if that is a first name, a last name, or just a nickname. We haven't been able to get close enough to pick up either a DNA sample or a fingerprint, but even if we could, according to Simpson, this Scully has never been seen without surgical gloves on his hands. What we do know, is that Sister Joan doesn't go anywhere without him."

"What about regular hangouts or local haunts," James asked.

"Neither she, nor he, leave the apartment building very much. Moreover, the building is far more than just a place where she lives; it seems they even record the television shows from somewhere within that structure."

"I've seen her shows," James said, "it sure looks like they regularly have thousands of people in the audience. How do they hold such crowds in a residential building, much less move them all in and out without getting unwanted neighborly attention?"

Elizabeth grinned, "Like so much else in that woman's world, the audience is just part of the make believe."

"I don't understand," he said.

"It seems that she broadcasts the shows in front of a green screen. The production people then add what looks like an audience later," Elizabeth said.

"Well, well," James said, shaking his head, "and the ones that seem to be *saved* during the show?" he asked.

"Also part of the electronically generated *make believe*," she said.

"Well," he said, smiling, "Thanks to you, we are not without some successes."

"The list of 19 phone numbers," she asked.

"The list of 19 phone numbers," he said. "We hit pay dirt with three of the numbers, we picked up actual base address locations and recent activity documents – a definite tie between Sister Joan's Miami address and Hornedo's art gallery in New Orleans."

"How about that," she said.

"With that nugget, we were able to cross check the phone messages we captured coming from the art gallery and learned that people both at the gallery and the Miami apartment communicated with each other at least one time a day for as far back as we could go, and from about six months before the bombing until the actual morning of the bombing there were multiple phone calls a day. Some days the number of contact was in double digits."

"That doesn't necessarily mean it was the two principals speaking, it could have been others within the two locations," she said.

"Yes, it could have been other people, but it wasn't. It was Sister Joan in the Miami apartment building and Arturo Hornedo in the art gallery," he said.

"How can you be so certain of that?" she asked.

"Because we were able to cross check a series of e-mails from each of their private computers with specific calls. There were e-mails that set up times for the calls and described what needed to be discussed on *secure lines*."

"You were able to hack into their computers?" she asked.

"Easy as pie," he said.

"Of all people, I would have thought they would have made that near impossible," she said.

"There is a portion of the building in which the art gallery exists, which so far has successfully blocked my efforts to hack in, but the gallery itself was relatively easy to access. Hey, after all this time with the Crew, you should know that the bigger they are, the more they think they are above it all — rules, regulations, hacking. That just makes it easier to get to them," he said.

"And the e-mail trail confirms their association?" she asked.

"It does that and more."

"A romantic association?" she asked.

"No, neither of them seems to need or want physical relationships. It is more likely that their dealings are all just business. *Monkey* business ... *dishonest* business ... but business none the less. Seems Sister Joan has come up with a really unique way to fleece her flock, and needed to be able to scrub and hide the fortune that most weeks exceeds a million dollars in cash – specific denominations of cash, $10, $20 and $50 bills to be exact. As it turned out, Arturo Hornedo knows how to launder cash better than most."

"So much cash?" she asked.

"So much cash," he repeated, "that's what makes her scam so powerful; she knows that checks and money orders leave trails that the IRS guys can follow, so she came up with a way to get cash instead. I've watched some of her shows, and she's a master at working cash out of her followers. At least three times during an average half hour broadcast, she reminds her viewers that there is special *stationery* that floats to the top of all piles, and if they write their needs and desires directly on what she calls a more easily recognizable 'writing paper,' it is more likely that God's little helpers will recognize it from the massive amount of messages 'the Lord' regularly receives from around the world."

"Special writing paper ... mounds of mail ... God," she said.

"Yes," he said with a broad grin, "if it wasn't so evil it would be brilliantly funny. Sister Joan tells her followers to write their hopes, wants, needs for God on bronze, silver or golden *parchment*. She *suggests* that they write their less time critical hopes for better days on a $10 bill – *bronze parchment;* more crucial needs for themselves or their loved ones on $20 bill – *silver parchment;* and when time sensitive health matters are involved, she told her followers that nothing gets quicker attention than $50 bills – *golden parchment*. Of course, since she regularly communicates with God, and God regularly communicates with her, who better for them to entrust those 'messages' with than her?"

Chapter 38

Sunday, January 6, 2019 — 5:19 a.m.
Hartsfield-Jackson Atlanta International Airport,
Security Division, Third Floor,
North Terminal, Blue Side

With Will back from New Orleans, Ivy scheduled an early morning meeting to allow the Seconds to review progress to date, and discuss how best to proceed.

Abi expressed frustration, "I agreed with Fritz," he said, "that a smaller, totally focused team such as ours; coming in without a preconceived agenda or departmental rivalry, *should* have been able to dig up a meaningful lead quicker than the teams of rivals or so called professional investigators with all of their clout and experience. But so far, we don't seem to be any closer than they are."

"I don't know," James said, "we might have more to show for our work than you think."

"What do you know that we don't?" Wanda said.

"For starters, the telephone scan Elizabeth was able to run when you were in Sister Joan's apartment has yielded some very useful information," James said, then walked them through the connection between Sister Joan and Arturo Hornedo, "Hard as it may be to believe, my initial suspect in the art fraud case is somehow tied to our current prime suspect in the Christmas Eve bombing here in Atlanta."

"I wouldn't believe it if it were in a novel or a movie so why should I believe it here and now?" Abi said.

"Believe it or not, the telephone records are what they are. These two people are linked ... no doubt about it," James said.

"I don't believe in coincidences; only fools and little children believe in coincidences," Abi said.

James looked around the table, "We have checked and rechecked the phone logs for each of the 19 separate telephone numbers caught up in Elizabeth's scan. We can document ongoing contact between two of those numbers and Hornedo's personal cell phone. *That* is an indisputable fact."

"You may be able to prove contact between the two numbers, but how can you be so certain that there has been contact between Sister Joan and Arturo Hornedo themselves," Abi asked.

"We have been able to hack into the personal computers being used by Hornedo, as well as the one that Sister Joan uses," James said, "and we counted 193 separate messages between those specific e-mail addresses, just between early October and the morning of the bombing. Of these 193, almost a third, were sent between the first week in November and Thanksgiving Day. This batch spreads a little light on the question that I have been asking since I got here, what the bomber meant by the 'earlier drops of blood.'"

"Forget for a moment that anything you learned from a hacked personal computer cannot be used in court, what did they discuss during that particular series of e-mails?" Wanda asked, “I have had my office dig through all reported crimes going back as far as 10 months before the Christmas Eve bombing. And they came up empty.”

“We went through the e-mails word by word. They were very careful in the words they used, there was never a reference to a pending crime – but there are some key excerpts I believe reference an earlier incident,” James said, as he passed out sets of documents to Wanda, Ivy, and Abi.

Pointing to the transcripts between Hornedo and Sister Joan, “I can get you copies of the entire e-mails, but for the sake of this discussion, these are specific comments in chronological order. First, we have a demand from her that he arrange to *liberate* – that is her word, *liberate* – an item which she says she wants in her hands before Christmas Eve. The next dozen or so excerpts are from follow up e-mails. The last message in this batch was sent and received on Thanksgiving morning. In this one, he reports back to her that his emissary failed to acquire the item. You will see a line from her final response, ‘there’s always plan B, if the primary objective cannot be met then I’ll substitute something else.’ He asks her what she is talking about, and she says it was going to be a Christmas Gift.”

“For whom,” Wanda asked.

“She never said, but my guess is that the items referred to as ‘left behind’ were the engraved Cross pen and the hair comb found in the taxi, but that is just a guess.”

“I can have my team do another search, but they are usually quite thorough and they found nothing that seemed to tie in with the ‘earlier warning’ comment referenced by the bomber,” Wanda said.

"What was the time range and geographic boundaries your people used?" James asked

"They went back 12 months and tightly scrutinized the past eight or 10 months. The search expanded to a hundred-mile radius around Atlanta," Wanda said.

"I would ask you to have them search again," James said, "this time add the greater New Orleans area, where Hornedo has his base of operations; Miami, where Sister Joan lives and works; and Pueblo, Colorado, where Joe Arridy was sent to the gas chamber. I would reel in the time period to about a hundred days before the blast."

Wanda reached for her cell phone and started to dial her office.

Abi said, "These two are much too smart to have done anything in their own back yard, but it certainly couldn't hurt to take another look. It might also help to look into the area where the radio station was based; the one that broadcast the call before the blast."

"Norfolk, Virginia," Ivy said.

"Abi is probably right about their not doing anything in or near where they call home," James said.

*****

A little more than an hour later, Wanda's phone rang. "Bingo!" she yelled, "they found a connection."

Chapter 39

Sunday, January 6, 2019 — 8:22 a.m.
Hartsfield-Jackson Atlanta International Airport, Security Division, Third Floor, North Terminal

The rest of the Seconds watched as Wanda frantically made notes on her legal pad. She hung up and smiled broadly, "They identified an incident that took place in Pueblo, Colorado, Thursday, November 22, just shy of five weeks before the Christmas Eve bombing. Seems two retired military men were found dead — maybe two murders, or a murder and an accidental death. According to the police report, there had been a struggle in the room in which their bodies were found. The room was in shambles, broken glass and upturned furniture all around the bodies, probably the result of a struggle of some sort. Near the bodies was an antique gun with documents tying it to the man who was credited with getting Arridy to confess. Police on the scene deduced that the two men must have been fighting over the handgun. One of the men was wearing rubber gloves, so they assumed he was trying to steal the pistol but that's just conjecture on their part."

"Was there any known connection between either man and Sister Joan," James asked.

"The local authorities would have had no reason to have checked that out, but my office is now looking into any possible connection. However, it fits like a glove with the e-mails you hacked, the ones where Sister Joan was demanding that Hornedo get something for her to give as a Christmas gift — we are guessing that would have been the handgun, but when that did not materialize, she left the Arridy engraved Cross pen and hair comb instead."

"Kind of a stretch," Ivy said, "how would people in Atlanta have even heard about a small burglary attempt in far off Colorado?"

"Nothing in this investigation makes sense," Abi said, "did they give you any further details?"

Wanda reviewed her notes, and then looked up with a blank expression, "You now know all that I know. I have asked for a copy of the full police report but my office doesn't think there is much more in the report that can help us with this investigation."

"Okay," Abi said, "let's set aside all reasonableness for just a second. *If* the two incidents were engineered by the same person, a big *if*, how do you explain the almost perfect planning of the bombing with such an amateurish attempt to steal the gun?"

"If we go back to the e-mails, then a strong case could be made for the two crimes *not* being planned by the same person. It is more likely that Sister Joan planned the bombing and someone else, possibly Hornedo, planned the robbery," James said.

*****

Hornedo first learned about the robbery gone bad on the internet. He called Sister Joan and told her as much as he knew.

She listened and then said "Thank you. Just send me your bill."

He was still talking when she hung up.

Sister Joan threw the phone against the wall and then called for Scully.

"I'm surrounded by amateurs," she said, and then she told him that the robbery did not go well.

Scully reminded her that he thought it was a bad idea to send anyone to steal the Sheriff Carroll gun, much less to send a complete novice such as Cruz. "I hated the idea from the very start and I told you so," he said.

Scully's voice was fading as the voices that helped her write her manifesto returned, *You should have done it yourself*, the deeper voice said, *You would have been successful if you handled it all by yourself. We suggested, then insisted, and finally, demanded that you take matters in your own hands but you ignored us Jessie Mae. Now you have no one to blame but yourself.*

"Stop it, stop it," she yelled, "don't call me Jessie Mae, I am Sister Joan to you, to everyone."

Scully stopped talking. *Who was she arguing with,* he thought. *He didn't call her Jessie Mae.* She was having a conversation with herself again. Lately, it was happening more and more often.

"I farmed it out to Arturo," she said.

"You told him that you were planning to leave it at the bomb scene?" Scully asked.

"Don't be stupid," she barked, "Why would I want him to know anything about the bombing? The last thing I need now is to be blackmailed." She turned her back to Scully and said, "I'm not blaming you."

"There isn't any blame to accept," Scully said, "I had nothing to do with it. You wanted to handle everything with Hornedo, personally, which is what you did."

She pushed Scully away, "I'm not talking to you, get out of here. I need to think – I don't know where he left the car I made available to him. It can be anywhere; I don't even know how to begin to search for it. If I am unable to find it, I will have to reimburse *someone* for 10s of thousands of dollars."

Part 3

Chapter 40

Tuesday, January 8, 2019 — 6:42 a.m.
Private waiting room located near
Critical Care entrance,
University Medical Center, New Orleans

Around a quarter to seven the new shift started to filter into the ICU. Stella was the first to wake. She had been keeping track of the shift changes, making notes on a small memo pad and was getting used to the procedures. She assigned nicknames to some of the regular staff members. Someone she had not seen before seemed to be arguing with one of the nurses. Stella woke Mason.

"There is something going on out there," she said.

"Is it Mr. Schless? Has there been a change in his condition?" he asked.

"I don't think so ... well, I don't know. But it looks like those two are talking about him, in German," she said, pointing to two people who seemed to be arguing just a matter of feet away from Schless' bed in the ICU. You know German, sort of, what are they saying?"

"Most of it's hard to hear because they are talking so low, but even if they screamed in my ear I wouldn't know the full meaning because I'm still learning."

"What did it sound like?" she asked.

"I am pretty sure that as the man kept pointing at Mr. Schless, he said something that sounded like, *Garaus ihm*."

"*So*, what does that mean?" she asked.

"I don't know," he said.

"How could you not know?"

"You want me to make something up? I don't know, okay?"

"Maybe they were just talking about one of the things they need to do to help him get better," she said.

"It really looks more like he is trying to get her to do something she doesn't want to do."

"Let's wake Elizabeth," Stella said, "she speaks a lot of languages, just tell her what you heard."

They gently tapped Elizabeth on the shoulder. She had fallen into a deep sleep in one of the lounge chairs. Stella whispered into her ear, "Elizabeth, wake up. I think two of the ICU workers are speaking in German about Mr. Schless. Can you tell me if I am right?"

Barely awake, Elizabeth stretched, and then asked, "Why do you want to know?"

"It is more about the way he said it than the words. He was holding on to her wrist, she seemed to be in pain."

"What did it sound like?" Elizabeth asked.

"*Garaus ihm*," Mason said, "what does that mean?"

"Finish him off," Elizabeth said.

"Finish him off?" Stella repeated, "Why would he say that?"

"He was pointing to Mr. Schless," Mason said, "why would he say that as he pointed to Mr. Schless?"

"Point them out to me again," Elizabeth said, still half asleep.

"They are over there," Mason said, pointing out toward the corridor.

Elizabeth glanced through the doorway. She saw an older woman and a huge hulk of a man in scrubs, at least a couple of sizes too small for him. His back was to her. The nurse began to walk away from him when he quickly turned and grabbed her arm. Elizabeth could now see his face, "Oh my God," she gasped. All the color drained from her face.

She pulled out her cell phone and walked into the bathroom as she dialed James' cell phone number.

Chapter 41

Tuesday, January 8, 2019 — 6:55 a.m.
Hartsfield-Jackson Atlanta International Airport,
Security Division, Third Floor,
North Terminal, Blue Side

James was meeting with the Seconds, when his cell phone began to vibrate. He glanced at the screen and said, "It's Elizabeth, she's at the hospital with Schless' family. Excuse me for just a moment."

He accepted the call.

"I am wide awake and in the middle of a nightmare," Elizabeth said.

"Calm down, is it news about Schless' condition?" he asked.

"No, it is my very own, very *real* nightmare."

"Talk to me," he said, "and not in 'B' movie dialogue."

"Dmitri Donskoy is standing less than 20 feet away from me," she said.

"Who?"

"Dmitri Donskoy, my so-called brother and, if everything I was told growing up is true, my *father* as well," she said.

“He is in New Orleans?”

“Yes, and he is in this very hospital, standing less than 20 feet away from me – standing in all of his glory between me and Bob Schless’ hospital bed.”

“I still can’t understand how the art dealer from New Orleans could have been tied to the chief suspect for the bombing here in Atlanta, and now you’re telling me that the Ukrainian rapist from your past may now be wandering the halls of the hospital where Schless is fighting for his life. This defies all belief.”

“I don’t know what to believe, all I know is that I am staring straight at him, this very second,” he said

“What is he doing?” James asked.

The neighbor’s little boy thinks he heard Dmitri talking in German to one of the nurses.”

“The 11-year old speaks German?” he asked.

“Among other things, yes, he speaks German,” she said, “But I need you to focus – Dmitri Donskoy is standing outside my door, and if he knows that I am here, none of the people in this hospital – much less this room – are safe from harm.”

“Let me think this through for a moment, first things first. Is Schless in harm as well?”

“Since he was pointing towards Bob Schless’ hospital bed and not me, I must believe that Bob Schless is his primary target right now,” he said.

"Okay, I need to get Ivy to call the police commander in New Orleans' 5th district to pull Dmitri out of there and quickly. I'll call you back. Meanwhile, keep out of sight. I'm sure you look a lot different than the last time he saw you, but you can't take any chances."

He hung up and dialed Ivy.

"Hi! I need you to do something, *now!"* he told her that the shooter who shot Schless is walking around the hospital in New Orleans and needs to be pulled out immediately before he finishes the job he started on Royal Street. He asked her to impress upon Greer the importance of getting Dmitri quickly shut away. "We can't have him communicating with anyone until we know more about why he is there, and what he is trying to do. Emphasize that he is dangerous and probably armed."

"I'll call right away," Ivy said.

James called Elizabeth back, "They have to charge him with something and offer him a lawyer, don't they?" she asked.

"If they want, they can 'misplace' him *and* his paperwork for at least a few hours. I asked Ivy to buy us as much time as she could. I hope he moves as quickly as we need him to."

"Wow," Elizabeth said, "she really did move fast, two of the largest and most muscular men I have ever seen just sauntered up to Dmitri and already have him in handcuffs and are leading him away."

"I'll get back to Ivy and ask her to have them pick up the person Dmitri was arguing with and keep her away from Dmitri as well as anyone else in the outside world. We don't want to take any chances," he said.

"Now that he is out of the way, I can take care of her. I'll call you back."

"No, don't leave the waiting room — we have no way of knowing if there are any more of them. Get the local police to handle her as well," he said. "Let's plan to speak again when that has been handled. Just make sure that second person does not get anywhere near Schless. Meanwhile, I'll brief the Seconds. When you call back I'll put you on speaker so that you can update them. Now, be careful."

James returned to the rest of the Seconds, and told them about the call he had just taken.

"My best guess is that somehow Hornedo was responsible for the ambush attack on Bob Schless. We already have more than enough proof that he is involved with Sister Joan and her criminal activities, possibly even this bombing. For all we know, this Dmitri person may also have something to do with the bombing." He turned to Wanda, "Can you make a formal request to have him and the person he was communicating with held incommunicado on suspicion of having played some role in the Christmas Eve bombing here in Atlanta? We don't want Dmitri alerting anyone that we are closing in on possible suspects?"

"Give me all of the details you have and I will get my office on it," Wanda said as she reached for her cell phone. Several minutes later, she held up both thumbs and nodded affirmatively. As she closed her phone she announced, "He will be shuffled from precinct to precinct for the rest of the day, today. All they could promise was 15 hours or so. Hopefully, by then we will have more to go on than we have right now."

Chapter 42

Tuesday, January 8, 2019 — 3:11 p.m.
the Crystal Palace, Collins Avenue,
Miami Beach, Florida

Scully's cell phone began to vibrate. He looked at the screen, hesitated, wondering if he should take the call or ignore it, he breathed a heavy sigh, then answered it and said, "This is Scully."

"I have been trying to get hold of her for an hour, what is going on there?" Hornedo said stiffly.

"And who is calling please?" Scully said, as he put the phone on speaker.

"You know damned well who it is you little turd, it is written right on that putrid little screen of yours. This is Arturo Hornedo — now, why is she ignoring my calls?"

Scully smiled, "She threw the phone against the wall the last time you two spoke. We are waiting for them to bring over another programmed unit."

"I need to speak to her, now!" Hornedo yelled.

"I'll try to find her and see if she is available," Scully said.

"I hate when you do that. You are *never* more than a few feet away from her — I know it, you know it, and you know that I know it. You think you're being funny, don't you? Now, hand her the phone and get out of the way, if you know what is good for you," Hornedo said.

"You can't threaten me. I work for her, not for you," Scully said.

"And don't you ever forget that. I would never allow you to slither around me the way you do around her. I will say this just one more time, you *will* hand her the phone and get out of the way," Hornedo yelled.

"Or what?" Scully said, defiantly.

"Or I will fly down there and personally pull your lungs out of your body through your nostrils – graphic enough for ya?" Hornedo screamed.

"I am not afraid of you," Scully said.

"Yeh, you're pretty brave at the other end of the telephone, come here and tell me how you aren't afraid of me."

"I'll think about it," Scully said, defiantly.

"While you are thinking, give her the phone. Do it now!"

Scully sneered, "Just a minute," he put the call on hold and leaned toward Sister Joan.

"It's *him,*" he said.

"I couldn't help but hear," she said with a smile.

Scully whispered something into her ear. She smiled, he giggled.

Sister Joan took the phone and pointed to the door; Scully closed the door and then took a seat opposite her.

"Only I can talk to Scully like that, I don't let anyone else talk to Scully like that, and you know it. Now, how about just telling me what is so important that you had to threaten him? Tell me before I bar you from ever calling me again," she said, clearly annoyed

"Dmitri is off the radar."

She was quiet for a while, and then quipped, "I am so sorry, but this isn't my day to keep watch over your oversized pit dog."

"If he has been caught doing something, anything, then none of us are safe, and that goes for that empty suit, Skippy, who is probably picking at his nails and making weird faces as he always does."

"His name is Scully," she said.

"Dmitri will sing loud and long to save his own hide," he said. "If that doesn't scare you, it should. It certainly scares me."

"So, what do you want me to do?" she said.

"Prepare to get out of town before they come for you — and they will definitely be coming for you. Hopefully, for your sake, there is still time." He sighed heavily, "We had such a good thing going here. It could have gone on forever — now you have real trouble on your hands."

"Dmitri is your problem, why are you trying to make it mine?"

"Dmitri knows about the Colorado incident, and now he is missing."

"I paid you royally for that little service, even if it was botched. I hate to repeat myself but, that is your problem, don't try making it mine."

"Dmitri is a loyal soldier. That is why I keep him around. However, he is also quite human, and if his disappearance is somehow linked to any of the work either you, or I, or we, have been doing then all bets are off. He will sing like a little birdie to save his own hide. I was willing to handle the Colorado matter for you because you are a good client, and up until recently, you haven't given me reason to doubt your ability to survive. However, *if* you had anything to do with that movie house incident, and *if* you still have plans to do that dumb thing in Las Vegas, you have become more of a liability to me than a source for revenue. At that point, you will move from current client status to a loose thread, and I always snip loose threads before they unravel the entire cloth. I am beginning to see you as a loose thread. You are playing with fire and I promise you, as God made little green apples, you will eventually get burned."

"Don't feel so sorry for that bumbler or for me," she said.

"I am not feeling sorry for either of you; I couldn't care less about him or you. You wanted whatever you wanted, well you got it. How is it now playing out for you? *Hmm*?"

"Revenge is sweet," she said.

"Maybe to little girls, or men from Mars, or that sniveling little disloyal turd who is probably sitting next to you listening in on this conversation, but not in the real world — or to truly sane and levelheaded people. In my world, there is no such thing as revenge, sweet, sour or in between ... and anyway, sweet revenge is an oxymoron. It is a contradiction of terms if there ever was one. At best, it is petty; at worst it can get you a whole lot of hurt. Here is a piece of free advice, I believe that getting even is far more satisfying than getting revenge."

"Don't be so dramatic, Arturo," she said.

"You opened the door," Hornedo screamed, "now it is for others to get their revenge against you. What I am concerned about, is that if they dig deep enough, and long enough, they might connect me to you and that is a concern worth my full attention."

"Always the 20/20 pragmatist," she said, "Maybe I should hang up since I have already heard this boring speech many times before."

The phone went dead.

"He hung up on me," Sister Joan said.

"Not a minute too soon," Scully said, "now, let's take his advice and get out while the getting is good."

"But I haven't finished my list yet," Sister Joan said.

"You won – what more do you need?"

"I need revenge, sweet revenge."

"Sweet revenge, my Aunt Tilly," Scully sputtered. "You beat them in court, you were found to be innocent, they can never ever charge you with that jerk's murder again, not in Atlanta, not anywhere in this great big country. You pulled off the bombing of the century. For most people, that would have been enough. Why can't you accept yes for an answer and stop while you are ahead? Just move on with your life."

"They needed to learn a lesson that they will never forget, if not for me then for poor Joe Arridy," Sister Joan said.

"Who cares what happened, or didn't happen 80 years ago?"

Chapter 43

Wednesday, January 9, 2019 – 3:27 a.m.
New Orleans Police Department Fifth District, North Claiborne Avenue, main interrogation room

Commander Greer moved quickly on Ivy's request and the call from the Georgia Attorney General to lose Dmitri in the system so as to deprive him of any form of communication, within or outside of the legal system. Without saying so in so many words or putting it in writing, both callers alluded to the possibility that the suspect might also be a "person of interest" in Atlanta's bombing.

The Commander had a long and celebrated history as a former commander of the Multi-Agency Gang and Street Gang units, as well as assignments in the Drug Enforcement Administration, the FBI Organized Crime Unit and the New Orleans Police Department's Vice Squad. He was a no nonsense law and order man. Murdering anyone in his district was unacceptable, but he took it quite personally that someone would come into his area of responsibility and try to assassinate an independent investigator. That was just a step away from trying to kill one of his own uniformed police men or women, and that was a line never to be crossed. Anyone who would attack a law enforcement person – uniformed or private – would be fully capable of bringing all sorts of harm to an average citizen.

He arranged for both suspects, Fiona Glattsman, the female hospital worker Dmitri seemed to be pressuring, and Dmitri, to be moved from district to district. He called around to alert the other commanders that these suspects were not to be officially charged, in order to walk the legal line against requiring them to offer access to a lawyer.

He asked his fellow commanders to keep the suspects busy answering the same basic questions, over and over again and to do whatever they could to slow the paper trail to a snail's pace, ultimately moving them on to the next precinct for similar treatment. By almost 3 a.m., Dmitri half walked and was half carried into the salmon and white colored cement block building housing the Fifth Police District: Commander Billy Greer's world. The woman followed less than a half hour later.

The commander shuttled back and forth between the two suspects. Early on in the questioning, it became clear to Greer that the woman was not involved with Dmitri. She was a German national who Dmitri learned was in the country illegally, which he tried to use against her to get her to add a drug to Schless' IV tube. As it turned out, her English was almost as bad as his German and so Schless was not further harmed.

Dmitri was placed in a small interview room and left for almost half an hour. Greer and one of the mayor's aides walked into the room and sat down opposite the suspect. Greer dropped an overstuffed manila folder onto the table in front of the not yet criminally charged *guest* of the precinct.

Speaking to the aide, Greer said, "We have here a Comrade Dmitri Donskoy; former member of the Russian Army with medal winning sharpshooter proficiency, former agent of the Russian KGB secret police enforcement unit, former mercenary soldier in Syria, former terrorist advisor to the Cuban Dictator Fidel Castro's brother, a prominent person of interest to various Law Enforcement Agencies around the world. This is *not* the kind of man you would hope your daughter might bring home with her for the holidays." Then, turning to face the suspect he said, "What say, Dmitri, have I left anything out?"

The suspect spat towards the two men and with as much defiance as he could muster at this hour, said, "I know my rights in America, and I am entitled to see a lawyer."

"That is true," Greer said, "but only after you have been accused of a crime. To my knowledge, you have not yet been accused of a crime, Comrade Donskoy."

"Then I should be free to go," Donskoy said.

"Of course you are free to go ... soon," the mayor's aide said.

Dmitri tried to stand.

Greer pushed him back into his seat, "Sit down."

"He said I could go soon," Dmitri said.

"Soon isn't the same as now," the commander barked.

"How soon?" Donskoy asked.

"After we get answers to a few questions," Greer said.

"What kind of questions do you ask a man who has not been charged with a crime and who you say can go free?" Dmitri asked.

"I didn't say you can go free, Mr. Donskoy. You asked me if you should be free to go and I said yes, you should. That is not the same as saying that you *can* go free now," the aide said.

"You're making no sense," Donskoy said.

"Life is often like that, Mr. Donskoy," Greer said.

"I'm thirsty," Donskoy said.

"It *is* kind of dry in here," Greer said, "Hey Fred," Greer said turning to the aide, "Let's grab a nice cold and refreshing drink." With that, both men stood and walked toward the door.

"Hey, what about me," Donskoy yelled, "I got a medical condition, I need to pee."

The aide turned around as he clutched the door knob, and said, "So pee, no one is stopping you. This is America. Generations of Americans have fought and died for you to have the right to pee."

Both men left the room and closed the door.

The Ukrainian threw his chair at the door and began beating his fists against the one-way glass.

A distorted voice came through the ceiling speaker demanding that he return the chair to the table and sit down.

Chapter 44

About 12 hours earlier ...
Tuesday, January 8, 2019 — 4:47 p.m.
Private waiting room located near
Critical Care entrance,
University Medical Center, New Orleans

A nurse walked into the waiting area and gently tapped Bonnie on the arm. “Mrs. Schless,” she said softly.

Bonnie opened her eyes and jumped up.

The nurse calmly whispered, “Please come with me.”

They walked out into the hall, Bonnie noticed that a curtain was circled around her husband’s bed as she followed the nurse into a small dimly lit room farther down the hall.

The nurse stayed with Bonnie a few minutes until the doctor joined them.

Bonnie looked at the doctor and with tears rolling down her cheeks said, “He’s gone, isn’t he?”

The doctor reached for her hand and said, “We tried everything to save him.”

“He’s gone?” she asked again.

There were a series of heart breaking sobs and then complete quiet as she held her hands tightly against her face.

*****

Elizabeth woke and noticed that Bonnie was not in the room. She stopped a nurse who led her to the room where Bonnie was now inconsolable. No one had to tell her, Elizabeth just knew, Bob Schless, her friend and coworker was dead.

Elizabeth wrapped her arms around Bonnie and tried to console her, but she knew that nothing, and no one would be able to console Bonnie at this moment.

The doctor offered her a sedative but that too was refused. She asked to see her husband's body and was taken to his bedside.

She kneeled down by the side of the bed and cradled his head in her arms.

Chapter 45

Wednesday, January 9, 2019 — 5:02 a.m.
New Orleans Police Department Fifth District, North Claiborne Avenue

The call from the hospital came into the Fifth District at 5:02 a.m.

"The out of town investigator was pronounced dead at 4:41 a.m.," the hospital administrator said, "I knew you would want to know."

Greer put the phone down with a heavy sigh. He turned to the mayor's aide and said, "Playtime is over. If this guy is the doer, than I want to throw the book at him."

"You don't have enough evidence yet, the case can't be made with the little you have so far," the aide said, "At the very least you need some iron clad evidence. A witness, something to prove he was at the scene, something ..."

"We have a witness," Greer interrupted.

"So, bring him or her in, if they make him as the shooter then we go to court."

"I am not so sure I want to do that," Greer said.

"You're not being consistent," the aide shot back, "either you think he is guilty and you want to get him charged and convicted, or you aren't completely certain and don't want him to be charged and convicted — either you have a witness or you don't ..."

"I have a witness," Greer said forcefully.

"*Soooo*?" the aide asked.

"So, he's 11 years old," Greer said.

"He's 11? Wasn't this 11-year old with an adult? Get the adult to testify."

"The adult was asleep at the time," Greer said.

"In *that* neighborhood," the aide shot back.

"He was with his father, but the father was asleep at the time. They are homeless, they sleep in doorways. One stands watch while the other sleeps. They alternate. You said it yourself; it isn't the safest of neighborhoods ..."

"Can't you protect the kid if he testifies?"

"You heard the jacket on that guy; this boy and anyone even remotely associated with him would have a target on their backs for the rest of their lives and maybe beyond. Would you put your kid in such a position?" Greer asked.

"So, without the kid there is no other evidence?" the aide asked.

They sat staring at each other when Greer jumped up, "Maybe there is."

Chapter 46

Wednesday, January 9, 2019 – 5:19 a.m.
New Orleans Police Department Fifth District, North Claiborne Avenue

Commander Greer reached for the phone and dialed Ivy Chan's cell.

Ivy was on her way to the Seconds' 6 a.m. meeting. She glanced at the screen and said, "Good Morning Billy, are you working late or starting early?"

"The former and I'm sick about it," he said.

"What can I do for my favorite New Orleans Fifth District Commander?" she asked.

"We are babysitting the Ukrainian here in New Orleans for the murder of an out of town investigator."

"You mean shooting; last I heard he was still alive," she corrected.

"That was before 4:41 this morning. Unfortunately, the investigator is now dead."

Ivy crossed her heart, "I'm so sorry to hear that."

"Me too," Greer said, "me too."

"One of his associates is working with us here in Atlanta on the Christmas Eve bombing," Ivy said.

"I didn't know that. But it is now a murder investigation here and I wonder if you can pull some strings and get me access to all of the closed-circuit footage in the immediate area of the ambush."

"But you have that power, Billy. You don't need me to do anything."

"I can't get it done as quickly as you can, and right now time might be against us. We have been playing musical chairs with this guy since late yesterday and the local DA thinks we may have muddied any case he might have been able to bring against him. The DA wants him to have legal representation. I am being shadowed by a mayor's aide right now, and all requests for access to the surveillance tapes now have to go from him, to the mayor, to the DA. I'm sure I will get the tapes eventually, but it would help more if it comes sooner rather than later."

"I'll ask the Homeland Secretary to step in. I am on the way to a meeting he will be attending. I think he will agree, and if he does you will have what you need within a very few hours."

"I owe you one," Greer said.

"No problem, Billy. You're one of the good guys, and I'm happy to be of help."

Greer hung up and turned to the mayor's aide, "You never heard that conversation, right?"

The aide smiled, "What conversation?"

Chapter 47

Wednesday, January 9, 2019 — 11:14 a.m.
New Orleans Police Department Fifth District, North Claiborne Avenue

Greg Poulakis, his wife Kennan, their daughter Riley and son Niko nervously walked into the Fifth District.

"Thank you for coming back for this," Greg said hesitantly to his wife.

"I would never let Niko go through this without a unified family to back him up," she said.

They walked into the building and asked to see Commander Greer.

A young policeman led the family into the commander's office.

After brief introductions all around, the commander sat down next to Niko and said, "You will be asked to pick the suspect out from a lineup of five men. Each of the five men loosely matches the description you gave us the day of the shooting. I will not lie or try to deceive you, although we will do everything in our power to protect you; merely by picking the suspect out of a lineup you may be opening yourself, and possibly your family, to future acts of revenge. Do you fully understand the possible risks involved?"

"Mr. Schless was a good guy and if I can help, I want to help," Niko said.

Commander Greer looked at Greg and Kennan and said, “You are alright with this?”

Greg answered, “Of course not, but we agree with Niko, we need to stand up for Mr. Schless, because he stood up for us. At least we know him — when he helped us, he didn’t know us or anything about us, but it didn’t stop him from doing the right thing. Now it is our turn.”

Greer repeated the question and asked Kennan to respond.

“My husband and son have told me about this Mr. Schless. Niko may only be 11 years old but, unfortunately, in his 11 years he has had to be part of all too many adult decisions. He wants to do this. It would be against everything we believe in — everything we have ever tried to teach our children — if we did not back Niko in this decision.”

Greer glanced toward the mayor’s aide who was sitting quietly in the corner of the room. The aide held up his hands and in an audible but low voice said, “They know the risks, so move on.”

“Okay, now the good news,” Greer said.

“There is good news?” Greg asked.

“Kind of good news, we only want you to confirm what we already know. We have ordered all of the closed-circuit footage from adjoining buildings. They will be in our possession shortly. I am confident that these images will place the suspect at the scene. They should clearly show him with a weapon and in the actual act of shooting through the glass passenger side window of the victim's car."

"Then why do you need Niko to do this?" Kennan asked.

"We want Niko's testimony just in case a good defense lawyer successfully keeps the surveillance footage from being entered into evidence. That could happen — rarely does — but it could, and the last thing we want is for this murderer to get off on a technicality."

*****

Both Kennan and Greg insisted that they and their daughter stay with Niko in the one way mirrored viewing room, "We are a family unit and we will do this as a family."

The commander told them that a court appointed lawyer for the suspect would have had the right to be present for this but because of Niko's age and the possible threat to each of you, Niko was granted the privilege of having a sitting judge in the room to protect the suspect's constitutional rights and also to make certain that no one was trying to influence Niko. Commander Greer walked out of the room and soon returned with an elderly gentleman. Young introduced the man as a currently sitting judge on the state's supreme court.

The judge shook the boy's hand, asked him if anyone has told him who to choose or what to say prior to entering this room or since.

Niko said that no one had told him what to say.

The judge then asked Niko if he knew the difference between a lie and the truth.

Niko said, "A lie is something that is made up. The truth is real. Lies are bad and people who lie are not good people." The judge smiled and sat down, nodding to Greer to continue.

Through the one-way window, they watched as five men, of similar height and build were led into the room on the other side of the glass partition. One by one they were asked to step forward, turn from side to side, and then step back. Niko walked closer to his side of the glass and watched intently.

"Can you ask them to say, 'Here is a late Christmas gift from your Secret Santa?'"

The judge asked Niko if that was what he heard before the victim was shot. Niko said that it was. Again, the judge nodded towards Greer to continue.

The commander stepped over to a microphone, turned it on and asked each of the five men to speak the sentence. One by one, each man stepped forward, spoke the sentence, then stepped back.

Niko began shaking, "It is the man in the middle, he did it, he shot Mr. Schless."

"Are you absolutely certain," the judge asked.

"Yes," Niko said, "He is the one who shot Mr. Schless, and then ran away. It was him alright."

Greer thanked Niko and said that he had arranged for the four of them to be driven to a local hotel at the city of New Orleans' expense, where they would be guarded around the clock until the authorities could determine if he would be needed to testify in open court as to what he saw. He added that anything they might need, food, essentials such as tooth brushes, night clothing, etc., would also be supplied at the city's expense. He said that he was aware that the parents were living apart and asked if two separate rooms would be required. Kennan looked at Greg, and then at Niko and Riley, and said, "That won't be necessary."

Chapter 48

Thursday, January 10, 2019 — 3:27 a.m.
New Orleans Police Department Fifth District, North Claiborne Avenue, interrogation room

Commander Greer, the mayor's aide, and the New Orleans District Attorney entered the small interrogation room. Dmitri Donskoy was in one of the metal chairs, leaning against the wall, his metal chair tipped back on its rear two legs.

The District Attorney spoke first as he sat down facing the Ukranian. "You're in big trouble Dmitri."

"I do not speak English," Dmitri said.

"Cut the crap, Dmitri, you have already been taped having had conversation with Commander Greer. You speak English, and pretending that you don't is an example of the kind of amateur games that will land you in even bigger trouble," the DA said.

"What do you mean *big* trouble?" he asked, settling his chair down on all four legs.

"Big trouble like the kind that comes from committing a murder in broad daylight with numerous closed-circuit television cameras, and plenty of eyewitnesses around," the DA said.

"I ain't done no such thing," Donskoy said.

“It happened in the 700 block of Royal Street, here in New Orleans.”

“So maybe I been there. But you can’t convince no one that I murdered anyone there,” he said.

The D.A put his attaché case on the table, unlocked both latches and said, “What if I told you that we have a series of photographs taken from closed-circuit cameras dotted along both sides of the 700 block?” He removed a thin folder and handed it to Greer.

The commander opened the folder and smiled, “You are quite photogenic, Dmitri. If you weren’t gonna die by lethal injection, you might have had a nice little film career.”

Donskoy glanced around the room, “I understand that closed-circuit pictures are real grainy. They could be pictures of anyone. But one thing is for certain, it ain’t me.”

“I also have an eyewitness who fingered you in a line up and is prepared to say in court, under oath, that it was you who lifted a gun, aimed, and shot Robert Schless twice — once through a closed passenger side window and the second time through the broken window, each at point blank range,” the DA said.

“You’re bluffing,” Dmitri said.

“I don’t bluff, Dmitri, I have you dead to rights and you know it.”

“You’re making a fool of yourself; in the lineup, we had you say the exact words you spoke just before you pulled the trigger, Dmitri," Greer said, "you are making this much harder for yourself."

"So how come you ain't charged me with nothin' yet."

"This discussion has only just begun, Dmitri," the DA said.

"You talkin' deal, here?"

"In order to discuss a deal you have to have something you can offer, and I don't know of anything you might be able to offer," the DA said.

"And if I ask for a lawyer?" he said, a bit less arrogantly.

"Let me understand, completely," the DA said, "Are you asking us *specifically*, for a lawyer or are you asking us in general, about the possible availability of a lawyer? Think about your answer before you speak it because, as you almost certainly already know, as soon as you request a lawyer all conversations between you and us, directly, will end – including the possibilities of a deal of any kind."

"You are just trying to confuse me," Dmitri said.

"I am just stating your rights. Although, I don't see anything a lawyer could offer up either. It looks like you are about to start a journey that will end with someone pumping a deadly concoction into your arm while you are strapped to a gurney at the end of death row."

"And what if I hand you the Atlanta, Christmas Eve bomber, on a silver platter?" Donskoy said.

“My jurisdiction does not include Atlanta. I am the New Orleans Parish District Attorney, New Orleans is my prime concern,” the DA responded, coldly.

“Come on, it’s been in all of the papers and all over the TV. The Christmas Eve Bomber,” Donskoy said, “be quite a win for you if you came up with the solution to that one.”

“Are you saying that you had something to do with that crime as well?” the DA asked.

Donskoy laughed, “Even if I did have something’ to do with that, which I don’t, you don’t think I would admit it to you, do you?”

“So, what are you saying, exactly?” the DA asked.

“I’m saying that I might know who did it. If I did know who did it, and was willing to share that information with you, would you be willing to toss the pictures and look away at this little matter?”

“It isn’t a little matter anymore, Dmitri. The man you shot died early yesterday morning. We are talking murder here — cold blooded murder — a crime punishable by a lethal injection.”

“So, no deal?”

“I didn’t say that, either.”

Donskoy slammed his hand on the table, “Don’t play with me, you interested or not?”

"You have been giving us a lot of maybes and 'perhapses,' Dmitri. You'll have to be a lot more forthcoming if you expect me to even consider moving from lethal injection to life in jail without parole."

The room went silent. Everyone in the room knew full well that the next person who spoke would be the loser.

Chapter 49

Thursday, January 10, 2019 – 4:17 p.m.
New Orleans Police Department Fifth District, North Claiborne Avenue

The entire Seconds team and the secretary quickly made arrangements to fly to New Orleans. They hoped that this would be the breakthrough they were looking for.

The governor of Georgia found out about it and called a press conference to announce that with his hard work and dedicated team of investigators an arrest was forthcoming, possibly as early as today. "The New Orleans police have just arrested a Ukrainian citizen who is a person of interest in the Christmas Eve bombing."

Realizing that such an announcement would now alert the prime suspects resulting in their making a run for it, Ivy asked the secretary to issue his own statement saying that there was nothing to the claims being made by the governor and then she asked the FBI director to put Sister Joan and Arturo Hornedo under a tight 24 hour watch and block all possible escape routes. She said the Seconds were on their way to interrogate this possible key witness and as soon as they have anything tangible against either or both Sister Joan and Hornedo, she would call in.

*****

They landed in New Orleans and quickly got into a waiting SUV. During the time in the air and now on the ground, they worked together structuring the best way to get the most out of this witness.

The van barely came to a stop at the curb in front of the police station when the three passenger doors opened and the Seconds leaped out, rushing toward the entrance. Commander Billy Greer was in the front lobby when they arrived.

“Where is he,” Wanda asked.

“I don’t know,” Commander Greer said, sheepishly.

“This is no time to joke around and we are definitely not in a laughing mood. Where is he?” Abi said.

“We don’t know,” Greer repeated, “Shortly after the Georgia governor made his announcement, a team of lawyers burst into this station house and demanded to see their client. We had no choice but to let them meet with him. The lead lawyer, Jeremy Stevens, is one of the best in the business and he lashed out at us 12 ways to Sunday. He demanded to know the charges; we said that for the moment he was being held as a material witness in a criminal investigation. ‘Then he is free to go. If not, charge him or let him go,’ Stevens kept saying. Ultimately, we had no choice – we had to let him go.”

The travel weary Seconds stood speechless.

Finally, Ivy spoke, “I’ve known you a very long time, Billy, you are a good cop and an honest commander. You had the surveillance photos in the local shooting, why didn’t you charge him with that?”

"No, we hadn't gotten all of the surveillance photos until just a few minutes ago. We only had the ones from the street corner but they were fuzzy and poorly lit. The mayor said it might not be a perfect match and wanted to have an independent lab give us an opinion."

"You had an eyewitness," Wanda said, "Didn't you?"

"The mayor said he didn't want an underage child's life to experience the kind of jeopardy he would surely face if we went public, and eventually his name would be made public. He said we could use it only to support the surveillance tapes. I may be wrong, but it sure looked like the mayor held up the tapes until he was sure that the suspect was out of this building. Kind of a *catch 22,* Stevens acted like he knew we were bluffing and called us on it."

"Well I'm telling you right now to put out an APB, and bring him back or I will make life more difficult for you and your team of Keystone Cops than you can believe," Wanda said.

"He's gone, Madam District Attorney," the commander said, "We all can be certain that he will not surface until, and unless he chooses — he is now wanted in a murder, and if, by your presence here, he is also being considered for the Atlanta bombing, you can bet he will be shuffled out of the country any way they can."

"Knowing this you let him go?" Wanda yelled.

"I had no other legal choice," he said.

James asked, "How long a lead do they have?"

"They have a little more than an hour," Greer said.

Almost simultaneously, Wanda, Abi, the secretary, and James stepped back and pulled out their cell phones. Wanda called the governor; Abi called the head of Mossad, Israel's foreign intelligence service, and quickly linked the call to a third line, the personal cell phone number for the head of their equivalent, the Shin Bet; the secretary called the president; and James scrolled down to Carmine DeStefano's personal cell number and dialed out.

Within minutes, James closed his phone, walked over to the secretary and said, "It is probably too late – there is a contract out for him. More than likely he is already dead."

Abi closed his phone and put it back into his pocket. He grabbed James' arm and whispered, "Maybe not."

The secretary said to Abi, "Don't even ask, chances are he has better sources than even you, and I know how good the Israeli spy network is."

"Maybe not," Abi repeated.

They all left Commander Greer standing and without a further word stormed out of the building. Ivy got into the front passenger seat of the SUV.

The secretary opened the back door for Wanda and then followed her into the back of the car.

Abi poked his head into the car and told the secretary that he and James would follow them in another car.

"What other car?" the secretary asked.

"That one," Abi said as a yellow taxi pulled up.

James stared at Abi, who smiled and said "You are going to have to trust me, Mr. James."

The secretary reminded Abi that the plane will be taking off as soon as they return to the airport.

"Don't wait for us," Abi said, "if we miss the plane we'll find our own way back."

The secretary gave Abi a quizzical look, "What are you up to, Abi?"

Abi whispered, "Trust me."

Abi led James into the taxi. James noticed that the driver did not match the photo on the taxi permit. He pointed to the permit and whispered to Abi, "The driver's photo ..."

Abi put his finger to his lips and said, "We are in good hands."

As the taxi pulled away from the limo, Wanda asked the secretary if he had any idea what was happening. The secretary looked concerned, "I would guess that Abi knows something that we don't."

"And you are alright with that?" Wanda asked.

"I'm not sure," he answered, shaking his head, "I'm just not sure."

Chapter 50

About an hour and a half earlier ...
Thursday, January 10, 2019 – 3:47 p.m.
the Crystal Palace, Collins Avenue,
Miami Beach, Florida

Scully's phone began to vibrate, he looked down at the screen and frowned, "What do you want now?"

"Give her the phone, *now,* and turn the television on for her."

"What station?" Scully asked.

"Any station, the governor of Georgia is holding a news conference and the wagons are beginning to circle," Hornedo screamed, "You damned fool, give her the phone."

Sister Joan reached for the phone, "What is it now," she asked.

"The governor is announcing that they have arrested someone of interest in the bombing case and he expected to close in on all who were responsible before the night is out."

"You think he was referring to Dmitri?" she asked.

"The governor's exact quote was, *'New Orleans police have just arrested a Ukrainian citizen who is a person of interest in the Christmas Eve bombing,'* now how many Ukrainian citizens do you think are in New Orleans today — of course he is referring to Dmitri. I told you that he fell off the end of the Earth. I also told you that if cornered, he would sing like a canary and he's probably doing that right now."

"I guess you want to run off to that island of yours."

"You bet I am going to get out, and if you and Skippy there have a brain between you, you will get out too. I can't believe I let you get me into this mess."

Scully turned on the television set, the governor was now taking questions.

"Given the fact that your term is all but over, do you have any misgivings about walking away after this major accomplishment, Gov. Harper?" asked a local reporter.

"I can't take *all* of the credit, Melissa. But yes, I will miss working for the great people of Georgia."

Scully turned down the sound.

"Well, you can do whatever you want but I'm not running, Arturo," she said.

"You won't get off so easy this time."

"I told them to expect seven examples of God's rage; I *will* give them seven examples of God's rage."

"Suit yourself," Hornedo said, "but God helps those who help themselves — see you in hell."

The line went dead.

Chapter 51

Thursday, January 10, 2019 — 3:37 p.m.
In a limo speeding toward the Henry Clay Avenue and Milan Street terminals in the Port of New Orleans

Jeremy Stevens was in the front passenger seat talking on his phone; Dmitri Donskoy was sandwiched between two hefty men in the backseat.

Stevens hung up and said, “How much did you tell them, Dmitri?”

“I said nothing to them,” Dmitri laughed, nervously.

“Come on, Dmitri, you know Arturo will not let anyone harm you, just tell me so that we can block their next move.”

“I swear, I told them nothing.”

“Arturo would not look well towards you if later he learns that you did leak, even a small detail, and you must know that he has enough influence in local government to eventually learn the full story. Tell us now and avoid a further loss of trust,” the lawyer persisted.

“I swear on my mother’s eyes,” Dmitri insisted.

“Okay, okay,” Stevens said. “Now, here is what we are going to do. We are heading toward the docks, we will get you on a freighter and you will be safe as long as you keep your mouth shut. Understand?”

"Don't lie to me, Jeremy — there is a contract out for me, isn't there?"

The lawyer stared back at Dmitri, then at the men on either side of him. Finally, with a deep sigh, he said, "Yes."

"I understand," Dmitri said, without emotion, "I would do the same. All I ask is for a chance to get Elizabeth Hillsonrat before I die. I give you my word, and Arturo knows that my word is golden; I will go quietly if you will only grant me that one wish."

Stevens dialed Hornedo. After a few moments, he handed Dmitri the phone.

"Arturo," Dmitri said, "All I ask is for the chance to get my revenge. She ruined my life; you can't let her survive me. I beg you."

There was silence for what seemed to Donskoy to be forever, "Okay, Dmitri," Hornedo said, "but not now. You are too hot right now. We will put you on the freighter and you will stay out of sight for six months, maybe a year. I can't take any chances. It is that or nothing."

"So I have your word that I will get my chance for revenge?" Dmitri asked.

Without a moment's delay, Hornedo said, "Yes, but only after you cool down. I will make sure they never get to the evangelist, and that is really the only way we can be tied to anything she is accused of doing. Once she is gone, their attention will move on to the next shiny object. At that time, you can have your request, but I want there to be no misunderstanding between us, as soon as you get this Elizabeth, you're a dead man, understood?"

"You will let me get rid of Elizabeth? You mean that?" Dmitri asked.

"Yeh, I mean that. This Elizabeth person was part of the group that had me under surveillance. She is as much an enemy of mine as she is of yours."

Staring at his crotch, Dmitri said, "I don't think she has done as much damage to you as she did to me. Not by a long shot."

"Okay," Hornedo said, "You win ... she took more from you than she took from me."

"So I have your word?" Dmitri asked.

"You have my word," Hornedo quickly added.

"Thank you," the condemned man said, softly.

*****

The car skidded to a stop as they came alongside an old freighter. "We will have to handcuff you so that the ship's captain can feel secure that you will not harm him or any of his crew," Stevens said. "You have quite a reputation and that was the only way we could get any vessel to even consider transporting you out of here."

The man to the right of Dmitri asked him to put his hands behind his back, Dmitri tried to talk his way out of it, but quickly realized that if he put up too much of an argument they would only kill him right here in the car. He put his hands behind his back and cuffs were quickly placed around his hands while the other man put leg irons on Dmitri's feet.

When I get out of these I'll kill you all, and then I'll come for Hornedo and finally for that crazy sister of mine, he thought.

The three men went up the gangplank while Stevens remained in the car; when they were about halfway up the two men backed away from Dmitri. As they did, someone from the shadows emerged and fired five bullets into Dmitri's back. Dmitri dropped to the floor. The shooter moved closer, put his gun up against Dmitri's temple, and shot once more. One of the men from the car took out a knife, cut off Dmitri's right hand, and quickly placing it into a plastic bag.

Stevens dialed Hornedo's cell number. When Hornedo answered, Stevens said, "It is done."

"I want his right hand as proof," Hornedo said.

"They have already bagged it, I'll have it to you within the hour."

"Good," Hornedo said, "Very, very good. Now let's give that phony holy roller something worth praying about."

Chapter 52

Thursday, January 10, 2019 — 5:32 p.m.
On route toward the home of Rabbi Stuart Baum, Metairie, Louisiana

Abi and Will James sat in silence as the taxi road along I-10 toward Metairie. Finally, it pulled into a long driveway about four miles from the main road.

Abi smiled, "We are here."

"And where is here?" James asked.

Abi told him that *here* is a state of mind. He opened the door and got out.

James remained inside.

Abi looked in and said, "Come, my friend, life is good, trust me."

Slowly James opened his door and got out of the car. Abi led him around the house into a free standing concrete structure.

Abi knocked on the front door twice, and then twice again. A small light could be seen in the door. Someone was looking through the eyehole in the door. Within seconds, the door opened and a tall young man with a sniper rifle hung around his neck opened the door and saluted as Abi entered.

Abi returned the salute and then said to James, “Welcome to one of the many Mossad safe houses in your country.”

Several additional guards seemed to come out of the woodwork; soon there were three men, each heavily armed, eager to shake Abi’s hand. A young woman was with them. She put her hand out to shake his hand and he pulled her closer to him and gave her a hug and a kiss on her cheek.

Abi asked one of the guards where they put the dessert.

“Come with me,” the lone woman said.

They walked down a well-lit hallway. Toward the end was a bright red door. The guard pulled out a ring of keys and unlocked the door, then swung it open. Seated on a metal chair was Dmitri Donskoy, stripped down to his underwear with the stub of his right arm stuck in a huge bucket of ice.

“I was told, by an unimpeachable source, that there was a contract out for him and he was murdered on the docks,” James said in amazement.

“You can’t always believe everything you hear, Will James,” Abi said.

They walked into the room. Abi slapped the back of Dmitri’s head, “Isn’t that true Mr. Donskoy?”

“But my source is unimpeachable ...” James repeated.

“Let’s just say your source was both right and wrong,” Abi said.

"Would you like to put some meat on those bones?" James asked.

"There was a contract out on little Dmitri, here, that is true. Arturo Hornedo paid plenty to make sure the contract would be completed to his satisfaction, and received this man's right hand as proof that the deed had been done. He was also shot a number of times, once with a powerful tranquilizer dart and then with a series of blanks — courtesy of this well-trained team. Meet Mr. Brown, the mission's *target locator*." One of the guards took a deep bow.

"Next, is Mr. Green, he was the *transporter*." Another of the guards nodded to James.

"Those two, Ms. Blue and Mr. Purple, would normally be the execution team, but in this instance, they were charged with keeping Dmitri alive long enough for you to decide what you wanted to do with him." The woman curtsied and the man saluted.

"I thought you never allowed women on your missions?" James said.

"Oh, her, she's no woman — she's my daughter," Abi said proudly.

"Mossad?" James asked.

"Mossad," Abi responded.

"Why didn't you tell the others, the Seconds?"

“I thought it best to allow them plausible deniability.”

“Even the secretary?” James asked.

“Especially the secretary,” Abi responded.

“And I don’t need plausible deniability?” James asked.

“Not as much as you may need revenge for your friend’s death.”

“Dmitri killed Bob Schless,” James asked.

“Ask him,” Abi said, pointing towards Dmitri.

Slowly, Dmitri nodded yes.

“No question in your mind?” James asked Abi.

“Not a doubt. He did it at Hornedo’s direction, but he is the one who actually did it. Now, if you will tell us what you want to do about that, we can get him dressed and ready to go.”

Chapter 53

Thursday, January 10, 2019 — 4:37 p.m.
the Crystal Palace, Collins Avenue,
Miami Beach, Florida

Sister Joan was on the floor pressing her knee against an overstuffed suitcase. She was frantically trying to get it to close, when Scully rushed into her bedroom.

"The car is downstairs by the curb. We really have to leave now," he said.

"Okay," she said, "this is the last piece. Help me close it and then run it down to the car — I'll be there soon."

Scully watched the evangelist. She had a cloth bag, rimmed with black fringes and a huge plastic daisy attached to its zipper pull in one hand, and with the other she was scooping up loose items from the top of her dresser and tossing them into a large purse. He stamped his foot down hard and demanded, "Now. We must leave now. You can buy whatever you have here, a thousand times over."

"I'll be there," she said, sternly.

"Jessie Mae, come with me, *now*."

She glared at him, "My name is Sister Joan to you and everyone else."

"Now," he insisted, "you must leave with me, *now*."

"You know that I don't like to be ordered around Scully. Watch it — you are on very weak ground."

He grabbed the cloth bag from her and threw it against the opposite wall, what looked like small shiny beads were now all over the floor.

"I said *now*!" he yelled.

*****

At the street level, the doorman loaded the last of the bags into the trunk of the limo as Scully held open the passenger side door for the evangelist. As soon as the doorman gently closed the trunk lid, Scully ran around to the driver's side and got into the car.

In his rearview mirror, Scully watched the doorman run into the building.

Sister Joan put her hand firmly on Scully's knee and said, "I am the Lord — you will serve me."

"You are a charlatan, and because you are my daughter I *have* served you. I will burn in hell until the end of time because of that."

Scully put the key in the ignition and gave it a half turn.

It was later reported that they could hear the blast and see the bright orange fireball from many blocks away

Chapter 54

Saturday, January 12, 2019 — 12:51 p.m.
The Statehouse, Atlanta

Governor Beau Harper took pride in never being late to a party, and this was definitely going to be *his* party.

Not only were all of the major print and electronic American news organizations represented in the briefing room today — including the largest thorn in his side: *those self serving demons from the 'not worth mentioning' New York Times,* but more than 60 foreign press passes were issued late in the morning after the governor's office announced that at precisely 1 p.m., today, Georgia's head of state would make an official statement about the end of the Christmas Eve Bombing Case.

*****

Exactly four minutes after the announcement was made public, the president of the United States personally placed a call to Harper's very private cell phone. He noticed the caller ID, "POTUS," and scowled; he thought only his wife had this number. *I guess Madam President is more resourceful than I had imagined,* he thought. He passed the phone to his aide and said, "Tell the she-devil that the governor will not be available until sometime after 3 p.m. today".

His aide put his hands up, "With all due respect, Beau — maybe *you* can say that to the president of the United States, but I can't."

The governor glared at the young man, “If I had as little courage as you are exhibiting right now I wouldn’t have been able to get out from under the covers most mornings.” He pulled the phone back and answered it. “Why, good morning Madam President. To what do I owe the pleasure of this call?”

“You cannot hold your little victory tour over the backs of those who did all of the work and you will *not* speak on this matter before I do at 3 o’clock today. Do you understand me?”

“Now, Madam President,” he said mockingly, “You don’t really want to talk to me like that, now, do you?”

“I am the president of these United States, you dishonest, degenerate, no-good, lame duck — and I will talk to you anyway I choose.”

“You may be the president for another thousand days or so, give or take a possible impeachment or two, but I am still the legally elected head of a very proud and, dare I say, influential state. I will hold a press conference when and where I choose. Do *you* understand *me*?”

The president was getting angry and didn’t care who knew it, “I will remind you that you are speaking to the person who received more individual votes than any person running for president in the history of this country; male or female, white or black, young or old. You, on the other hand, ‘Gov. Barbecue and Biscuits,’ also ran for president, and as I remember, you were beaten like a drum. I will also remind you that I am president of all 50 United States, of which Georgia’s schools ranked 23rd in safety and 39th in school system quality. One last *little* reminder, whoever in hell you think *you* are — when the president of the United States calls, she expects her wishes to be granted *immediately*."

Without a beat, the governor said, "I seem to have made you angry, 'Madam Catfish and second rate Barbecue.' Good, very good indeed. Now, let me remind *you* that our triple 'A' credit rating makes us number one where it counts. How about we continue this little love fest of ours at 3 p.m. today, when nothing of any importance will be taking place so I can give you all of the time and attention you deserve. Right now, I have a press conference to prepare for."

There was a click and the phone went dead.

The president slammed the phone down. She turned to her assistant and said, "He hung up on me, that arrogant son of a ..."

"Remember what you always tell me," Mindee Daniele broke in, "never get mad — get even."

"You're missing the point," the president said, "It has nothing to do with me; I don't give two shakes about what that old goat thinks of me. It is disrespectful to the office of the president, and I can't — I won't — let him get away with it."

"You must know that you can't win a gutter fight with him. The gutter is his turf." The president's aide said.

"So, what are you suggesting, I kiss his ..."

"No," the aide broke in again, "I suggest you make him wonder. I suggest you play with his head a little. I suggest you call him back and tell him you think he should do whatever he thinks is right. Just remind him that he who speaks last, wins, and you will be speaking at 3 p.m. today; and if he then speaks after you, there will be a follow up from you or one of your many surrogates, because the President of the United States *always has the last word.*"

The president smiled broadly, "That might be the best advice I have ever been given."

"That's why you keep me around."

"So that's why," the president teased.

*****

The governor stood patiently just outside of the briefing room with one hand on the door knob, staring at the Patek Philippe Calibre 89 pocket watch in his other hand. As the unique watch alarm sounded, he took a deep breath, flashed his well-practiced smile, and strolled into the crowded press room with the air of confidence that comes from knowing that he can buy and sell anyone else in his world many times over and he *doesn't really need anyone – anymore.* Then the face of the president crossed his mind and for a brief moment the smile was replaced by a flash of anger.

How dare she speak to me like that? He thought, *I was a power in this state and in this party before she was a twinkle in her daddy's eye.*

He stood in front of the bank of microphones, many with the distinctive logos or "flags" of the nation's broadcasting networks. Still holding the pocket watch, with its 18-karat white gold reflecting against the camera lights, he tried but couldn't push the president out of his thoughts. He mechanically waved and pointed at no one in particular, glancing back and forth at the intricate face of the watch. When the second set of chimes could be heard, signaling exactly 1 p.m., he slipped the watch into his jacket pocket, tapped on one of the microphones and said, "Ladies, Gentlemen, thank you for coming here today. I do not think you will leave disappointed – as we say in one of this great state's two endearing mottos, 'Wisdom, Justice, Moderation' – Georgia's sons and daughters contributed mightily with their collective wisdom, sense of justice, and seasoned use of moderation until the successful capture and extinction of those demons from hell who dared to do the unthinkable on our holiest of holy Christmas Eve."

A strikingly beautiful young woman stood and said, "Scarlett Madison, WGKA-AM Talk 920, governor, the Department of Homeland Security claims that the ultimate solution was the result of a collaboration of specially selected security specialists working independently, can you confirm that?"

"I am very proud to tell you," Harper said, "that the contributions from the dedicated and highly competent Georgia law enforcement departments, led by our state police and of course some other agencies were responsible for quickly identifying and putting an end to the appalling and gruesome animals that tried, but failed, to bring us to our knees. Now, if you will all kindly hold your questions for the moment, I would like to read a short statement. I assure you that not one person will leave this room without the answers to each and every question on their minds."

He put on a pair of gold rimmed eye glasses, and reading from a series of three by five index cards, he said, "I was in constant touch with the lead team of investigators from minutes after the bomb went off until just before I came out to brief you all here today. Less than five minutes ago, I spoke with the state adjutant general to compliment him and his team on a job well done ..."

He looked up and saw the photographers and reporters beginning to pack up. "Say," he said to the CNN reporter, "What is going on here?"

"We have been preempted, Mr. Governor," one of the other reporters yelled.

"By whom," he asked.

"The White House, our signal is being switched to the White House Press Room. Seems the president is about to speak and so our feed was cut.

The governor smiled, *Son of bitch,* he thought, *that mean old lady won after all.* Rather than being angry he took out his cell phone and called the White House. Mindy Danielle answered the president's personal line.

"Tell her I respect her for stickling to her guns."

"No hard feelings?"

"None, she won fair and square. But remind her that she might have the last word, but my memoir will be out before hers — and I know a few dillies that will help sell a bunch of books."

He hung up.

Chapter 55

Saturday, January 12, 2019 — 4:22 p.m.
The Varsity drive in, North Avenue, NW, Atlanta

Ivy arranged for a table for the five of them to be set up in one of the storerooms of the famous Varsity drive in. Each of the Seconds sat down and placed their orders with the night manager.

Abi stretched his arms up and out, "I'm anxious to get home but I don't look forward to getting on a plane in a few hours and flying through the night."

"Why not stay over, you could catch a plane in the morning," Ivy said.

"No defendable reason to prolong my visit here, and if you want to know the truth I really prefer my own bed, my own covers, and most of all, my own pillows," Abi said.

"I am still bothered by Arturo Hernado. I'd feel much better if we found even a small clue as to where he went and how he got there," James said.

"He can't stay hidden forever," Wanda said.

"I don't know, he has found ways to fade into the woodwork before, and is just cagy enough to have worked out more than one escape plan in advance," James said.

"You're the man with the deep dark sources," Abi said, "Can't you find a way to get the answer to that?"

"Maybe we got all his accounts, maybe we didn't. The ones we did identify were left intact, but we can never be certain that we identified every account in his control, which would determine how long he can stay off the grid," James said. "He helped launder a lot of money for Sister Joan and probably many others. It would not have been too hard for him to skim off enough from the top of those transactions to last him a dozen life times."

"Do you really believe that he has the personality to fold up his tent and never be seen or heard from again," Ivy asked.

James just shook his head, "I just don't know."

"He seemed to be the only one of them all who wasn't motivated by a need for revenge," Wanda said.

"I don't know about that," James said, "At a time when he should have been concerned more with his own survival, he chose to stop long enough to take out the Ukrainian – and more than likely Sister Joan for added measure."

"We do not know that for a fact," Wanda said.

"We know that he got Dmitri pulled out of custody with the help of his longtime lawyer, and that Dmitri was later found floating, face down, next to a garbage scow," James said.

"Without anything tangible to connect the dead body to Hornedo, you can't be certain that he either did it or had it done," Wanda said, "we certainly couldn't make a legal case."

As if lost in thought he kept stacking and restacking his french fries. "According to Commander Greer, given a little more time, he might have been able to make a deal with Dmitri to trade immunity or at least a slap on the wrist for getting firm evidence against Sister Joan and maybe even Hornado," James said.

"Be honest," Abi said, with a sly wink at James, "You are haunted by this nothing burger art dealer because you think he was one of the people responsible for your friend's death; right or wrong?"

"I wouldn't call him a nothing burger, but yes, James said, "Schless – I have to stop calling him that – *Bob*'s murder will haunt me for as long as I live. From here I fly to Connecticut for Schless, excuse me, for *Bob*'s funeral. His wife has asked me to speak at the funeral, but for the first time in my life I am speechless."

"Just say what is clearly in your heart," Ivy said.

The night manager brought a tray of plastic water glasses, each filled halfway with what he said was champagne. "We apologize for the shoddy barware, but the boss wanted you all to know that he and everyone he holds dear thank you for whatever you might have done in taking down those animals. The governor says he did it all, but we here in Atlanta have been living with that old crook too long to think he would ever take valuable time away from lining his own pockets to do anything good for the rest of us, especially with just a few days to go in his term."

The secretary handed a glass to each of the Seconds, and took the last one for himself. Clicking glasses first with

Ivy, then James, then Wanda, and finally with Abi, he said, “I know that the president of the United States would want me to thank each of you for your service to this country, this state, this city. I can think of a lot of better ways to start a New Year but no better a group to start it with.”

They all lifted their glasses, and then clicked theirs against each of the others. Before they could drink the liquid Abi said, “One more thing, may we never meet like this again and החברים שלך יכול לקבל חיים ארוכים וזכרונות קצרים שלך אויבים.”

“Which means?” Ivy asked.

Abi tossed his head back and swallowed the liquid in a single gulp, gave a small burp and said, “Which means, ‘May your friends have long life and your enemies short memories.’”

*****

As they were walking towards the door Abi pulled James aside.

For what it is worth, מוות מותיר על שברון הלב .אף אחד לא יכול לרפא, אהבה מותיר זיכרון .אף אחד לא יכול לגנוב.

“Which means?” James asked.

“Which means, ‘death leaves a heartache, no one can heal; love leaves a memory, no one can steal.’”

“An old Israeli saying?” James asked.

Abi laughed, “It comes from a headstone I once saw in Ireland.”

They embraced and wished each other safe travels.

Chapter 56

Saturday, January 12, 2019 — 11:43 p.m.
Bradley International Airport,
Windsor Locks, Connecticut

As soon as his plane landed, James picked up his rental car and went directly to the Schless home. He spoke to Bonnie earlier in the day and she suggested that he stay over so that they could all go to the church together in the morning. He agreed so that he could spend some time with Bonnie and the boys and planned to leave a company check to cover the funeral arrangements as well as for a cushion to help Bonnie through the difficult days ahead. As he drove into their driveway, Mark came out to the car and asked if he could have a private moment with him.

"Of course," James said.

They walked into the garage and Mark hit the remote to close the overhead door. He waited for the door to drop down all the way and then turned towards James and punched him hard in the stomach followed by a left jab to James's jaw. The punches didn't seem to take James by surprise but the force of the blows did. He stumbled backwards, hitting the wall with a thud.

"Come on," Mark yelled, "Hit me back."

"I am not going to hit you Mark," James said.

Another jab to the stomach, "Hit me back, hit me back" Mark said again and again.

"I told you, I am not going to hit you," James repeated, with a slight grimace.

"Damn you, hit me back," Mark demanded.

"I will not fight with you, Mark," James said.

Mark hit him again, this time pushing him to the ground.

Mark stood over James, taunting him, "Put your hands up and fight like a man."

"I told you, I am not going to fight you," James repeated as he slowly got up off the floor and dusted himself off. "I told you that I wasn't going to fight you and I meant it. You're angry – I understand that; you have good reason to be angry."

"I'm angry at you," Mark screamed.

"Yes, at me," James said.

Mark reared his left hand and started to swing, but James grabbed Mark's wrist and slightly twisted it back, forcing Mark to his knees.

"Hit me, fight back. I want you to fight back," Mark said, tears running down his cheeks.

James released mark's wrist and sat down on the floor next to the grieving boy.

“You took my father away from us,” Mark said.

“No, a gunman took your father away from you.”

James leaned forward, put his arms around Mark, and said, “I understand, I do, I understand.”

“I don’t want your understanding, I want my father back, Mark said, tears continuing to stream down his face.

“I want him back too. He was my best friend, Mark. I loved your father as if he were my brother. We spoke each and every day since all the way back to our teens.”

“Then why didn’t you protect him? Why did you let him die? I hate you ... I hate you. I will never forgive you for taking him away from us.”

“I didn’t take your father away Mark, but I do accept responsibility for him not being around anymore, which is why I will not hit you back. I deserve all you can send my way and more.”

The connecting door between the house and the garage opened and Bonnie poked her head out. James waved her away; she nodded and went back into the house and closed the door. She returned several minutes later with a wet cloth for each of them. Sitting down on the floor between Mark and James she said, “I have an idea what this is all about and I am asking each of you to put whatever is going on here away. Not just for now, or today, or until we bury Bob — but forever. You each loved Bob, but this is no way to show that love. If he were alive right now, he would be telling you the same thing.”

"If he was alive and here right now," Mark said, under his breath, "we wouldn't have a reason to fight."

Bonnie gave her oldest son a shove, "There is more than enough hurt in this house right now, I am full up, I can't take any more."

"You're taking his side?" Mark asked.

"There are no sides anymore; you *are* going to each pull together." She put her hands up to her face and began to cry.

Chapter 57

Sunday, January 13, 2019 — 6:43 a.m.
The Schless family's church,
Waterbury, Connecticut.

The square block area, covered by the church the Schless family has attended for much of the time they have lived in Connecticut, stood gleaming in the sun this cold morning in January. The parking area which surrounded the building began to fill up well before 6 a.m. Most people huddled in their cars with the heat up to high while a few milled around the steps.

Will James, Bonnie, her three sons and their wives planned to arrive at the church well before the services were scheduled to begin so that they could say their final goodbyes to Bob. As their cars drove into the parking area they were surprised to see how many people were already there.

Elizabeth was parked in one of the few marked spaces directly in front of the main entrance steps. She got out of her car when she saw them arrive. She went directly to Bonnie, circled her arms around the grieving woman and whispered, "Whatever you need, anything, anytime, anywhere, all you have to do is ask. You know that, don't you?"

Bonnie kissed her on her cheek and said, "Thank you."

"You must also know that me, Will, and everyone else who worked with Bob are going to be really persistent pests and will huddle around you until we are each certain that you are okay and can make it on your own," Elizabeth said.

"I guess it is just what Bob would have done if the situation was reversed," Bonnie said with a weak smile.

The two women walked slowly towards the front entrance where Father David was waiting to greet Bonnie.

*****

Elizabeth was standing in the back of the church. James walked over to her and gave her a hug. "I want you to know something."

She gave him a warm smile, "I know, you will miss him, we will all miss him."

"I will miss him every day of my life," James said softly, "but I wanted to talk to you about something else." He leaned closer and whispered in her ear, "Dmitri will never ever harm you again."

"I know," she said, "I heard how the art dealer had him murdered."

"I murdered him."

With a shocked expression on her face she said, "You wouldn't kill an ant – I don't know anyone less violent than you. You don't even own a gun."

"I killed him," he repeated.

She leaned forward, gave him a kiss on the cheek, "Sure you did."

*****

The priest walked toward the coffin and said, “We are here to honor our friend and neighbor, Robert Schless.”

The Schless sons spoke from their hearts. Mark spoke first, sharing that his Dad taught him how to be a “glass half full type of person” and to appreciate other people, places and things. He talked about how he acquired a love of all things sports as well as the ability to laugh at anything and everything from his dad. “I learned that getting lost is a great way to find new things. My dad’s perseverance through tough times showed me that you need to keep moving forward, and things will work out. His dedication to supporting his family taught me responsibility, and his ability to start home projects without finishing them carried straight on to his son,” he waived towards the casket, “thanks for that *‘half-job Bob,’* and sorry to my wife Lauren!”

Mark’s brothers Will and Tom talked about how Bob became the role model, not only for them but for so many of their friends, “Teaching us all right from wrong and how to value hard work at work, and good play time out of work.”

Bob’s brother and sister and a number of Bob’s longtime friends spoke about Bob’s uniqueness. The last one just said, “You will be missed old friend,” then quoting Dylan Thomas, “‘Do not go gentle into that good night.’”

Each speaker went over to Bonnie before and after their remarks to embrace her and let her know that they will be there for her.

Bonnie bent down and picked up a large binder filled with family photos that she brought to the church from her home. She walked towards the casket, lifted the cover, bent down to kiss her husband one last time, and then gently placed the binder in the casket and lowered the lid. She turned to Father Dave who was watching with a puzzled look on his face.

"It would have been the one thing he would have grabbed if our house ever went up in flames," she said, "of course after all humans and family pets were safely out."

Father David asked if anyone else would like to say a few words. So many people began walking toward the alter that the priest put his hands up — "may I ask for only the closest of friends and relatives to speak, or this service might flow into the middle of next week." There was a rustle of voices, but only a few returned to their seats.

"Then please keep your comments short as a courtesy to each of those who would also like to speak here today," Father David said.

About an hour later, after a series of reminders to be brief, a little girl about 10 years old stood up and nervously raised her hand. Father David nodded towards her.

Looking around and then directly towards the priest she said, "My name is Stella Zimmer. Mr. Schless is ...," she paused and gave a deep sigh, "Mr. Schless *was* my neighbor and friend for as long as I can remember. I would like to speak about him and how very much he will be missed."

Looking at Bonnie and then Father David, she asked, "Is that okay?"

Bonnie stood up and went to the little girl, opened her arms and threw them around her. "Of course that is okay," Bonnie said.

The little girl took a crumpled sheet of paper out of her pocket, looked it over and then refolded it and stuffed it back into her pocket.

She walked toward the closed coffin. John Zimmer, her dad, stood silently behind her.

"Dear Mr. Schless," she began, "This is Stella Blu, remember me? I want to tell you that you are, were, will *always* be in my heart and on my mind."

The other mourners stretched to hear what this little girl was saying.

"I don't think my dad will mind my saying that you were like another father to me. Every time I saw you, it put a smile on my face, or at least that's what my dad used to say. No matter what would happen to me, you always had a way of comforting me – making me smile, making me know that 'it wasn't the end of the world.'" She smiled, "You always told me that 'the only thing that can be the end of the world is the end of the world, and this problem, whatever it was, was not even close to being the end of the world.'" She put her hands up to her face and began to cry.

Mason stood up and walked over to put his arms around his sister.

Two youngsters and two adults had been standing against the wall in the back of the church. As John, Mason, and Stella returned to their seats, the four walked over to the casket. The young boy spoke first, "Hello, Mr. Schless, I'm Niko Poulakos. My dad and I met you in New Orleans. You were very kind to us. You didn't have to be so nice – no one else had been that nice – but you were, and I'm just very sorry that we will never be able to thank you to your face. It isn't fair that such a caring and generous guy like you should be dead. I just wanted you to know that if I ever get a chance to help someone the way you helped my dad and me – and the food shelter, I'll do it because of you."

The man put his hand gently on the boy's shoulder and turned to face the people, "Hello, my name is Greg Poulakos and I would like to share a short story with you about the man we came here to honor. Not long ago, my family was struggling to deal with the aftermath of Katrina. I was having trouble finding regular work, and my son Niko and I were getting a bit discouraged about our situation. Mr. Schless saw us huddled in a doorway. A lot of people must have also noticed us there, but only Mr. Schless took the time to check up on us. Unlike so many other busy people, when he asked how we were doing, he actually waited for an answer. We were human beings to him. When he learned about our plight, he stepped in and showed true generosity by arranging for us and others at the local Salvation Army Mission to have fresh food. He turned just another hopeless day into a New Year's Eve party. He never once made it feel like charity, if anything he made it sound as if *we* were helping *him* by taking the food off of his hands. I can't stress how much his acts of kindness meant to us. Individually, and as a family, we are so very, very sad about his death. He was a very good man and I don't think any member of our family will go a single day from now on without thinking about him. The impact his acts of kindness have made on each of us will never be forgotten, and will always be appreciated. Rest in peace 'Good Samaritan.'"

Once again, Father David asked if anyone else would like to say a few words. Will James and Elizbeth were seated in the fourth row. Elizabeth said, "You should say something."

"What's the use? He can no longer hear anything I might have to say."

"You should say something. Speaking here ... now ... is not for the dead — it is for the living."

"I ... I can't Elizabeth, I just can't."

"If you do not get up now, you will regret it for the rest of your life."

Will patted her hand, "I can't. I wouldn't know how to start, much less how to finish."

Elizabeth gently touched Will's cheek, "Just say what is on your heart."

Father David again asked if anyone else would like to say a few words.

Will hesitantly stood up and then slowly made his way through the row and out to the closed casket. He stood silently for several minutes and then with his head bowed he pulled a clump of tissues from his pocket, dabbed at his eyes, blew his nose, sighed, and then began, "We met at the Federal

Correctional Facility in Oakdale, Louisiana. I was sent there because I had hacked into the computer system at the Department of Defense. Bob was sent there because he had committed one too many petty crimes and had punched a federal marshal." He smiled, "We might never have met if his left jab was as weak as my left jab.

"The very first time I met Robert Schless was one of the scariest days of my life. I was about 16 years old – going on 12; he was about 18 years old – going on 40. He was street wise and able to charm his way into, or out of any situation ... and I mean *any situation*. I, on the other hand, lacked any charm whatsoever, or skills, or even the basic survival instincts that would have enabled me to have a better than point zero, zero two percent chance to get out of there alive." He smiled and then laughed, "Yes, *'point zero, zero two percent chance to get out of there alive'* – those were the first words Robert Schless ever said to me, *'and the only reason your chances are that high,'* he went on to say, *'is because I am being seen talking to you right now.'*"

James looked up and met Elizabeth's eyes, tears were welling up as she nodded affirmatively toward him.

"What happened next was typical Robert Schless. He leaned closer to me and whispered, *'punch me in the face, as hard as you can.'* All I could do was stand there and stare at him. He then repeated what he had just said, *'punch me, punch me hard, in the face, do it now.'* So I did. Then I closed my eyes because I knew I was about to die, but when I opened my eyes he was on the floor with his hands up like he was surrendering. It wasn't until later that day that he told me that the other toughs would probably stay out of my way now – maybe not forever, but long enough to give me time to work on the weakest left jab he had ever seen. That was how we met." His voice was beginning to break, "That was 51 years ago, and until he was ambushed on the streets of New Orleans, he and I spoke almost every day since that first meeting. He was the brother I never had.

"When we first got out of jail," he was now speaking in spurts, "A very good guy is down and out, I can't adequately describe the loss I am feeling right now."

Silence filled the church for several minutes, and then he said, "You must have read about the running of the bulls in Spain; well early in July, right after we got out of jail, Schless," he looked nervously at Bonnie, "I mean Robert, still in his teens at the time, got it into his head to go backpacking in Europe. The next thing I knew, he was at the Festival of Saint Fermín in Pamplona. He called me and left his phone on so that I could hear what he was experiencing. All I could make out over his heavy breathing were loud and disjointed sounds; I could picture that damned fool running through the streets barely in front of some raging bulls with his mobile phone up in the air. I was in the safety of some dingy little take out Chinese restaurant at the time of this call. I told him he was either the bravest person I had ever known, or the absolute dumbest, stupidest, ignoramus of a jerk – and I hung up on him. He called back – imagine, he must have been running at full speed with a crowd of other fearless jerks trying to get out of the way of a herd of angry, nervous, dangerous bulls, and yet he found a way to dial me back; *'You gotta experience this with me'* he kept yelling into the phone. To this day, I don't know how he made it out of there alive."

"During those months in prison I taught him everything I knew about computers. Something he probably never used or needed. He taught me how to survive in life, in general, and in the real world, in particular. Things that have served me well during all these years; he was everything a good and caring friend could be.

"He was a real trouper. He never once complained. Well, maybe once. The week before his death he was on his way to Nashville to attend a special concert in honor of Bill Monroe and the Bluegrass Boys. The very last time we spoke he said he would go to New Orleans to finish my assignment even though he would now be forced to pass up the concert, something he would miss for the rest of his days on earth." Tears were now streaming his face, "It is my hope and prayer," he bowed his head and rubbed the tears away, "My hope ..." he stopped again, took a deep breath, "It is my hope that as soon as he passed the pearly gates, he was escorted to a front row seat to hear Bill Monroe perform, just for him.

"We shared happy times and sad times and never once ... not for a single second, did I doubt that if Bob Schless was in your corner, you didn't need anyone else. I am so thankful that he entered my life — and stayed for more than half a century."

Staring down at the coffin he said, "I love you Bob Schless, and I know that wherever you are right now, you are charming the angels. They don't have a chance."

He blew his nose, shifted from his right foot to his left, and then said, "The English poet, Robert Southey once said, *'The loss of a friend is like that of a limb; time may heal the anguish of the wound, but the loss cannot be repaired.'*"

As he started to walk back to his seat he absentmindedly put his hand in his pocket and pulled out a handful of M&M peanut candies. He walked back to the casket and carefully placed two blue M&M's on top of the casket. "See," he said to the casket, "I did listen to you. No more fruits and roots."

*****

The priest stood and said, "One of Robert's greatest pleasures was music. His son, Mark and one of his dearest friends, Stella Zimmer have arranged for a blue grass band to perform now, in honor of a life fully lived and a man who will surely be missed."

Chapter 58

Sunday, January 20, 2019 — 10:41 a.m.
The White House

ט ו בשבט שמח, אב שלום *Hello Abi, and happy Tu B'Shevat*, the president said.

"Madam President, my own mother doesn't pronounce it so well, but I am sure you know that Tu BiShvat is a very minor holiday in the Jewish calendar."

"The New Year of the Trees is minor? Where are your priorities, dear Abi?"

"Somehow, I cannot believe that you stopped in the middle of your busy day to acknowledge one of the four New Year holidays mentioned in the Mishnah, Madam President."

אני אוהב עצים, אני עוצר באמצע יום עסוק כדי לוודא שחזרת הביתה בסדר וגם להודות לך על העזרה שלך *I love trees and I am also stopping in the middle of a busy day to make sure you got back home all right, and also to thank you for your help.*

"I would never disappoint such a good and old friend, Madam President. But for the record, I really didn't do very much. You had a lot of talented people and they did all of the heavy lifting, believe me. By the way, you speak Hebrew? Where did you learn to speak so fluently?"

אני לא יודע איך שוטפת אני מדבר אבל למדתי לדבר עברית מתוך כבוד השכנים שלי, רבים מהם הם ממזרח אירופה. *I don't know how fluently I am speaking but I learned how to speak Hebrew out of respect for my neighbors, many of whom are from Eastern Europe.*

אתה מדבר יפה בשם שיקסע *You speak pretty good for a shiksa.*

שיקסע או אישה? *A shiksa or a woman?*

"So, to what do I owe the pleasure of this call," he asked.

"I know that you and some members of your government have been using the services of an American money launderer," she said.

"His or her name?" he asked.

"Come on, Abi, give me some respect here, you know who I'm talking about."

"And if I were to say that I do, what would you want me to do with or for that person?"

"Let's say, it would be very helpful if he went on a long and well-earned vacation for at least as long as I am in the White House."

"I've told you before, you are one tough broad and maybe the toughest man in your government," he said.

Can I just be one of the best *women* in my government," she asked, demurely.

"With all due respect, do you believe that women are better than men?"

“מנהיג ישראלי גולדה מאיר אמר פעם, ‘if שנשים טובות יותר מאשר גברים, איני יכולה לומר. אבל אני יכול להגיד לך כי הם בהחלט לא יותר גרוע.’” *Israeli leader Golda Meir once said, “if women are better than men, I cannot say. But I can tell you that they are definitely not worse.”*

Chapter 59

Thursday, January 24, 2019 — 9:18 p.m.
Main cabin, luxury private plane, on route to Bermuda

Arturo Hornedo was the sole passenger in the Cessna CJ2525-P twin-engine jet aircraft on route to Bermuda. He sat staring out at the blackness, considering his options and how best to get back at the rest of those who doomed him to what promised to be a life in hiding.

In the cockpit was a military trained and seasoned pilot with more than 20-years experience flying for major commercial airlines, handpicked to Hornedo's strict specifications. *He has to be counted on to take this entire mission to his grave. I don't want any tell-all books or spilling of his guts to the Feds; he has to be one thousand percent reliable. I also want the very best possible pilot in that seat, I don't want anyone learning on my dime — he has to be free of any, and all, physical or mental or temperamental conditions that might lead him to fly us into the ocean.*

When Hornedo first contracted with Miguel Ángel Cervantes, known throughout the underworld as *Guía de oro*, the golden guide, Hornedo knew the cost would be high, but even he gasped at the price Cervantes demanded. "You need me now, you pay a lot. You can wait until mañana, it costs you less. If you can leave when it is most convenient for *me*, you have a little negotiation power. But, my friend, if you want me to have my very best pilot sitting in place twiddling his thumbs with such a fancy and dependable aircraft by his side until you get the urge to fly into the sunset ... well, that costs a little more."

Hornedo was required to pay double to have the plane and pilot camp out in a secluded hangar on the outskirts of Lakefront Airport, about five miles northeast of New Orleans's central business district, ready to lift off on an hour's notice, for the past two and a half weeks.

"What good is having money if you don't use it to ensure a secure way out of town before *La Chota* comes knock, knock, knocking on your door?" Cervantes said with a toothy grin, "And after all, we are not bank robbers, rapers, traitors or infanticides, we are just businessmen ... like you; are you not just a businessman Señor Hornedo?"

Hornedo knew full well that there was absolutely no chance he would be able to talk the cost down. Cervantes ran an exclusive shuttle service for members of the underworld. As the brother in law of the current head of the Gulf Cartel, he was able to pick and choose his clientele, as well as set his prices according to whim, *his* whim. He was also quite capable of cutting Hornedo's throat and leaving him for the vultures to find.

*****

Hornedo had just fallen asleep when the noise of things crashing around him woke him. Something was terribly wrong; the plane seemed to be in a dive.

It was a struggle but he made his way to the cockpit, the pilot was out cold. Alarms were now blasting throughout the plane. They were losing altitude, "No, no," he screamed, "this isn't happening!" Hornedo disconnected the pilot's seat belt and shoulder harness and pushed him to the side.

Hornedo had some basic small plane training but not recently and never on this particular type of aircraft. He feverishly pushed and pulled the switches and dials and then concentrated every ounce of energy on pulling back on the controls but the plane was still gliding downward.

There was a sudden movement which propelled him backwards, causing him to slam against the back wall, then forward, hitting his head against the side wall.

When he regained consciousness, he was in total darkness. He tried to feel around but something was holding him down. It was cold and damp, "I guess I didn't die because this can't be the fires of hell," he said aloud.

ישנן גרסאות רבות של גיהנום, מר Hornedo *There are many versions of hell, Mr. Hornedo,* said a voice close by.

Acknowledgements

It was during a signing event for my previously published novels in this *Will James Mysteries* series, *The Jefferson Files* and *The Hidden Treasure Files,* that a woman said she would love to be a character in one of my books, “I bet you couldn’t make up some of the things I have experienced ...” she said. *What a good idea*, I thought. That evening I came up with a way to bring everyday people into future story plots.

I created a drawing — a simple message: no purchase necessary — here’s a chance to become immortalized in a future novel ... *if I draw your name you will be a character in my next book*. My plan was to create a character with the same name as the one drawn. In addition, I planned to interview the winner and make their character mirror the personality and natural individuality of the chosen person. It would be my responsibility to do all of this without breaking the natural flow of the story line.

The concept was so quickly accepted by the public, that before long I accumulated close to a thousand entries and that number grew from there. People of all ages entered which was fine because my mail has been coming from readers as young as 9 years of age all the way up to 91.

The first name drawn, Stella Zimmer, turned out to be only 9 years old. Adding a young character to a mystery can be doubly challenging. To my pleasant surprise, when Stella responded to my first series of questions, she proved to be so interesting that I had plenty to work with. Rather than slow the storyline down I think her character added a lot to the mix.

Stella is one very special 9-year old girl. Imagine, a 9-year old with musical preferences ranging from The Eagles, the Grateful Dead, Frank Zappa, Led Zeppelin to The Beatles and the Steve Miller Band. More than *just* a fan and consumer of music, she is also a performer, playing the saxophone and guitar in her school band.

Stella is also a student of Tae Kwan Do and skilled at skiing, swimming, sailing, diving, fishing, hunting, bike-riding, roller skating, golf, dodge ball, and extremely accurate with a pellet gun. She is currently learning Spanish and German. In addition, Stella helps to care for a *few pets* ... a cat named Simon Goldfinger, a dog named Archie, a goat named Gerty, and a sheep named Mama. (Stella lives on a family farm.)

Would this have described you or many people you know at the tender age of 9? I don't know about you, but I'm winded just by listing all of her interests and extracurricular activities.

After I drew Stella's name and bombarded her with my interview questions, I remembered what an absolute delight it was speaking with her and Mason, her 11-year old brother, during my appearance at the 2016 "Big E," (the Eastern States Exposition/State Fair, in Springfield, Mass.). I can't say that I remember each and every person I spoke with during this massively attended event but I did remember Stella and Mason, when they stopped by my signing table. What made them stand out for me was that even though they were very young, they already exhibited a natural poise and maturity and basic intellectual curiosity few develop well into adulthood. These are very special young people.

As this novel began to take shape, I decided to also add her brother, and to a lesser degree, her parents, to the storyline. As it turned out, Mason is also quite a unique individual; already active in sports, music and a beginning student of the German language. According to those who know him best, "everyone loves Mason." I think you will as well.

For this novel, I also held a second drawing. This time the winner was Niko Poulakis, also very young, just a week after his name was drawn Niko celebrated his 11th birthday.

Niko's activities include a love for animals. He told me that one of the jobs he would like to have when he grows up is zookeeper. He is currently active in his area's 4H club. Like Mason Zimmer, Niko is also learning to read and speak Spanish.

The original intent was to closely mirror the winner's characteristics and way of life. Niko and his family are portrayed in this novel as homeless due to the after effects of a natural disaster. In reality, the Poulakis family is *not* homeless, but they were willing to go along with the premise. Keep in mind as you read the story that the Poulakis family is *only* homeless between the covers of this novel.

I thank Stella Zimmer and Mason Zimmer and Niko Poulakis, and their families for allowing me to weave them into this work of fiction. In my opinion, this novel is far better than it would have been without the characters they inspired. (You, the reader, will be the ultimate judge of that.)

I'm always interested in what *you*, the reader, think. Please send your comments to Mherman194@prodigy.net. I personally answer every letter I receive.

Martin Herman

Bloomfield, Connecticut, February 26, 2017

Final thoughts —
what is fact and what is fiction?

Of all the mail I receive two questions surface the most: how long does it take me to write a book and what is fact and what is fiction in the books I write.

In reality, the writing is the quickest and easiest part. The initial time spent creating and shaping my characters followed by weeks, sometimes months of research, is what prolongs the process. In the case of the first novel in this series, *The Jefferson Files*, the time span from beginning to end was almost 10 years. Thomas Jefferson has been my hero since 6th grade, and so I wanted to make certain that I got the parts about him as correct as possible.

As far as what is fact and what is just the product of my overactive imagination; the following is meant to help address that for this novel:

Prologue
Pete's Landing Bar and Grill is a real place near the Pueblo Memorial Airport, Pueblo, Colorado. It is open until 3 a.m. as stated in this chapter.

There is indeed a real home on Desert Candle Drive, in Pueblo, Colorado, with all of the specifications and features of the home described in this chapter — all the way to the selling price. I did a search for the most expensive, *new homes*, available for sale at the time I wrote this section. As this is being written this house is still for sale and, according to the local real estate agent, a "steal at the price!"

The actual house is near the Colorado State University and the Walking Stick Golf Course.

Everything written about the gun in this section is based on verifiable fact. It was owned by Sherriff Carroll, the same person who was part of the posse that captured the infamous Barker/Karpis Gang; the same person who claimed that Joe Arridy confessed to him; and the same person who was featured in about a hundred detective and crime magazine articles.

It was given to Carroll by J. Edgar Hoover.

Part 1/Chapter 1

The movie theater referenced in this chapter is based on the famous Plaza Theater at 1049 Ponce De Leon Avenue., NE, in Atlanta. Designed by George Harwell Bond and opened in 1939, it is Atlanta's longest continually operating and only independent movie theater. (Bond also designed the first shopping center with off-street parking in Atlanta.)

When I was researching this novel, the route from the theater, on Ponce de Leon Avenue, NE, to the Greyhound Bus Station, at 232 Forsyth St., took about 18 minutes.

Part 1/Chapter 3

It is a fact that Hartsfield-Jackson Atlanta International Airport began its life on April 16, 1925 with a 287-acre area which had been an abandoned auto racetrack before. It was named Candler Field after the property's former owner, Asa Candler, a former Mayor of Atlanta and the businessman who initially purchased the rights to the Coca-Cola formula from its founder.

It is also true that in the mid-1950s, a hangar on the outskirts of the Hartsfield-Jackson Atlanta International Airport was used to store military vehicles.

The U.S. Army Criminal Investigation Laboratory, referred to in this chapter is a real entity; located at the former Fort Gillem in Forest Park, Georgia, it provides forensic laboratory services to the Department of Defense as well as other federal investigative agencies. It is the only full service forensic laboratory in the Department of Defense and trains special agents and investigators from all four branches of the United States military and manages the government's criminalistics and visual information programs.

Part 1/Chapter 4

The 2016 U.S. presidential election was decided well before this book went to press. Portraying the president of the United States in this novel as a woman was neither meant to forecast the results of the 2016 United States election nor to discount the actual election results. That was fact and the bulk of this novel is fiction.

Part 1/Chapter 6
Israel actually can build an emergency field hospital in 12 hours. They have done so in various parts of the world after natural disasters.

The *San* people, also known as Bushmen or Basarwa, are members of various indigenous hunter-gatherer people of Southern Africa, whose territories span Botswana, Namibia, Angola, Zambia, Zimbabwe, and South Africa.

As any native New Yorker over the age of 50 will tell you, *yes*, there is indeed such a place as Yonah Shimmel: it is a specialty bakery/restaurant. Yonah Shimmel Knishes have been a New York City ethnic delicacy since 1890. Shimmel originally sold knishes – Eastern European filled pastries – from a pushcart along the lower East Side of Manhattan. Eventually the business was moved into a small store front on the south side of Houston Street. It moved one more time to its present location at 137 East Houston Street, New York City in 1910.

You don't have to be quite as old to also know about Katz's Deli, a kosher style New York City Deli on the lower east side of Manhattan. A few blocks up the same street, at 205 East Houston Street, New York City, is Katz's Deli. Don't try to finish their Corned Beef or Pastrami sandwich along with their really good french fries in a single sitting; it is possible, but not so easy.

Part 1/Chapter 7
Neither the Old or the New Testament records a list of the "seven deadly sins," although there are references to various sins throughout The Bible, and a listing of sins in Proverbs 6:16-19 and Galatians 5:19-21.

The seven deadly sins were originally based on a list of eight principal vices. The list was developed in the fourth century by the mystic Evagrius Ponticus, whose work inspired the writings of monk and ascetic John Cassian.

In the sixth century, Pope Gregory I changed Cassian's list of eight vices into the list of seven deadly, or cardinal, sins of Roman Catholic theology:

Pride, Greed, Lust, Envy, Gluttony, Anger, and Sloth. Gregory viewed these as capital, or principal, sins in that many other sins came from them.

Part 1/Chapter 8
Pálinka is a traditional fruit brandy in the Carpathian Basin, known under several names, and invented in the Middle Ages. Traditionally limited to fruit spirits mashed, distilled, matured and bottled in Hungary.

Part 1/Chapter 9
Atlanta's busy airport – Hartsfield–Jackson, is on land originally owned by Asa Candler. (In 1888, Candler purchased the original formula for Coca-Cola from its inventor for $550), the land used for the airport had an earlier life as an auto racetrack – the Atlanta Speedway. It had been abandoned when a portion of the space was turned into the city's first airport.

It is factual that there is a U.S. Army Criminal Investigation Lab, (USACIL), in Metro Atlanta's Gillem Enclave. USACIL, formerly Fort Gillem, is generally recognized to be *the* authority for battlefield forensics, it had been initially set up to supply worldwide forensic support and train special agents for all branches of the U.S. military. As of the writing of this novel it was the only Department of Defense full-service forensic laboratory in the world.

Part 1/Chapter 10
On April 16, 2013, a group of marksmen reportedly entered an underground vault for the Pacific Gas and Electric Company's Metcalf Transmission Substation, in Coyote, California, near San Jose, and "shot out" six AT&T fiber-optic telecommunications lines. A half hour later, the snipers began firing at the power station, destroying 17 giant transformers and six circuit breakers. The attack resulted in almost $15.5M in damages, in 2013, dollars and resulted in the station being shut down for 27 days.

Fortunately, the power supply to Silicon Valley was not disrupted because other power sources were used to make up for the loss; but it did act as a reminder of just how vulnerable our power grid is to possible attack.

Part 1/Chapter 13
With the help of my old friend, Ric Francis, we came up with 700 block, Royal Street, New Orleans for the art gallery in this chapter. That choice locked me into the Fifth Police District for the storyline.

Part 1/Chapter 14
There are a number of Western Union offices in and around New Orleans. The one chosen for this novel is a 24-hour Western Union office outside of Crowder Blvd.

Part 1/Chapter 18
The references to the Joe Arridy case are based in fact.

Joe Arridy was born April 15, 1915, his parents were each other's first cousins, having immigrated to the United States from Syria. They settled in Pueblo, Colorado. Joe Arridy had an IQ of 46. According to his comments and actions, it was clear that he was mentally disabled.

When he was 21, Arridy was found wandering around the Cheyenne train yards where he was picked up for questioning about the rape and murder in Pueblo of Dorothy Drain, a 15-year old school girl. He was interrogated by Sheriff George Carroll, a nationally famous former member of the posse that caught the infamous Ma Barker Gang. Arridy confessed to the crime along with other crimes it now seems he couldn't have committed. Doctors examined him and at a sanity hearing they said he was an imbecile, their clinical terminology, for someone who has the mental capacity of a child between 4 and 6 years of age; "more capable than an idiot, but not quite as mentally able as a moron."

He was tried and after deliberating for only 28 minutes the jury found him guilty, recommending he get the death penalty. On January 6, 1939, when he was 23 years old, the State of Colorado executed him in the gas chamber in Cañon City, Colorado.

Seventy-two years later, in 2011, when evidence was made available showing that he wasn't even in Pueblo when the crime was committed and so his confession was almost certainly coerced, the sitting governor, Bill Ritter, posthumously pardoned him.

Sheriff Carroll's hand gun, with the identifiable pearl grip and metal eagle emblem, reportedly given to him by J. Edgar Hoover, was passed down to relatives after his death.

In this novel, all comments about this case, Sheriff Carroll's gun, Joe Arridy in particular, are completely based upon published reports by people at the time of the murder and since.

The connection made to the fictitious character, Sister Joan, created in this novel is **not** true.

Part 1/Chapter 19
Joe Arridy's prison number actually **was** 19845.

It is a fact that the Georgia Historic Preservation Act of 1980 was passed to create a basis for local government to protect historic resources within their jurisdictions.

Part 1/Chapter 20
Verti Marti, is a famous 24/7 deli on the corner of Royal and Governor Nicholls Streets. As mentioned in this chapter, it was destroyed by a six-alarm fire in mid-2010. It was also totally rebuilt and reopened eight months later, to the day. Some of the plywood sheets used to cover the storefront after the fire and during the reconstruction was retained to preserve the "love notes" and best wishes by the restaurant's many loyal customers.

In this chapter I introduce Niko Poulakis and his father Greg. Later I bring in Niko's mother, Kennan and his sister Riley to the story.

Niko entered the second drawing I held to *be a character in a future novel.* Although each of the characters with the same names as those in the Poulakis family are purely fictitious, I tried my best to infuse a real voice in my characters, especially those of the drawing winner and ultimately his family; having said that I want to stress that the Poulakis family is definitely **not** homeless nor are they from New Orleans, as depicted in this fictitious novel. They each wrote a good portion of the words the characters bearing their names, speak in this novel.

One of the largest supermarket chains in New Orleans is Schwegmann Giant Supermarkets.

Part 1/Chapter 23
University Medical Center would be the health care facility where people from the *700 Block* with medical emergencies would be brought.

Part 2/Chapter 24
The *L-32*, described in this chapter, is a figment of my imagination. To the best of my knowledge, it does not exist.

Part 2/Chapter 28
In this chapter I introduce Stella Blu Zimmer, who won the very first drawing in my contest to be a character in a future novel. When I first learned that Stella was only 9 years old, I wondered how I could properly work her into my storyline. Then I learned more about her and how very special and active and interesting a young person she was. Now I can't imagine this novel without her.

During the research process, I realized that there could be a meaningful place in the storyline for Stella's brother, Mason as well. He too added a unique value to the storyline.

I extend to Stella and Niko, in particular, and Mason, and the Zimmer and Poulakis families in general, a huge thank you for their cooperation and general good nature during the writing of this novel.

Part 2/Chapter 32
Although the "place" Donetsk in the Ukraine is a real place and is factually described, the characters said to be from this place within this novel are entirely fictitious.

I chose the town of Donetsk, in the Ukraine as the birthplace for Elizabeth Hillsonrat, a member of the investigation team and Dmitri Donskoy, one of the three major villains, after a great deal of research. I wanted a real location with a wide-ranged history to draw upon in this novel and possibly in future novels within this series. I found Donetsk to be everything I wanted and more. It has been a hot bed of Russian mafia activities, and an important industrial and mining town. It was reported to have been where the Soviets sent captured German scientists during and after World War II — and the official home of the Russian Space program, *Roscosmos*. With all of that in its history, it is more than likely that it also had extensive KGB activities over the years. That fit nicely within the story I was constructing.

Part 2/Chapter 33
Balkan 176º, is an actual product. Everything said about it in this chapter is true. It is a Serbian triple-distilled grain vodka with 88 percent alcohol by volume. It is hand crafted in small batches. Its packaging carries 13 health warnings, and when first shipped to the western countries — and possibly to this day — the label had 15 warnings about its potency ... including one in Braille.

Part 2/Chapter 36
The *Entico 76 Signal Tracking* device mentioned in this chapter is, to the best of my knowledge, just a figment of my imagination.

Part 3/Chapter 54
The *Patek Philippe Calibre 89* pocket watch described in this chapter is one of the most valuable watches in the world. Only four of these were made in 1989 to celebrate the company's 150th anniversary. It has 1,728 components, including a thermometer, and a star chart. One unit each was made in white gold, one in yellow gold, one in rose gold and one in platinum. The gold units were made with 18-karat (75 percent) gold. Initially each watch was valued at about $6M. The value has risen since.

Part 3/Chapter 55
Dining at the *Varsity Drive In* is an Atlanta tradition. Although there is more than one location, the main site is responsible for more retail sales of Coca-Cola, on an annual basis than any other single location in the world, a record which has stood for many years.

Part 3/Chapter 57
I take pride in mixing verified facts within my fictitious mysteries. On very rare occasions I take literary license and throw reality to the wind. This chapter contains an example of my doing just that. In this chapter, Will James recalls conversations between him and Bob Schless over mobile phones when Schless was running the Festival of Saint Fermín in Pamplona. This event would have taken place in the late 1960s when both Schless and James were each in their late teens. Mobile phones didn't reach the masses until almost 30 years later when satellites were put into place by a company called Iridium in 1998. They also produced the first hand-held satellite phones, which were smaller and less cumbersome than the earlier "bag" phones.

Part 3/Chapter 59
The choice of aircraft for Arturo Hornedo's getaway was also the result of an extensive research project. I wanted an aircraft that was currently available for general aviation, one of the 75 most expensive airplanes in this niche category, and a plane that *might* be used by an underground shuttle service because only one crew member would be required to pilot it and it could maneuver short runways and hard to access landing strips.

The *Cessna CJ2525A twin-engine jet* filled the bill to a T.

The Gulf Cartel, *Cártel del Golfo*, referred to in this chapter is known to exist. It is a Mexican criminal syndicate and drug trafficking organization specializing in kidnapping, extortion, human trafficking, assassination, protection rackets, prostitution, and money laundering. Believed to have been in operation since the 1970s, it is one of the oldest known criminal groups in Mexico, and is based in Matamoros, Tamaulipas, across the border from Brownsville, Texas.

The phrase, "We are not bank robbers, rapers, traitors or infanticides" spoken by a fictitious character in this chapter is actually the cartel's official motto – yes, they have an official motto.

About the author

Martin Herman was born and raised in Brooklyn, New York. He has lived and/or worked in most major marketing areas, here and abroad.

His business career includes line and field responsibilities as a marketer, retailer, distributor, wholesaler, and manufacturer of branded premium consumer products.

Since 1999, he has had an active executive business consulting practice, working with entrepreneurs in new start-up businesses as well as owner/managers of troubled, mature companies.

He has been writing since he was 11 and selling short stories under a variety of pen names since he was 13. A lifelong obsession with news and newsmakers led him to write his first full length historical mystery novel, *The Jefferson Files*, published in February, 2015, a few months shy of his 75th birthday. It was followed the next year by *The Hidden Treasure Files*.

This is the third in the *WILL JAMES MYSTERY* series.

He prefers to write at night and during long business trips on airplanes and extended periods in airports and hotel rooms.

He lives in Bloomfield, Conn., halfway up a small mountain with a breathtaking view of the Connecticut countryside.

Website: martinhermanauthor.com

E-mail: mherman194@prodigy.net

Blog: https://mhermanwriter.wordpress.com/
Facebook: Martin Herman-Writer

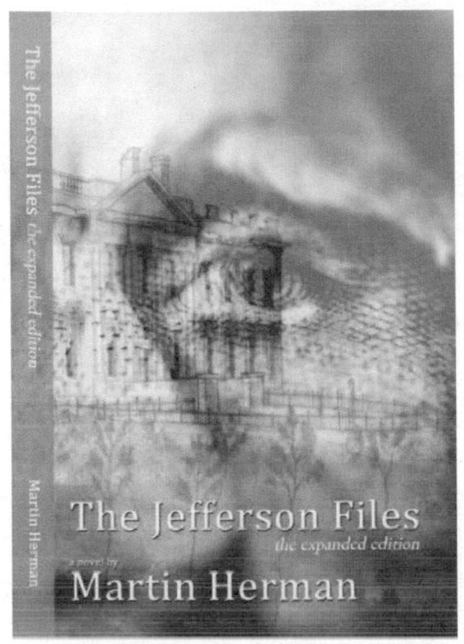

Also by Martin Herman:
The Jefferson Files – the expanded edition
ISBN 978-1-945211-00-3 PRINT

A deeply entrenched secret society arranges for a dissident within their organization to be brutally murdered and left floating in the Potomac River, within clear site of the Jefferson White House. The secret society is challenging Jefferson to either deal with them as equals, or suffer the consequences.

Almost 200 years later, after discovering a lost diary written at the time of the crime, three college students and a world class computer hacker begin unraveling the modern day offenses of the secret society.

By digging up this 200-year old crime, the students attract the attention of the modern day leader of the secret society who then threatens their very existence. Rather than retreat, the students fight back.

You will not be able to put this book down until the end ... the end ... the final, final end.

If you usually can guess the ending of a mystery within the first third or so of a novel, you will *not* be able to do it this time. You will be kept guessing until the very last page.

Some of *The Jefferson Files* reviews:

Marvelous Read By S Mazurick
"… a fascinating and engaging read ... At times I needed to remind myself that it's fiction, because the author does such a fantastic job capturing the reader … great intertwining the 1800s to 2009 ... very creative."

I loved how the book told of two parallel stories ... By E Donovan
"… included mystery and suspense … loved the ties to New Jersey which made the story that much more realistic. Can't wait to read the next adventure from this writer …"

A MUST READ!! Well written. By K Thorne
"… loved the book … a real page turner …"

Gripping page-turning thriller with outstanding historical references By jw
"… I picked this book up, as a fan of Jefferson and couldn't put it down … the book touched on patriotism, ethics, family … you can tell how meticulously the author researched his subject. the characters were compelling and well written … story line is totally engrossing. I hope there is a sequel!"

Highly recommend! By BritChik
"… so engaging that it inspires you to read more on the topic … takes you to many locations and times throughout history … author has done an excellent job making it all come together, a testament to the writer's ability … the fictional elements were both tense and exciting. Highly recommend."

Well done and interesting … a good read. By K Stevens
"Wonderful writing … loved the pace and attention to detail. The author had me at chapter one … Nice work …"

Loving both history and murder mysteries, book does a fantastic job of combining the two. By Mei
"… draws you into the setting quickly and skillfully … keeps you there until the end … easy and enjoyable read …"

A true page-turner! By A Hon
"… immediately engaged … fast-moving … excellently written … great attention to detail … great read …"

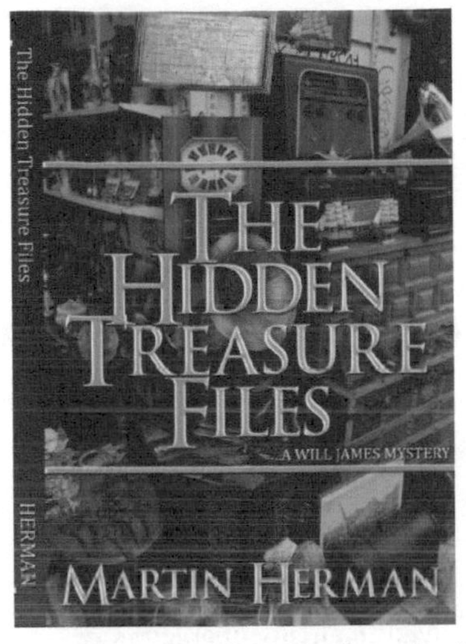

Also by Martin Herman:
The Hidden Treasure Files

ISBN 978-1-945211-01-0 PRINT

In *The Hidden Treasure Files*, the second in the current series of *Will James Mysteries,* the resourceful data breach expert/quick-witted investigator and his crew are asked to help unravel a mystery that begins in a Brooklyn antique store's weekly auction and ends in the most unlikely of locations.

It should have triggered many questions when one specific auction, which rarely draws more than a handful of onlookers, attracts a packed room of possible bidders. But the questions only start when the auctioneer offers up a prohibition era permit in a battered old wooden frame. It was one of many items he acquired in an estate purchase.

Hoping he would wind up with something between 50 cents and a dollar for what he considered to be "*... a piece of junk,*" he starts the bidding at $2.00. To his surprise and amazement, two separate people quickly bid the price up to $100,000. "Who would pay $100,000 for this," he asks himself, "What do they know that I don't?"

When the head of the New York Mafia family also shows interest in the item, the auctioneer becomes convinced that he has a hidden treasure on his hands.

If you think you know how this will end you are very, very wrong. As with all Will James Mysteries, the numerous twists and turns will keep you guessing until the very last page.

Some of *The Hidden Treasure Files* reviews:

The book is wonderful by A Wilcox
"The Hidden Treasure Files is amazing ... I can't stop reading it … love the different lifestyles of the characters … made me want to keep reading more and more"

Excellent book by D Taylor
"… lots of twists & turns … kept me interested ... loved the many characters & their backgrounds, most of all the hidden treasures we have inside of us ...

The plot was engaging and kept me reading by M Harris
"At his signing event, the author predicted that if I kept reading to page 10, I would be hooked, and he was right …
the many plot twists kept it interesting, a few I saw coming, many I didn't … loved the characters, particularly enjoyed their interesting background stories … a nice twist to have a mystery without a murder …"

A great escape and entertaining in every way by J Stone
"… such a 'feel-good' ending doesn't come with every story, real or fiction …"

---

can't put it down! by I Walker
"I would love to one day be a character in one of Herman's books"

**Your comments and suggestions are always welcomed. Please contact the author at: mherman194@prodigy.net
Visit our website:
martinhermanauthor.com**